SWEET LITTLE LIES

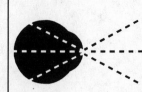

This Large Print Book carries the
Seal of Approval of N.A.V.H.

A HEARTBREAKER BAY NOVEL

Sweet Little Lies

Jill Shalvis

THORNDIKE PRESS
A part of Gale, Cengage Learning

GALE
CENGAGE Learning·

Farmington Hills, Mich • San Francisco • New York • Waterville, Maine
Meriden, Conn • Mason, Ohio • Chicago

GALE
CENGAGE Learning·

LIBRARY OF CONGRESS CATALOGING-IN-PUBLICATION DATA

Names: Shalvis, Jill, author.
Title: Sweet little lies : a Heartbreaker Bay novel / by Jill Shalvis.
Description: Large print edition. | Waterville, Maine : Thorndike Press, 2016. |
 Series: Thorndike Press large print romance
Identifiers: LCCN 2016020747| ISBN 9781410492531 (hardcover) | ISBN 1410492532
 (hardcover)
Subjects: LCSH: Large type books. | GSAFD: Love stories.
Classification: LCC PS3619.H3534 S94 2016 | DDC 813/.6—dc22
LC record available at https://lccn.loc.gov/2016020747

Published in 2016 by arrangement with Avon Books, an imprint of HarperCollins Publishers

Printed in Mexico
1 2 3 4 5 6 7 20 19 18 17 16

CHAPTER 1
#KEEPCALMANDRIDEAUNICORN

Pru Harris's mom had taught her to make wishes on pink cars, falling leaves, and brass lamps, because wishing on something as ordinary as stars or wishing wells was a sign of no imagination.

Clearly the woman standing not three feet away in the light mist, searching her purse for change to toss into the courtyard fountain hadn't been raised by a hippie mom as Pru had been.

Not that it mattered, since her mom had been wrong. Wishes, along with things like winning the lotto or finding a unicorn, never happened in real life.

The woman, shielding her eyes from the light rain with one hand, holding a coin in her other, sent Pru a wry grimace. "I know it's silly, but it's a hit-rock-bottom thing."

Something Pru understood all too well. She set a wriggly Thor down and shook her arms to try and bring back some circulation. Twenty-five pounds of wet, tubby, afraid-of-his-own-shadow mutt had felt like seventy-five by the end of their thirty-minute walk home from work.

Thor objected to being on the wet ground with a sharp bark. Thor didn't like rain.

Or walking.

But he loved Pru more than life itself so he stuck close, his tail wagging slowly as he watched her face to determine what mood they were in.

The woman blinked and stared down at Thor. "Oh," she said, surprised. "I thought it was a really fat cat."

Thor's tail stopped wagging and he barked again, as if to prove that not only was he all dog, he was big, *badass* dog.

Because Thor — a rescue of undetermined breed — also believed he was a bullmastiff.

When the woman took a step back, Pru sighed and picked him back up again. His old man face was creased into a protective frown, his front paws dangling, his tail back to wagging now that he was suddenly tall. "Sorry," Pru said. "He can't see well and it makes him grumpy, but he's not a cat." She gave Thor a *behave* squeeze. "He only acts like one."

Thor volleyed back a look that said Pru might want to not leave her favorite shoes unattended tonight.

The woman's focus turned back to the fountain and she eyed the quarter in her hand. "They say it's never too late to wish on love, right?"

"Right," Pru said. Because they did say that. And just because in her own personal experience love had proven even rarer than unicorns didn't mean she'd step on someone else's hopes and dreams.

A sudden bolt of lightning lit up the San Francisco skyline like the Fourth of July. Except it was June, and cold as the Arctic. Thor squeaked and shoved his face into Pru's neck. Pru started to count but didn't even get to One-Mississippi before the thunder boomed loud enough to make them all jump.

"Yikes." The woman dropped the quarter back into her purse. "Not even love's worth getting electrocuted." And she ran off.

Pru and Thor did the same, heading across the cobblestone courtyard. Normally she took her time here, enjoying the glorious old architecture of the building, the corbeled brick and exposed iron trusses, the big windows, but the rain had begun to fall in earnest now, hitting so hard that the drops bounced back up to her knees. In less than ten seconds, she was drenched

9

through, her clothes clinging to her skin, filling her ankle boots so that they squished with each step.

"Slow down, sweetness!" someone called out. It was the old homeless guy who was usually in the alley. With his skin tanned to the consistency of leather and his long, wispy white cotton-ball hair down to the collar of his loud pineapples-and-parrots Hawaiian shirt, he looked like Doc from *Back to the Future,* plus a few decades. A century tops. "You can't get much wetter," he said.

But Pru wasn't actually trying to dodge the weather, she loved the rain. She was trying to dodge her demons, something she was beginning to suspect couldn't be done.

"Gotta get to my apartment," she said, breathless from her mad dash. When she'd hit twenty-six, her spin class instructor had teasingly told her that it was all downhill from here on out, she hadn't believed him. Joke was on her.

"What's the big rush?"

Resigned to a chat, Pru stopped. Old Guy was sweet and kind, even if he had refused to tell her his name, claiming to have forgotten it way back in the seventies. True or not, she'd been feeding him since she'd moved into this building three weeks ago. "The

10

cable company's finally coming today," she said. "They said five o'clock."

"That's what they told you yesterday. And last week," he said, trying to pet Thor, who wasn't having any of it.

Another thing on Thor's hate list — men.

"But this time they mean it," Pru said and set Thor down. At least that's what the cable company supervisor had promised Pru on the phone, and she needed cable TV. Bad. The finals of *So You Think You Can Dance* were on tomorrow night.

" 'Scuse me," someone said as he came from the elevator well and started to brush past her. He wore a hat low over his eyes to keep the rain out of his face and the cable company's logo on his pec. He was carrying a toolbox and looking peeved by life in general.

Thor began a low growl deep in his throat while hiding behind Pru's legs. He sounded fierce, but he looked ridiculous, especially wet. He had the fur of a Yorkshire terrier — if that Yorkshire terrier was fat — even though he was really a complete Heinz 57. And hell, maybe he *was* part cat. Except that only one of his ears folded over. The other stood straight up, giving him a perpetually confused look.

No self-respecting cat would have allowed

such a thing. In fact, the cable guy took one look at him and snorted, and then kept moving.

"Wait!" Pru yelled after him. "Are you looking for 3C?"

He stopped, his gaze running over her, slowing at her torso. "Actually," he said. "I'm more a double D man myself."

Pru looked down at herself. Her shirt had suctioned itself to her breasts. Narrowing her eyes, she crossed her arms over her decidedly not DDs. "Let me be more clear," she said, tightening her grip on Thor's leash because he was still growling, although he was doing it very quietly because he only wanted to pretend to be a tough guy. "Are you looking for the person who lives in *apartment* 3C?"

"I was but no one's home." He eyed Thor. "Is that a dog?"

"Yes! And *I'm* 3C," Pru said. "I'm home!"

He shook his head. "You didn't answer your door."

"I will now, I promise." She pulled her keys from her bag. "We can just run up there right now and —"

"No can do, dude. It's five o'clock straight up." He waved his watch to prove it. "I'm off the clock."

"But —"

But nothing, he was gone, walking off into the downpour, vanishing into the fog like they were on the set of a horror flick.

Thor stopped growling.

"Great," Pru muttered. "Just great."

Old Guy slid his dentures around some. "I could hook up your cable for you. I've seen someone do it once or twice."

The old man, like the old Pacific Heights building around them, had seen better days, but both held a certain old-fashioned charm — which didn't mean she trusted him inside her apartment. "Thanks," she said. "But this is for the best. I don't really need cable TV all that bad."

"But the finals of *So You Think You Can Dance* are on tomorrow night."

She sighed. "I know."

Another bolt of lightning lit the sky, and again was immediately followed by a crack of thunder that echoed off the courtyard's stone walls and shook the ground beneath their feet.

"That's my exit," Old Guy said and disappeared into the alley.

Pru got Thor upstairs, rubbed him down with a towel and tucked him into his bed. She'd thought she wanted the same for herself, but she was hungry and there was nothing good in her refrigerator. So she quickly changed into dry clothes and went back downstairs.

Still raining.

One of these days she was going to buy an umbrella. For now, she made the mad dash toward the northeast corner of the building, past the Coffee Bar, the Waffle Shop, and the South Bark Mutt Shop — all closed, past The Canvas tattoo studio — open — and went straight for the Irish Pub.

Without the lure of cable to make her evening, she needed chicken wings.

And nobody made chicken wings like O'Riley's.

It's not the chicken wings you're wanting, a small voice inside her head said. And that was fact. Nope, what drew her into O'Riley's like a bee to honey was the six-foot, broad-shouldered, dark eyes, dark smile of Finn O'Riley himself.

From her three weeks in the building, she knew the people who lived and/or worked here were tight. And she knew that it was in a big part thanks to Finn because he was the glue, the steady one.

She knew more too. More than she should.

"Hey!" Old Guy stuck his head out of the alley. "If you're getting us wings, don't forget extra sauce!"

She waved at him, and once again dripping wet, entered O'Riley's where she stood for a second getting her bearings.

Okay, that was a total lie. She stood there *pretending* to get her bearings while her gaze sought out the bar and the guys behind it.

There were two of them working tonight. Twenty-two-year-old Sean was flipping bottles, juggling them to the catcalls and wild amusement of a group of women all belly up to the bar, wooing them with his wide smile and laughing eyes. But he wasn't the one Pru's gaze gravitated to like he was a rack of double-stuffed Oreo cookies.

Nope, that honor went to the guy who ran the place, Sean's older brother. All lean muscle and easy confidence, Finn O'Riley wasn't pandering to the crowd. He never did. He moved quickly and efficiently without show, quietly hustling to fill the orders, keeping an eye on the kitchen, as always steady as a rock under pressure, doing all the real work.

Pru could watch him all day. It was his hands, she'd decided, they were constantly moving with expert precision. He was busy, way too busy for her, of course, which was only one of the many reasons why she hadn't allowed herself to fantasize about him doing deliciously naughty, wicked things to her in her bed.

15

Whoops. That was another big fat lie.

She'd *totally* fantasized about him doing deliciously naughty, wicked things to her in bed. And also out of it.

He was her unicorn.

He bent low behind the bar for something and an entire row of women seated on the barstools leaned in unison for a better view. Meerkats on parade.

When he straightened a few seconds later, he was hoisting a huge crate of something, maybe clean glasses, and not looking like he was straining too much either. This was in no doubt thanks to all that lean, hard muscle visible beneath his black tee and faded jeans. His biceps bulged as he turned, allowing her to see that his Levi's fit him perfectly, front *and* back.

If he noticed his avid audience, he gave no hint of it. He merely set the crate down on the counter, and ignoring the women ogling him, nodded a silent hello in Pru's direction.

She stilled and then craned her neck, looking behind her.

No one there. Just herself, dripping all over his floor.

She turned back and found Finn looking quietly amused. Their gazes locked and held for a long beat, like maybe he was taking

16

her pulse from across the room, absorbing the fact that she was drenched and breathless. The corners of his mouth twitched. She'd amused him again.

People shifted between them. The place was crowded as always, but when the way was clear again, Finn was still looking at her, steady and unblinking, those dark green eyes flickering with something other than amusement now, something that began to warm her from the inside out.

Three weeks and it was the same every single time . . .

Pru considered herself fairly brave and maybe a little more than fairly adventurous — but not necessarily forward. It wasn't easy for her to connect with people.

Which was the only excuse she had for jerking her gaze away, pretending to eye the room.

The pub itself was small and cozy. One half bar, the other half pub designated for dining, the décor was dark woods reminiscent of an old thatched inn. The tables were made from whiskey barrels and the bar itself had been crafted out of repurposed longhouse-style doors. The hanging brass lantern lights and stained-glass fixtures along with the horse-chewed, old-fence baseboards finished the look that said

17

antique charm and friendly warmth.

Music drifted out of invisible speakers, casting a jovial mood, but not too loud so as to make conversation difficult. There was a wall of windows and also a rack of accordion wood and glass doors that opened the pub on both sides, one to the courtyard, the other to the street, giving a view down the hill to the beautiful Fort Mason Park and Marina Green, and the Golden Gate Bridge behind that.

All of which was fascinating, but not nearly as fascinating as Finn himself, which meant that her eyes, the traitors, swiveled right back to him.

He pointed at her.

"Me?" she asked, even though he couldn't possibly hear her from across the place.

With a barely there smile, he gave her a finger crook.

Yep. Her.

Chapter 2

#TAKEMETOYOURLEADER

Pru's brain wondered what her mom would've said about going to a man who crooked his finger at her. But Pru's feet didn't care, they simply took her right to him.

He handed her a clean towel to dry off. Their fingers brushed, sending a tingle straight through her. While she enjoyed that — hey, it was the most action she'd gotten in a very long time — he cleared her a seat.

"What can I get you?" His voice was low and gravelly, bringing to mind all sorts of inappropriate responses to his question.

"Your usual?" he asked. "Or the house special?"

"What would that be?" she asked.

"Tonight it's a watermelon mojito. I could make it virgin-style for you."

He saw God knew how many people day in and day out, and on top of that the two of them hadn't spoken much more than a few words to each other, but he remembered what she liked after a long day at work out on the water.

And what she didn't. He'd noticed that she didn't drink alcohol. Hard to believe that when he had a pub menu, a regular alcoholic beverage menu, and also a special menu dedicated solely to beer, he could keep it all straight. "You kept track of my usual?" she asked, warmed at the idea. Warmed and a little scared because she shouldn't be doing this, flirting with him.

"It's my job," he said.

"Oh." She laughed at herself. "Right. Of course."

His eyes never left her face. "And also because your usual is a hot chocolate, which matches your eyes."

Her stomach got warmer. So did some of her other parts. "The virgin special would be great, thanks."

The guy on the barstool next to her swiveled to look at her. He was in a suit, tie loosened. "Hi," he said with the cheerfulness of someone who was already two drinks into his night. "I'm Ted. How 'bout I buy you an Orgasm? Or maybe even" — wink, wink — "multiples?"

Finn's easy, relaxed stance didn't change but his eyes did as they cut to Ted, serious now and a little scary hard. "Behave," he warned, "or I'll cut you off."

"Aw, now that's no fun," Ted said with a toothy smile. "I'm trying to buy the pretty lady a drink, is all."

Finn just looked at him.

Ted lifted his hands in a sign of surrender and Finn went back to making drinks. Soon as he did, Ted leaned in close to Pru again. "Okay now that daddy's gone, how about Sex On The Beach?"

Finn reached in and took Ted's drink away. "Annnnd you're out."

Ted huffed out a sigh and stood up. "Fine, I gotta get home anyway." He flashed a remorseful smile at Pru. "Maybe next time we'll start with a Seduction."

"Maybe next time," she said, picking one of the sweet, noncommittal smiles from her wide repertoire of smiles that she used on the job captaining a day cruise ship in the bay. It took a lot of different smiles to handle all the people she dealt with daily and she had it down.

When Ted was gone, Finn met her gaze. "Maybe next time?" he repeated.

"Or, you know, never."

Finn smiled at that. "You let him down easy."

"Had to," she said. "Since you played bad cop."

"Just part of the service I offer," he said, not at all bothered by the bad cop comment. "Did you have to cancel your last tour today?"

So apparently he knew what she did for a living. "Nope. Just got back."

"You were out in this?" he asked in disbelief. "With the high winds and surf alerts?"

His hands were in constant motion, making drinks, chopping ingredients, keeping things moving. She was mesmerized by the way he moved, how he used those strong hands, the stubble on his jaw . . .

"Pru."

She jerked her gaze off his square jaw and found his locked on hers. "Hmm?"

A flash of humor and something else came and went in his eyes. "Did you have any problems with the high winds and surf out there today?"

"Not really. I mean, a little kid got sick on his grandma, but that's because she gave him an entire bag of cotton candy and then two hot dogs, and he wolfed it all down in like two seconds, so I'm not taking the blame there."

He turned his head and looked out the open doors facing the courtyard. Dusk had fallen. The lights strung in pretty ribbons over and around the wrought iron fencing and fountain revealed sheets of rain falling from the sky.

She shrugged. "It didn't start raining until I was off the water. And anyway, bad weather's a part of the job."

"I'd think staying alive would be a bigger part of the job."

"Well yes," she said on a laugh. "Staying alive is definitely the goal." Truth was, she rarely had problems out on the water. Nope, it was mostly real life that gave her problems. "It's San Francisco. If we didn't go out in questionable weather, we'd never go out at all."

He took that in a moment as he simultaneously cleaned up a mess at the bar and served a group a few seats down a pitcher of margaritas, while still managing to make her feel like he was concentrating solely on her.

It's his job, her brain reminded her body. But it felt like more.

From the other side of the pub came a sound of a plate hitting the floor. Finn's eyes tracked over there.

One of his waitresses had dropped a dish, and the table she'd been serving — a rowdy group of young guys — were cheering, embarrassing her further.

Finn easily hopped over the bar and strode over there. Pru couldn't hear what he said but the guys at the table immediately straightened up, losing their frat boy antics mentality.

Finn then turned, crouched low next to his waitress, helped her clean up, and was back to the bar in less than sixty seconds.

"You've got an interesting job," he said, coming back to their conversation like nothing had happened.

"Yes," she said, watching as the waitress moved to the kitchen with a grateful glance in Finn's direction. "Interesting. And fun too." Which was incredibly important to her because . . . well, there'd been a very long stretch of time when her life hadn't been anything close to resembling a good time.

"Fun." Finn repeated the word like it didn't compute. "Now there's something I haven't had in a while."

Something else she already knew about him, and the thought caused a slash of regret to cut through her.

Sean came up alongside Finn. The brothers looked alike; same dark hair, same dark green eyes and smiles. Finn was taller, which didn't stop Sean from slinging an arm around his older brother's neck as he winked at Pru. "You'll have to excuse grandpa here. He doesn't do fun. You'd do better to go out with me."

Sean O'Riley, master flirt.

But Pru was a master too, by necessity. She'd had to become well versed in dealing with charming flirts at work. It didn't matter if it was vacationers, tourists, or college kids . . . they all got a kick out of having a female boat captain, and since she was passable in the looks department and a smartass to boot, she got hit on a lot. She always declined, even the marriage proposals. *Especially* the marriage proposals. "I'm flattered," she said with an easy smile. "But I couldn't possibly break the hearts of all the women waiting for their *cocktail* fantasies to come true."

"Damn." Sean mimed a dagger to the heart but laughed good-naturedly. "Do me a favor then, would ya? If you're going to take this one for a spin" — he elbowed Finn — "Show him how to live a little and maybe take him for a walk on the wild side while you're at it."

Pru slid her gaze to Finn, which was how she caught the quick flash of irritation as Sean sauntered off. "You need help living a little?" she asked him lightly. Not easy to do since her heart had started pounding, her pulse racing, because what was she doing? Was she really playing with him? It was a bad idea, the worst of all her bad ideas put together, and she'd had some real doozies over the years.

Don't be stupid. Back away from the cute hottie. You can't have him and you know why.

But the troubling train of thought stopped on a dime when Finn laughed all rumbly and sexy, like maybe he saved it for special occasions.

"Actually," he said, "I've lived plenty. And as for taking a walk on the wild side, I wrote the book on it." He leaned on the bar, which brought him up close and personal. Eyes locked on hers, he stroked a strand of wet hair from her temple.

She went still, like a puppy waiting for a belly rub, staring up at him, her heart still pounding, but for another reason entirely now. "What changed?" she asked, whispered really, because she was pretty sure she knew what the catalyst had been and it was going to kill her to hear him say it.

He shrugged. "Life."

Oh how she hated that for him. Hated it, and felt guilty for it. And not for the first time when she felt overwhelmed and out of her league, she opened her mouth and put her foot in it. "You know, in some circles

26

I'm known as the Fun Whisperer."

He arched a brow. "Is that right?"

"Yep," she said, apparently no longer in control of her mouth. "The fun starts right here with me. I specialize in people not living their lives, the ones letting their life live them. It's about letting stuff go, you see." Seriously. Why wasn't her mouth attached to a shut-the-hell-up filter?

Finn smiled and blew half her brain cells. "You going to teach me how to have fun, Pru?" he asked in that low, husky voice.

Good God, the way her name rolled off his tongue had her knees wobbling. She could see now that his eyes weren't a solid dark green, but had swirls of gold and brown and even some blue in them in the mix as well. She was playing with fire and all her inner alarms were going off.

Stop.

Don't engage.

Go home.

But did she do any of those things? No, she did not. Instead she smiled back and said, "I could knock the ball out of the park teaching you how to have fun."

"I have no doubt," he murmured, and blew all her remaining brain cells.

CHAPTER 3
#GOBIGORGOHOME

It wasn't until Finn shifted away to help one of his servers that Pru let out a shuddery breath. *I'm known as the Fun Whisperer?* She smacked her own forehead, which didn't knock any sense into her. Ordering her hormones to cool their jets, she turned away to take in the rest of the pub.

She was immediately waved over to the far end of the bar, which she'd missed when she'd first come in because hello, she'd honed in on Finn like a homing pigeon.

Informally reserved for those who lived and worked in the building, this end of the bar was instant camaraderie as someone you knew was always there to eat or drink with.

Tonight that someone was Willa, sole proprietor of the South Bark Mutt Shop, a one-stop pet store on the southwest ground-floor corner of the building.

Willa eyed a still very wet Pru and without

a word pushed a plate of chicken wings her way.

"You're a mind reader," Pru said and slid onto the seat next to her.

Willa laughed at the squishy, watery sound Pru made when she sat. "When you live in a city that's all hills and rain and soggy rainbow flags you learn really fast what's valuable. An umbrella with all its spokes . . . and a man who believes in happily-ever-afters."

Pru laughed. "Aw. You believe in fairy tales."

Willa smiled, her bright green eyes dancing. If you took in her strawberry red hair cut in layers framing her pretty face and coupled it with her petite, curvy frame, she looked like she belonged in a fairy tale herself, waving her magic wand. "You don't believe the right guy's out there for you?"

Pru took a big bite of a mouth-watering chicken wing and moaned. Swallowing, she licked some sauce off her thumb. "I just think I'd have better luck searching for a unicorn."

"You could wish on the fountain," Willa said.

The fountain in their courtyard had quite the reputation, as the woman she'd seen earlier had clearly known. The 1928 four-

29

story building had actually been built around the fountain, which had been here in the Cow Hollow district of San Francisco for fifty years before that, when the area still resembled the Wild West and was chock-full of dairies and roaming cattle.

Back then only the hearty had survived. And the desperate. Born of that, the fountain's myth went that a wish made here out of true desperation, with an equally true heart, would bring a first, true love in unexpected ways.

It'd happened just enough times over the past hundred plus years that the myth had long since become infamous legend.

A big hand set a mouth-watering looking watermelon mojito mocktail in front of her, the muscles in his forearm flexing as he moved. Pru stared at it for a beat before she managed to lift her gaze to Finn's. "Thanks."

"Try it."

She obediently did just that. "Oh my God," she murmured, pleasure infusing her veins. "What's in it?"

He smiled mysteriously, and something warm and wondrous happened deep inside her.

"Secret recipe," he said while she was still gaping up at him. He turned to Willa. "And your Irish coffee."

Willa squealed over the mountain of whipped cream topping the glass and jumped up to give Finn a tight squeeze.

Pru knew that they were very tight friends and it showed in their familiarity with each other. It didn't seem sexual at all so there was no need for jealousy but Finn definitely let down his guard with Willa. And it was *that*, Pru knew, that gave her the twinge of envy.

Finn waited until Willa sat and attacked her drink before he spoke again. "Your girl Cara tried to con Sean into a drink last night."

Willa, who'd just spooned in a huge bite of the cream, grimaced. She always had three or four employees on rotation at her shop, all of them some sort of rescue, many of them underage. "She have a fake ID?"

"Affirmative," Finn said. "He cut it up on my orders."

Willa sighed. "Bet that went over like a fart in church."

Finn lifted a shoulder. "We handled it."

Willa reached out and squeezed his hand. "Thanks."

Finn nodded and turned his attention back to Pru, who'd sucked down a third of her drink already. "You need your own

31

order of chicken wings?"

What she needed didn't involve calories. It involved a lobotomy. "Yes, please."

"You warming up yet?"

Yes, but that might've had more to do with his warm gaze than the temperature in the room. "Getting there," she managed.

The barest of smiles curved his mouth.

Idle chitchat. That's all this was, she reminded herself. They were just like any other casual acquaintances who happened to be in the same place at the same time.

Except there was nothing casual about her being here. Finn just didn't know it.

Yet.

She'd have to tell him eventually, because this *wasn't* a fairy tale. And she absolutely would tell him. But as a rule, she tended to subscribe to the later-is-best theory.

She realized he was watching her and she squirmed in her seat, suddenly very busy looking anywhere and everywhere except right into his eyes because they made her think about things. Things that made her nipples hopeful and perky.

Things that couldn't happen.

As if maybe he knew what he could do to her with just one look — or hey, it wasn't like her wet white shirt was hiding much — the corners of his mouth quirked.

Which was when she realized that Willa had stopped eating and was staring at the two of them staring at each other. When Willa opened her mouth to say something, something Pru was quite certain she didn't want said in front of Finn, she rushed to beat her friend to it. "On second thought, can I double that order of chicken wings?"

"Sure," Finn's mouth said.

Stop looking at his mouth! She forced herself to look into his eyes instead, those deep, dark, mossy green eyes, which as suspected, was a lot like jumping from the frying pan into the fire. "Um, I think that's my phone —" She started digging through her purse. Wrapping her fingers around her cell, she pulled it out and stared at the screen.

Nothing. It was black.

Dammit.

Finn smiled and walked away, heading back to the kitchen.

"Smooth," Willa said and sipped her Irish coffee.

Pru covered her face, but peeked out between her fingers, watching Finn go, telling herself she was completely nonplussed by her crazy reaction to him, but the truth was she just wanted to watch his very fine ass go.

"Huh," Willa said.

"No," Pru said. "There's no *huh.*"

"Oh, honey, there's a *huge* huh," Willa said. "I work with dogs and cats all day long, I'm fluent in eye-speak. And there's some serious eye-speak going on here. It's saying you two want to f—"

Pru pointed at her and snagged the last chicken wing, stuffing it into her mouth.

Willa just smirked. "You know, it's been a long time since I've seen Finn look at a woman like he just looked at you. A real long time."

Don't ask. *Don't ask* — "Why's that?" She covered her mouth. Then uncovered her mouth. Then covered it again.

Willa waited, eyes lit. "Not that *that* wasn't fun to watch, but are you finished arguing with yourself?"

Pru sighed. "Yeah."

"Finn's got a lot going on. Keeping the pub's head above water isn't easy in today's economy. Plus he's slowly renovating his grandparents' house so he can sell it and move out of the city —"

Pru's heart stopped and she swallowed a heavy bite of chicken wing. "He wants to leave San Francisco?"

"To live, yes. To work, no. He loves the pub, but he wants to live in a quieter place and get a big, lazy dog. And then there's his biggest time sink — keeping Sean on the straight and narrow. Add all of that up and it equals no time for —"

"Love?"

"Well, I was going to say getting lucky," Willa said. "But yeah, even less time for love."

Pru turned her head and watched Finn in action, taking care of his employees, his customers, his brother . . .

But who took care of him, she wondered as he worked his ass off, running this entire place and making it look easy while he was at it.

She knew it wasn't about making time. It was about what had happened eight years ago when he'd been just barely twenty-one. Her gut twisted, which didn't stop her from eating her entire plate of chicken wings when it came.

An hour later she left the bar warm, dry, and stuffed. Night had fallen. The rain had tapered off. With the clearing of most of the clouds, a sliver of a moon lit her way. The courtyard was mostly empty now, the air cool on her skin. Pots of flowers hung from hooks on the brick walls and also the wrought iron lining parts of the courtyard. During the day, the air was fragrant with the blooms but now all she could smell was the salty sea breeze.

A few people were coming and going, either from the pub or cutting through for a shortcut to the street and the nightlife the rest of the Cow Hollow and Marina area offered. But the sound of street traffic was muted here, partially thanks to the fountain's water cascading down to the wide, circular copper dome that had long ago become tarnished green and black. A stone bench provided a quick respite for those so inclined to stop and enjoy the view and the musical sound of the trickling water.

Pru stopped, staring at the coins shining brightly from the tiles at the bottom of the fountain. What was it the woman from earlier had said? *Never too late to wish for love . . .*

On a sudden whim, she went through her purse, looking for her laundry money. Pulling out a dime, she stared into the water. *A wish made here out of true desperation, with an equally true heart, will bring a first, true love in unexpected ways.*

Well, she had the desperation. Did she have the true heart? She put a hand to it because it did hurt, but that might've been the spicy chicken wings.

Not that it mattered because she wasn't

going to wish for herself. She was going to wish for true love for someone else, for a guy who didn't know her, not really, and yet she owed him far more than he'd ever know.

Finn.

She closed her eyes, sending her wish to . . . well, whoever collected them. The fountain fairy?

The Karma Fairy?

The Tooth Fairy?

Please, she thought, *please bring Finn true love because he deserves so much more happy than he's been dealt.* And then she tossed in the dime.

"I hope you find him."

Pru gasped and whirled around to face . . . Old Guy.

"What's his name?" he asked.

"Oh," she said on a low laugh. "I didn't wish for me."

"Shame," he said. "Though it doesn't really work, you know that, right? It's just a propaganda thing the businesses here in the Pacific Pier building use to draw in foot traffic."

"I know," Pru said, and crossed her fingers. *Please let him be wrong . . .*

"I tried it once," he told her. "I wished for my first love to return to me. But Red's still

37

dead as a doornail."

"Oh," Pru breathed. "I'm so sorry."

He shrugged. "She gave me twelve great years. Shared my food, my bed, and my heart for all of them. Slept with me every night and guarded my six like no other." He smiled. "She'd bring me game she'd hunted herself when we were hungry. She followed me everywhere. Hell, she didn't even mind when I'd bring another woman home."

Pru blinked. "That's . . . sweet?"

"Yeah. She was the best dog ever."

She reached out to smack him and he flashed a grin. "Don't be ashamed of wishing for love for yourself, sweetness," he said. "Everyone deserves that. Whoever he is, I hope he's worthy."

"No, really, it's not —"

"Or she," he said, lifting his hands. "No judging here. We all stick together, you know what I'm saying? Take Tim, the barista at the coffee shop. When he decided to become Tina a few years back, no one blinked an eye. Well, okay, I did at first," he admitted. "But that's only because she's hot as hell now. I mean, who knew?"

Pru nodded. Tina had made her coffee just about every morning for three weeks now, and on top of making the best muffins in all of San Francisco, she was indeed hot

38

as hell. "I'm not wishing for me though. I'm wishing for someone else. Someone who deserves it more than me."

"Well, then," he said, and patted down his pockets, coming up with a quarter, which he tossed in after her dime. "Never hurts to double down a bet."

CHAPTER 4
#CAREFULWHATYOUWISHFOR

Two days later Finn was at his desk pounding the keys on his laptop, trying to find the source of the mess Sean had made of their books while simultaneously fantasizing about one sexy, adorable "fun whisperer," and how much he'd like her to fun whisper him. He was a most excellent multitasker.

He liked that sassy smile of hers. He liked her easygoing 'tude. And he really liked her mile-long legs . . .

He was in the middle of picturing them wrapped around him when he found the problem.

Sean had done something to the payroll that had caused everyone to get fifty percent more than they had coming to them. Finn rubbed his tired eyes and pushed back from his desk. "Done," he said. "Found the screwup. You somehow managed to set payroll to time and a half."

Sean didn't say anything and Finn blew

out a breath. He knew that sometimes he got caught up in being the boss and forgot to be the older brother. "Look," he said, "it could've happened to anyone, don't take it so hard —"

At the sound of a soft snore, Finn craned his neck and swore.

Sean lay sprawled on his back on the couch, one leg on the floor, his arms akimbo, mouth open, dead asleep.

Finn strode over there and exercised huge restraint by kicking his brother's foot and not his head.

Sean sat straight up, murmuring, "That's it, baby, that's perfect —" When he saw Finn standing over him, he sagged and swiped a hand down his face. "What the hell, man. You just interrupted me banging Anna Kendrick."

Anna Kendrick was hot, but she had nothing on Pru Harris. "You're not allowed to sleep through me kicking your ass."

Sean didn't try to dispute the fact that Finn could, and had, kicked his ass on many occasions. "Anna Kendrick," he simply repeated in a devastated voice.

"Out of your league. And why the hell don't you sleep in your own office? Or better yet, at home."

Home being the Victorian row house they

shared in the neighborhood of Pacific Heights, half a mile straight up one of San Francisco's famed hills.

"I've got better things to do in my bed than sleep," Sean muttered and yawned. "What do you want anyway? I've cleaned my room and scrubbed behind my ears, *Mom.*"

"I'm not your damn mom."

This earned him a rude snort from Sean. Whether that was because Finn had indeed been Sean's 'damn mom' since the day she'd walked out on them when they'd been three and ten, or simply because Finn was the only one of them with a lick of sense, didn't matter.

"Focus," Finn said to his now twenty-two-going-on-sixteen-year-old brother. "I found the error you made in the payroll. You somehow set everyone to time and a half."

"Oh shit." Sean flopped back to the couch and closed his eyes again. "Rookie mistake."

"That's it?" Finn asked. "Just 'oh shit, rookie mistake'?" He felt an eye twitch coming on. "This is a damn partnership, Sean, and I need you to start acting like it. I can't do it alone."

"Hey, I told you, I don't belong behind a desk. My strength's in front of the customers and we both know it."

Finn stared at him. "There's more to running this place than making people smile."

"No shit." Sean cracked open an eye. "Without me out there hustling and busting my ass to charm everyone into a good time every night, there'd be no payroll to fuck up."

"You think that's all this pub is, a good time?" Finn asked.

"Well, yeah." Sean stretched his long, lanky body, lying back with his hands behind his head. "What else is there?"

Finn pressed his fingers against his twitching eye so that his brains couldn't leak out, but what did he expect? Back when he'd been twenty-one, he'd been as wild as they came. And then suddenly he'd found himself in charge of fourteen-year-old Sean when their dad had gotten himself killed in a car accident. It'd been hell, but eventually Finn had gotten his act together for both his own and Sean's sake. He'd had to.

When Sean had turned twenty-one last year, they'd opened the pub to give them both a viable future. And if Finn's other goal had been to keep Sean interested in something, *anything,* he couldn't very well now complain that Sean thought life was all fun and games.

"How about making a living?" Finn asked.

"You know, that little thing about covering our rent and food and other expenses, like your college tuition? What are you now, a third-year sophomore?"

"Fourth I think." Sean smiled, though it faltered some when Finn didn't return it. "Hey, I'm still trying to find my calling. This year probably. Next year tops. And then the good times really start."

"As opposed to what you're doing now?"

"Hey, we work our asses off."

"You work part-time at a pub, Sean. By the very definition of that, you're having fun every single day."

Sean snorted. "Seriously, man, we need to redefine your definition of fun. You're here twenty-four seven and you know it. You should've let Trouble show you what you're missing. She's cute, and best yet, she was game."

"Trouble?"

"Yeah, man. The new chick. Don't tell me you weren't feeling her. You made her a virgin version of our special. You don't do that for anyone else ever."

True. Also true was that he'd been drawn in by Pru's warm, shiny brown eyes. They matched her warm, shiny brown tumble of long hair, and then there was her laugh that always seemed to prove Pavlov's theory.

Except Finn's reaction wasn't to drool when he heard it.

"Did you know she's a ship captain?" Sean asked. "I mean that's pretty badass."

Yeah, it was. She drove one of the fleet ships out of Pier 39 for SF Bay Tours, a tough job to say the least. Finn's favorite part was her uniform. Snug, fitted white Captain's button-down shirt, dark blue trousers that fit her sweet ass perfectly, and kickass work boots, all of which had fueled more than a few dirty-as-fuck daydreams over the past three weeks.

He'd never forget his first glimpse of her. She'd been moving in, striding across the courtyard with a heavy box, her long legs churning up the distance, that willowy body with those sweet curves making his mouth water. She had her mass of wavy hair piled on top of her head — not that this had tamed the beast because strands had fallen into her face.

Yeah, he'd felt her from day one, and though she often sat at the end of the bar he reserved for his close-knit friends, he hadn't spoken much to her until two nights ago.

"She offered to show you a good time and you turned her down," Sean said, shaking his head in mock sadness. "And you call yourself the older brother. But yeah, you were probably right to turn her down. Would've been a waste of her efforts, seeing as you have no interest in anything remotely resembling a good time."

"I didn't turn her down."

"Flat, dude."

Finn hoped like hell Pru hadn't taken it that way, because he sure hadn't meant it like that. "I was working."

"Always are," Sean said. "Whelp" — he stood and stretched again — "this has been fun, but gotta run. The gang's hiking Twin Peaks today. First to the top gets number one draft pick in our fantasy football league. You should come."

"I won the league last year," Finn said.

"Uh huh. Which means we'd totally try to push you off the trail and sabotage your ascent. So you should definitely come."

"Wow, sounds like a real good time," Finn said. "But there's this . . ." He pointed to his desk and the mountain of work waiting on him.

Sean rolled his eyes. "You know what all work and no play makes you, right?"

"Not poor?"

"Ha-ha. I was going to say not laid."

This was unfortunately true but Finn

turned back to his desk. "Kick ass out there."

"Well, duh."

CHAPTER 5

#DIDIDOTHAT?

Hours later, Finn was still at his desk when Sean sauntered back in, hot, sweaty, and grinning. He helped himself to Finn's iced soda, downing it in three gulps. "Asses have been kicked," he said.

"No way did you beat Archer," Finn said. No one beat Archer at anything physical. The man was a machine.

"Nah, but I got second draft pick."

Annie, one of the three servers coming on shift for the night, stuck her head in. "Already filling up out front," she told them both.

"Got your back, darlin'," Sean said and set Finn's now empty glass back onto his desk. "Always."

Annie smiled dreamily at him.

Sean winked at her and slid out of the office before Finn could remind him of their *no sleeping* with the hired help policy. Swearing to himself, Finn grabbed his iPad and followed. He intended to go over inventory, but was immediately waved to the far end of the bar.

Sitting at it were some of his closest friends, most of them having been linked together in one way or another for years.

Archer lifted his beer in a silent toast. The ex-cop worked on the second floor of the building running a private security and investigation firm. He and Finn went back as far as middle school. They'd gone to college together. It'd been Archer who'd been with him in their shared, tiny frat boy apartment the night the cops had come to the door — not because Finn had been caught doing something stupid, but because his dad had just died.

Next to Archer sat Willa. Bossy as hell, nosy as hell, and loyal as hell, Willa would give a perfect stranger the shirt off her back if Finn and Archer didn't watch her like a hawk.

Spencer was there too. The mechanical engineer didn't say much, but when he did it was often so profound the rest of them just stared at him in shock and awe. Quiet, although not particularly shy or introverted, he'd recently sold his start-up for an undisclosed sum and hadn't decided on his next step. All Finn knew was that he was clearly unhappy.

Since pushing Spence was like trying to push a twenty-foot-wide concrete wall over, they'd all unanimously decided to let it be for now. Finn knew he'd talk about it when he was good and ready and nothing could rush that. For now he seemed . . . well, if not miserable, at least better, and was currently stealing French fries on the sly from Elle's basket.

Elle was new to the group but had fit right in with the exception of Archer. Finn didn't know what was up, but the two of them studiously avoided each other whenever possible. Everyone but Elle was in shorts and tees, looking bedraggled, a little sweaty and a whole lot dusty. Elle hadn't gone on the hike. She didn't do dirt. Or excursion. Dressed to kill as always, she wore a royal blue sleeveless sheath and coolly slapped Spence's hand away from her fries.

He grinned in apology but the minute Elle's back was turned, he stole another. Only Spence could do that and live.

Haley was there too, an intern at the optometrist's shop on the ground floor of the building. But Finn's gaze went directly to the last person sitting there, just as dusty as everyone but Elle.

Pru.

"Got suckered into the hike up Twin Peaks, huh?" he asked.

She smiled the smile of someone who was very proud of herself.

He grinned back. "Number four?" he guessed.

Her smile widened. "Three."

Whoa. Finn turned to Spence, who shrugged. "On the way there, I calculated out who and what everyone's going to pick in the draft," Spence said. "All I needed was the fourth pick, so I didn't see any reason to go crazy out there."

"You did that on the way there," Finn repeated, a little awed.

"Actually, I worked it out in my head before we even left."

Elle looked at Spence. "Remember when you told me to tell you when you were acting like that kid that no one would want to be friends with?"

Spence just grinned and stole another fry.

"She looks so delicate," Willa said and jabbed a thumb in Pru's direction. "Totally thought I could take her." She shook her head. "She wiped the trail with me."

"You do a lot of hiking?" Finn asked Pru.

"Not lately." She lifted a shoulder and sipped at what looked like a plain soda. "I haven't had time," she said demurely. "I'm out of shape."

Archer laughed. "Don't believe that for a second. This girl can move when she's got inspiration, and apparently she takes her fantasy football seriously. You should've seen those long legs in action."

Oh, Finn had. In his sexual fantasies.

"Why didn't you go?" she asked. "Didn't want to show off *your* long legs?"

Archer choked on beer. "I like her," he announced.

Finn didn't take his eyes off Pru. Hers were lit with amusement, which went well with the streak of dirt across her jaw. There was another over her torso, specifically her left breast. "I have great legs," he said.

"Uh huh."

"I do. Tell her," he said to the room.

Spence shrugged noncommittally. "Archer's are better."

Archer grinned. "Damn straight."

Elle let out a rare smile. "I like her too," she said to Archer.

"It's not about my legs," Finn said to Pru. Shit, and now he sounded defensive.

"Maybe you should prove it," she said casually and Archer choked again.

Willa bounced up and down in her seat, clapping. "It's like Christmas!"

"We're keeping her, right?" Spence asked.

"Hey," Sean said, bringing them another pitcher of beer. "If a lady wanted to see my legs, I'd show her. Just sayin'."

Asshole.

Pru turned expectantly back to Finn and he had to laugh. "What, right here?" he asked in disbelief.

"Why not?" she asked.

"Because . . ." Jesus. How had he lost control of this conversation? "I am not dropping trou right here," he said stiffly, and great, because now he sounded like he had a stick up his ass.

"Maybe he hasn't shaved," Willa said. "That'd keep me from dropping trou. I only shaved from my knees down. My thighs are as hairy as a lumberjack's chest, which is why I'm wearing capris and not short shorts. You are all welcome."

Elle nodded like this made perfect sense.

"Gonna have to prove it to the lady," Archer said ever so helpfully to Finn. "Drop 'em."

He was an asshole too.

Willa grinned and tapped her hands on the bar in rhythm and began to chant. "Drop 'em, drop 'em . . ."

The others joined in. Shit. They were *all* assholes.

Pru leaned in over the bar and gave him a

come here gesture. He shifted close and met her halfway, stilling when she put her mouth to his ear.

"No one but me can see behind the bar," she whispered.

It took a moment to compute her words because at first all he could concentrate on was the feel of her lips on his ear. When she exhaled, her warm breath caressed his skin and he had to remind himself that he was in a crowded bar, surrounded by his idiot friends.

She smiled enticingly.

"Not happening," he said on a laugh. At least not here, with an audience. He wondered if she'd still be playing with him if they were alone in his bed. Or if that was too far away, his office . . .

Her hair fell into his face and a stubborn silky strand stuck to the stubble on his jaw. He didn't care. She might be streaked with dirt but she smelled amazing.

He was mid-sniff when she whispered, "Fun Whisperer, remember?"

"Maybe I'm commando," he whispered back and was gratified by her quick intake of breath and the darkening of her eyes. "Either way," he said, "I don't drop trou on the first date."

She bit her lower lip and let her gaze drop

over him, probably trying to figure out if he was telling the truth about going commando.

Then her phone buzzed and she flashed him a grin as she stepped aside to answer it.

Sean came close and nudged him as they both watched Pru talk into her cell. "That's the woman for you."

"No," Finn said. "She's not. You know I don't date women in the building."

"Which would be a great rule if you ever left the building."

"I leave the building." To get to and from work, but still. He resented the implication that his life wasn't enough as is.

Elle shoved her glass under Sean's nose. She didn't like beer on tap. "Earn your keep, bar wench."

Sean rolled his eyes but took the glass. "What do you want, your highness? Something pink with an umbrella in it, I suppose?"

"Do I look like a college coed to you?" she asked. "I'll take a martini."

He grinned and shifted away to make it for her.

Willa came around to Finn's side of the bar. She was tiny, barely came up to his shoulder, but she was like a mother cat when riled. He knew better than to go toe to toe with her, especially when she was giving him The Look. But he wasn't in the mood. "No," he said.

"You don't even know what I'm going to say."

"You're going to say I'm being a stupid guy," Finn said. "But newsflash, I am a guy and sometimes we're stupid. Deal with it."

"I wasn't going to say that." She paused when he slid her a look and she sighed. "Okay, fine, I was. But you *are* being stupid."

"Shock," he said.

She put her hand on his arm until he blew out a breath and looked at her again.

"I'm worried about you," she said softly. "You've got yourself on lockdown. I know this place has taken off and you're so busy, but it's like Sean is the one having all the fun with it and you're just . . . letting him. What about you, Finn? When is it going to be about you?"

He turned and watched Sean work his magic charisma on a gaggle of young twenties at the other end of the bar. He'd never gotten to be just a kid. The least Finn could do was let him be twenty-two. "He deserves it."

"And you don't? You're working like crazy and just going through the motions."

True or not, he didn't want to hear it. "You want anything to eat?"

She sighed, getting the message, which was part of why he loved her so much. "No, thanks, I've gotta go. Gotta get up early tomorrow for a wedding. I've got a cake to make and flowers to arrange."

He found a smile. "Another dog wedding?"

In on the joke that she made more money off dog tiaras and elaborate animal weddings than grooming and pet supplies, she laughed. "Parrots."

Finn laughed too and gave her a hug goodnight. As she walked away, his gaze automatically searched for Pru. The gang was all moving to the back room and she was with them, heading for either the pool table or the dartboards. It was tourney night.

He took some orders and flagged down Sean to pass them off. "Fill these for Workaholic, Playboy, and Desperado at your four, five, and six o'clock." He turned and caught Pru staring at him. She'd come back for the bag of leftover chicken wings she'd forgotten.

"Workaholic, Playboy, and Desperado?" she asked.

"Customers," Sean explained.

"We all have nicknames?" she asked.

"No," Finn said.

"Yes," Sean said. And then the helpful bastard pointed out some more in the place. "Klutz, Pee-Dub, and Woodie."

"Pee-Dub?"

Sean grinned. "He's an old friend with a very new wife. He's Pussy-Whipped. PW, which cuts down to Pee-Dub. Get it?"

"I'm sorry to say I do," she said, laughing. "And Woodie?"

Sean smiled. "Would you like me to explain that one to you?"

Finn reached out, put his hand over Sean's face and shoved.

"Hey, she asked," he said, voice muffled.

"What's my nickname?" Pru asked.

Shit. This wasn't going to end well. "Not everyone has a nickname," he said.

She narrowed her eyes. "Spill it, Grandpa."

Sean snorted.

Even Finn had to laugh. "Well it *should* be Pushy."

"Uh huh," she said. "Tell me something I don't know. Come on, what do you two call me?"

"Your first day in the building, it was Daisy," Sean told her. "Because you were holding flowers."

"From my boss for my new place," she said. "What changed?"

"We saw you feeding our homeless guy, so we switched it to Sucker."

"Hey," she said, hands on hips. "He's a nice guy and he was hungry."

"He's hungry because he makes pot brownies," Finn said. "They give him the munchies. And just so you know, we all feed him too. He's got food, Pru. He's just got a good eye for the sweet cuties who are also suckers."

She blushed and he laughed.

"So I'm Sucker? Really?"

"Nope," Sean said. "You're Trouble with a capital T."

Finn shook his head at him. "Don't you have some orders to fill?"

Sean laughed and walked off, leaving him with Pru.

"I'm not a *lot* of trouble," she said.

His gaze slid to her mouth. "You sure about that?"

"Completely." And then she flashed him an indeed trouble-filled smile.

And that's when he knew. *He* was the one in trouble. Deep trouble. "What can I get you?" he asked, his voice unintentionally husky.

"I was sent over here to get a set of darts."

"You play?" he asked, digging some out of a drawer.

"No, but I'm a quick learner. I can do this."

He felt yet another laugh bubble up. "Good 'tude," he said. "Tell Spence to go easy on you, darts are his game. And don't bet against Archer. He grew up a bar rat, you can't beat him."

She bit her lip. "He said he was new at darts."

"Shit," Finn said. "He already conned you, didn't he?"

"No worries," she said. "I've got this."

He watched her go, shook his head, and then got busy making drinks because Sean was very busy flirting with Man-eater at one of the tables, even though she had already eaten him up and spit him out just last month.

When Finn looked up again after fulfilling a bunch of orders, half an hour had gone by and some serious chanting was coming out of the back room.

"Bull's-eye, bull's-eye, bull's-eye . . ."

He whistled for Sean. "Need two mojitos," he said and dried off his hands before heading out from behind the bar.

"Hey, I'm busy," Sean complained. "Getting some digits over here. Where are you

60

going — Hey, you can't just walk away, you — *Hell*," he muttered when Finn didn't slow.

He entered the back room hoping like hell Archer wasn't taking advantage of Pru. She had a sweet smile, and even though he knew she had a mischievous side and a unique ability to change the energy in a room for the better, she was no match against his friends.

And more had shown up, including some of Archer's coworkers, all of whom were either out of the military or ex-cops. He could see Will and Max up there, both skilled as hell in darts and women.

Shit.

Pru was at the front of the room, at the first of three dart boards. She was blindfolded, dart in hand, tongue between her teeth in concentration as Will spun her around.

Spun her around?

He had time to think *what the fuck* before Will let her go and Pru threw her dart.

And nailed Finn right in the chest.

CHAPTER 6
#DONOTTRYTHISATHOME

At the collective shocked gasp of the room, Pru ripped off her blindfold and blinked rapidly to focus her vision. And what she focused in on with horror was the dart stuck in Finn's pec, the quill still quivering from impact.

Archer and Spence had their phones out and were taking pics with big grins but Pru saw nothing funny about this. "Oh my God," she whispered as she ran to him. *"Oh my God."* Panic blocked her throat as she gripped his arms and stared at the dart. "I hit you!"

"Bull's-eye," he said, looking down at it sticking out of his chest. "Not bad for a beginner."

He was joking. She'd hit him with a dart and he stood there joking. *Good God.* She wished for a big hole to swallow her up, but as already proven, she'd never had much luck with wishes. "I'm so sorry! Do we pull it out? Please, you've got to sit down." She was having trouble drawing air into her lungs. "You need to stay still. You could have a cracked rib or a pierced lung." Just the thought of which had her vision going cobweb-y. "Someone call 911!" she yelled.

Finn calmly pulled out the dart. "I'm fine."

But she wasn't, not even close. The tip of the dart was red. *His blood,* she thought as she felt her own drain from her face.

That's when the red stain began to spread through his shirt, blooming wide. She was living the worst scary movie she'd ever seen. "Oh, God, Finn —" She was freaking out, she could feel herself going cold with fear as she again tried to push him into a chair and put both hands over the blood spot to apply pressure at the same time.

He stood firm, not budging an inch as he captured her hands in his and bent a little to look into her eyes. "Breathe, Pru."

"But I — You — I'm so sorry," she heard herself say from what seemed like a long way off. "I wished for true love, not death, I swear!"

"Pru —"

She couldn't answer. There was a buzzing in her ears now, getting louder and louder, and then her vision faded to black.

Pru came to with voices floating around her head.

"Nice going, Finn. You finally got a good one on the line and you kill her." Archer, she thought.

"She's got a tat," someone else said — Spence? — making Pru realize her shirt had ridden up a little, exposing the compass on her hipbone, the tattoo she'd gotten after her parents' death, when she'd been missing them so much she hadn't known how to go on without them. The world had become a terrifying place, and all alone in the world she'd needed the symbol of knowing which direction to go.

"Finn's more of a piercing kind of guy," Spence said.

"I bet today he's more of a tat guy," Archer said.

"Hell, I'm sold," Spence said.

Pru shoved down her shirt and opened her eyes. She was prone on a couch with a bunch of disembodied faces hovering over her.

"She's pretty green," Spence's face said. "Think she's going to hurl?"

Willa's face was creased into a worried

frown. "No, but I don't think she's moisturizing enough."

"Does she need mouth-to-mouth?" Sean.

"Out. All of you." The low but steely demand came from Finn and had all the faces vanishing.

Pru realized she was in an office. Finn's, by the look of things. There was a desk, a very comfortable couch beneath her, and on the other side of it, a large picture window that revealed a great view of the courtyard and the fountain.

She narrowed her eyes at the fountain, sending it *you're dead to me* vibes. Because really? She'd wished for love for Finn and instead she'd stabbed him with a damn dart.

Gah.

Finn was shoving people out the door. When they were gone, he leaned back against his desk to look at her, feet casually crossed, hands gripping the wood on either side of his hips. He was hot, even in a pose of subdued restraint as he watched her carefully while she sat up. "Easy, Tiger."

"What happened?" she asked. When she struggled to stand, he pushed off from the desk, coming to her.

Crouching at her side, he stopped her, setting his hands on her thighs to hold her still. "Not yet."

"How did I get here?"

"You fainted," he said.

"I most definitely did not!"

His lips twitched. "Okay, then you decided to take a nap. You weren't feeling the whole walking thing so I carried you."

She stared at him, horrified. "You carried me?"

"That bothers you more than the fainting in front of a crowded bar?" he asked. He shrugged. "Okay, sure, we can go with that. Yes, I picked you up off the floor and carried you. Not that I don't make sure the floors are clean mind you, but there's clean and then there's clean, so I brought you to my couch."

"Ohmigod," she gasped, "I hit you with a dart!"

He was still crouched at her feet. Close enough for her to push his hands from her and start tugging up his shirt, needing to see the damage. "Let me see. I'm a halfway decent medic — which I realize is hard to believe given I ended up on your floor — but I promise, I know what I'm doing." She couldn't shove his shirt up high enough. "Off," she demanded.

"Well usually I like to have a meal first," he said, "and get to know each other a little bit —"

"Off!"

"Okay, okay." He reached up and pulled the shirt over his head.

Pru nearly got light-headed again but this time it wasn't the blood. He had a body that . . . well, rocked hers. Sleek and hard-looking, he had broad shoulders, ripped abs, sinewy pecs — one of which had a hole in it an inch from his right nipple. A fact she knew because she'd leaned in so close her nose nearly brushed his skin.

"Feel free to kiss it better," he said.

"I'm checking to see if you're going to need a tetanus shot!" But good Lord, she'd done this to him. She'd put a hole in his perfect, delectable bod —

"Are you going to pass out again?" he asked.

"No!" Hopefully. But to be sure, she sat back. Just for a second she promised herself, and only because replaying the night's events in her mind was making her sweat. "First-aid kit," she said a little weakly.

"What do you need?" he asked, voice deep with concern.

"Not for me, for you!" She sat up again. "You could get an infection, we need a first-aid kit!"

He blew out a sigh, like maybe she was being a colossal pain in his ass. But he rose to his feet and walked toward a door behind his desk. The problem was now she could see his back, an acre of smooth, sleek skin, rippling muscles . . .

He vanished into a bathroom and came back with a first-aid kit, and then sat at her side on the couch. Before he could open it up, she took it from his hands and rummaged through. Finding what she needed, she poured some antiseptic onto a cotton pad and pressed it against the wound.

He sucked in a breath and she looked up at him. "Getting hit with a dart didn't make you blink an eye," she said. "Neither did ripping it out like a He-man. But this hurts?"

"It's cold."

This got a low laugh out of her. She was trying not to notice that her fingers were pressed up against his warm skin as she held the cotton in place, or that her other hand had come up to grip his bicep. Or that his nipples had hardened.

Or that she was staring at his body, her eyes feeling like a kid in a candy shop, not quite knowing where to land. Those pecs. That washboard set of abs. The narrow happy trail that vanished into the waistband of his jeans, presumably leading straight to his —

"I think I'm all disinfected now," he said, sounding amused.

With a jerky nod, she set the cotton pad aside and reached for a Band-Aid. But her hands were shaking and she couldn't open the damn thing.

His fingers gently took it from hers. Quickly and efficiently, he opened it and put it on himself. "All better," he said and quirked a brow. "Unless . . ."

"Unless what?"

"You changed your mind about kissing it all better?"

That she wanted to do just that kept her from rolling her eyes again.

He laughed softly, which she assumed was because the bastard knew exactly what he did to her.

"So," he said. "You were right. You really do bring the fun. What's next?"

"Hitting you over your thick head with this first-aid kit," she said, closing the thing up.

"You're violent." He grinned at her. "I like it."

"You have a very odd sense of humor." She stood on legs that were still a little wobbly. "I really am sorry, Finn."

"No worries. I've had worse done to me."

"Like?"

"Well . . ." He appeared to give this some thought. "A woman once chucked a beer bottle at my face." He pointed to a scar above his right eyebrow. "Luckily I ducked."

She gaped at him. "Seriously?"

He shrugged. "She thought I was Sean."

"Well that explains it," she said and had the pleasure of making him laugh.

His laugh did things to her. So did the fact that he was still shirtless. "Do you have another shirt?" she asked.

"One without a hole in it, you mean?"

She groaned. "Yes! And without blood all over it." She bent and scooped up his fallen shirt. "I'm going to buy you a new one —" she started as she rose back up and . . . bumped into him.

And his bare chest.

"Stop," he said kindly but firmly as his hands came up to her shoulders. "I'm not all that hurt and you've already apologized. It wasn't even your fault. My idiot brother should never have allowed blindfolded darts. If our insurance company got a whiff of that, we'd be dumped."

But Pru had a long habit of taking on the blame. It was what she did, and she did it well. Besides, in this case, her guilt came from something else, something much, much worse than stabbing him with a dart and she didn't know how to handle it. Especially now that they were standing toe to toe with his hands on her.

Tell him, a voice deep inside her said.

But she was having trouble focusing. All she could think about was pressing her mouth to the Band-Aid. Above the Band-Aid. Below the Band-Aid. Wayyyyy below the Band-Aid . . .

She didn't understand it. He wasn't even her usual type. Okay, so she wasn't sure what her type was exactly. She hadn't been around the block all that many times but she'd always figured she'd know it when she saw it.

But she was having the terrible, no-good, frightening feeling that she'd seen it in the impenetrable, unshakeable, unflappable, decidedly sexy Finn O'Riley.

Which of course made everything, *everything,* far worse so she closed her eyes. "Oh God. I could have killed you."

Just as her parents had killed his dad . . .

And at *that* thought, the one she'd been trying like hell to keep at bay, the horror of it all reached up and choked her, making it impossible to breathe, impossible to do anything but panic.

"Hey. *Hey,*" Finn said with devastating gentleness as he maneuvered her back to sitting on the couch. "It's all okay, Pru."

She could only shake her head and try to pull free. She didn't deserve his sympathy, didn't deserve —

"Pru. Babe, you've got to breathe for me."

She sucked in some air.

"Good," he said firmly. "Again."

She drew in another breath and the spots once again dancing in front of her eyes began to fade away, leaving her view of Finn, on his knees before her, steady as a rock. "I'm okay now," she said. And to prove it she stood on her own. To gain some desperately needed space, she walked away from him and walked around his office.

His big wood desk wasn't messy but wasn't exactly neat either, a wall lined with shelves on which sat everything from a crate of pub giveaways like beer cozies and mouse pads, to a big ball of Christmas lights.

Pictures covering one wall. His brother. His friends. A group shot of them on the roof of the building, where people went for star gazing, hot summer night picnicking, or just to be alone on top of the world.

There were a few pics of Finn too, although not many, she saw as she moved slowly along the wall, realizing the pics got progressively older.

There were several from many years ago.

Finn in a high school baseball uniform. And then a college uniform. He'd played ball for a scholarship and had been destined for the pros — until he'd quit school abruptly at age twenty-one when he'd had to give everything up to care for his younger brother after the death of his father.

She sucked in a breath and kept looking at the pictures. There was one of Finn and a group of guys wearing no shirts and backpacks standing on a mountaintop, and if she wasn't mistaken, one of them was Archer.

Another of Finn sitting in a souped-up classic-looking Chevelle next to a GTO, a pretty girl standing between the cars waving a flag. Clearly a pre-street-race photo.

Once upon a time, he'd indeed been wild and adventurous. And she knew exactly what had changed him. The question was, could she really help bring some of that back to him, something she wanted, *needed,* to do with all her heart.

Chapter 7

#WAFFLESAREALWAYSTHEANSWER

Finn watched Pru's shoulders tense as she looked at the pictures on the walls, and wished she'd turn his way so he could see her face. But she kept staring at the evidence of his life as if it was of the utmost importance to her. "You okay?" he asked.

She shook her head. Whether in answer to the question or because whatever was on her mind weighed too heavily to express, he had no idea. Turning her to him, he watched as her long lashes swept upward, her eyes pummeling him with a one-two gut punch.

And going off the pulse racing at the base of her throat, she was just as affected by him, which was flattering as hell but right now he was more concerned about the shadows clouding her eyes. "You're worried about something," he said.

She bit her lower lip.

"Let me guess. You forgot to put the plug in your boat and it might sink before your next shift."

As he'd intended, her mouth curved. "I never forget the plug."

"Okay . . . so you're worried you've maimed me for life and I'll have to give up my lucrative bartending career."

Her smile faded. "You joke," she said, "but I *could* have maimed you if I'd thrown higher."

"Or lower," he said and shuddered at the thought.

She closed her eyes and turned away again. "I'm really so very sorry, Finn."

"Pru, look at me."

She slowly turned to face him. There were secrets in her eyes that had nothing to do with the dart thing, and a hollowness as well, one that moved him because he recognized it. He'd seen it in the reflection of his own mirror. Moving in close, he reached for her hand, loosely entangling their fingers. He told himself it was so that he could catch her again if she went down but he knew the truth. He just wanted to touch her.

"I'm sure you have to get back out there —" she started.

"In a minute." He tugged her in a little so that they were toe to toe now. And thanks to her kickass boots, they were also nearly mouth to mouth. "What's going on, Pru?"

he asked, holding her gaze.

She opened her mouth but then hesitated. And when she spoke, he knew she'd changed whatever she'd been about to say. "Looks like your life has changed a lot," she said, gesturing to the pictures that Sean had printed from various sources, stuffed into frames, and put out on the shelf in chronological order the day after they'd opened the pub.

When Finn had asked him what the hell, Sean had simply said "not everyone is as unsentimental as you. Just shut up and enjoy them — and you're welcome."

Over the past year new pictures just showed up. More of Sean's doing. Finn got it. Sean felt guilty for all Finn had given up to raise him, but Finn didn't want him to feel guilty. He wanted him to take life more seriously.

"It's changed some," he allowed cautiously to Pru. He didn't know how they'd gotten here, on this subject. A few minutes ago she'd been all sweetly, adorably worried about him, wanting to play doctor.

And he'd been game.

"It looks like it's changed more than some," she said. "The fun pics stopped."

"Once I bought the pub, yeah," he said.

He'd had different plans for himself.

76

Without a maternal influence, and their dad either at work or mean as a skunk, he and Sean had been left to their own devices. A lot. Finn had used those years to grow up as fast and feral and wild as he could. Yeah, he'd been an ace athlete, but he'd also been a punk-ass idiot. He'd skated through on grades, which luckily had come easy for him so his coaches had been willing to put up with his crazy ass to have him on the team. His big plan had been to get drafted into the big leagues, tell his dad to go fuck himself, and retire with a big fat bank account.

It hadn't exactly gone down like that. Instead, his dad had gotten himself killed in a car accident that had nothing to do with his own road rage — he'd been hit by a drunk driver.

Barely twenty-one, Finn might've kept to his plan but Sean had been only fourteen. The kid would've been dumped into the system if Finn hadn't put a lock down on his wild side, grown up, and put them both on the straight and narrow.

It'd been the hardest thing he'd ever done, and there'd been lots of days he wasn't entirely sure he'd succeeded.

"Well I probably should . . ." Pru trailed off, gesturing vaguely to the door. But she didn't go. Instead she glanced at his mouth.

As far as signs went, it was a good one. She was thinking of his mouth on hers. Which seemed only fair since he'd given a lot of thought to the same thing.

" 'Night," she whispered.

"Night," he whispered back.

And yet neither of them moved.

She was still staring at his mouth, and chewing on her lower lip while she was at it. He wanted to lean in and take over, nibbling first one corner of her mouth and then the other, and then maybe he'd take a nibble of her plump lower lip too, before soothing it with his tongue. Then he'd work his way down her body the same to every last square inch of her —

"Right?" she asked.

He blinked. So busy thinking about what he wanted to do to her, about the sounds she might make as he worked her over with his tongue, he'd not heard a word she'd said. "Right."

She nodded and . . . walked away.

Wait — what the hell? He grabbed her hand and just barely stopped her. "Where are you going?"

"I just said I really should go and you said right."

Not about to admit he hadn't listened to

a word she'd said because he'd been too busy mentally fucking her, he just held onto her hand. "But you're the Fun Whisperer. You have to stay and save me, otherwise I'll go back to work."

"A real wild man," she said with a smile.

He gave another tug on her hand. She was already right there but she shifted in closer, right up against him.

She sighed, as if the feel of him was all she'd wanted, and then she froze. Her eyes were wide and just a little bit anxious now as she stared into his. "Uh oh."

Granted, it'd been awhile but that wasn't the usual reaction he got when he pulled a woman in close. "Problem?"

"No." She bit her lower lip. "Maybe."

"Tell me."

She hesitated and then said, "My mom taught me to show not tell." And then her hands went to his chest, one of them right over the Band-Aid, which she touched gently, running her fingers over it as if she wished she could take away the pain. "I just need to see something . . ."

"What?"

Her gaze dropped to his mouth and again she hesitated.

Tenderness mixed with his sudden pervasive hunger and need, a dizzying combina-

79

tion for a guy who prided himself on not feeling much. "Pru —"

"Shh a second," she whispered. And then closing the gap, she brushed her lips over his.

At the connection, he groaned, loving the way her hands tightened on him. She murmured his name, a soft plea and yet somehow also a demand, and he wanted to both smile and tug her down to the couch. Trying to cool his jets, trying to let her stay in charge, he attempted to hold back, but she let out this breathy little whimper like he was the best thing she'd ever tasted. Threading his fingers through her hair, he took over the kiss, slow, deeper now, until she let out another of those delicious little whimpers and practically climbed his body.

Yeah, she liked that, a whole hell of a lot, and he closed his arms hard around her, lifting her up against him for more. He'd known they had something but this . . . this rocked his world. Hers too because they both melted into it, tongues sliding, lips melding, bodies arching into each other in a slow rhythm.

The door to the office suddenly opened and Sean stood there, face tilted down to his iPad. "We've gotta problem with inventory —" he said, still reading. "Where the hell's the — *Oh,*" he said, finally looking up. "Shit. Now I owe Spence twenty bucks."

Finn resisted smashing in his brother's smug smile, barely, mostly because he didn't want to take his eyes off Pru who'd brought her fingers up to her still wet lips, looking more than a little dazed.

Join my club, babe . . .

"Sorry if I interrupted the sexy times," Sean said, not looking sorry at all. He smiled at Pru. "Hey, Trouble."

"Hey," she said, blushing. "I've got to go." She turned in a slow circle, clearly looking for her purse, finding it where he'd dropped it on the couch. She slung it over her shoulder and without actually making eye contact with either of them, said a quick " 'night" and headed to the door.

Finn caught her, brushing up against her back. "Let me walk you home —"

"I live only two flights up," she said, not looking at him. "Not necessary."

Right. But it was more than her safety he'd been worried about. She'd been with him during that kiss, very with him, but now there was a distance again and he wanted to breach it.

"If there's any complications from where I tried to kill you," she said to the door. "You need to —"

"I won't. I'm fine." He let his mouth brush her ear as he spoke and he could feel the shiver wrack her body.

"Okay then," she said shakily, and was gone.

Finn turned to Sean.

Who was grinning. "Look at you with all the moves. They grow up so fast."

"You ever hear of a thing called knocking?" Finn asked.

Sean shrugged. "Where's the fun in that?"

"Is everything about fun?"

"Yes!" Sean said, tossing up his hands. "Now you're getting it!"

Finn turned away and eyed the spot between the couch and the desk where he'd just about dragged Pru down to the floor and ended his long dry spell by sinking into her warm, sweet body. "What's the problem with the inventory?"

"It's down, the whole system's down."

Finn snatched the iPad and swiped the screen to access the data. "And you're just now telling me? Are you kidding me?"

"Yes," Sean said.

Finn lifted his head and stared at Sean. "What?"

His brother flashed a grin. "Yes I'm kidding. Funning around. Fucking with your head. I came back here because Archer and

Spence sent me in here to spy on you and Trouble. We bet twenty bucks. They thought you might be making a rare move."

Jesus.

"Not me though," Sean said. "I figured you're so rusty you'd need some pointers. And here's your first one — lock the door, man. *Always.*"

Finn headed toward him but Sean danced away with a grin. "Oh and pointer number two — you got your shirt off and that's a good start, but it's the pants that are the important part." He was chortling, having a great ol' time.

Finn smiled at him, shoved him out the door, and slammed it on his smug-ass face.

Then he hit the lock.

"*Now* you lock it?" Sean asked through the wood, rattling the handle. "Hey. You do know I nap on that couch. Tell me you didn't do it on the couch."

Finn turned away and headed to his desk.

Sean pounded on the door once. "You didn't, right?"

Finn put on his earphones and cranked some music on his phone. And then headed to his desk to wade through the mountain of work waiting on him.

Pru got to work extra early the next morning. It was month end and though Jake did his best to see that his boat captains didn't drown in paperwork, some of it was unavoidable. She wanted to catch up but she hadn't slept well and her eyes kept crossing. Finally, she caved and set her head down on her desk.

Just for a minute, she told herself . . .

Finn pressed his body to hers and she moaned as his hands stroked up her sides, his thumbs brushing over her nipples. She arched into him and he kissed her like it was an art form, like he had nothing more important to do than arouse her and he had all the time in the world to do it. She clutched at him and he ground his lower body into her, letting her feel how aggressively hard he was. Aching for him, she tangled her hands in his hair, kissing him deeper until he groaned into her mouth. "Please," she begged.

"Hell yeah, I'll please." His voice was sexy rough and she held tight, anchoring her hips against his as he slid a hand down her belly and into her panties.

He groaned again and she knew why. She was wet and on fire for him.

Breaking the kiss, he nibbled her ear. "Pru," he said in that deliciously gruff tone. "You have to wake up."

She jerked awake and sat straight up, realizing she'd fallen asleep at her desk doing the dreaded paperwork. "Wha . . . ?" she managed.

Finn was crouched at her side, fully dressed, and breathing a little ragged.

And that's when she realized something else — her hand was stroking what felt like a very impressive erection behind his jeans.

She snatched it back like she'd been burned and he dropped his head and gave a rough laugh. Ignoring how his laugh did funny things to her belly and parts south, she cleared her throat. "Sorry."

"Don't be. Best greeting ever."

"Okay, that was your fault," she muttered, her face heating. "That's what you get for waking me from a deep sleep."

"I'm not sure if you could call that sleep." He lifted his head. He was smiling, the smug jerk. "Jake let me in, pointed me in the direction of your office, which was unlocked. You were moaning and sweaty. I moved in to see if you were okay and you molested me."

She groaned and thunked her head to her desk a couple of times. "Why are you here?" she moaned. "Other than to rudely wake me up from the only action I've had in far too long?"

He laughed. *Laughed.* She gave some

thought to killing him but then she realized he was holding a brown bag from which came the most delicious scent.

"Stopped by the waffle shop for breakfast," he said and lifted the bag. "Thought of you."

She went still. "Chocolate and raspberry syrup?" she asked hopefully, willing to let bygones be bygones for a sugar and carb load.

"Of course."

She didn't ask how he knew her kryptonite. Everyone she knew worshipped at the magical griddle inside the magical food cart outside their building that a woman named Rayna ran. Pru snatched the bag from Finn and decided to forgive him. "Do not think that this means we will be reenacting what I was dreaming about."

"Absolutely not," he said.

She paused, her gut sinking to her toes unexpectedly. "Because you don't think of me that way?"

He paused as if carefully considering his next words, and she braced herself. She was good at rejection, real good, she reminded herself.

Apparently deciding against speaking at all, Finn rose to his full height. Since she was still in her chair, this put her face right about level with the part of his anatomy she'd had a grip on only a moment before.

He was still hard.

"Does this look like disinterest to you?"

She swallowed hard. "No."

"Any further questions?"

"Nope," she managed. "No further questions."

Nodding, he leaned over her and brushed his mouth across hers. "Ball's in your court," he said and then he was gone.

Chapter 8
#ALLTHECOOLKIDSAREDOINGIT

Pru got up the next morning at the usual time even though it was her day off. She pulled on her tank top and yoga capris and shoved her feet into her running shoes. "I hate running," she said to the room.

The comforter on her bed shifted slightly and she pulled it back to reveal Thor, eyes closed.

"I know you're faking," she said.

His eyes squeezed tight.

"Sorry, buddy, you're coming with me. I ate that entire *huge* waffle Finn brought me yesterday. And I realize you don't care if you can fit into a pair of skinny jeans without your belly rolling over the waistband, and you don't even know who Finn is, but trust me, you wouldn't have been able to resist him or the waffle either."

Thor didn't budge.

"A doggie biscuit," she said cajolingly. "If you get up right now I'll give you a doggie

88

biscuit."

Nothing. This was probably because he knew as well as she did that she was out of doggie biscuits. She would have just left him home alone but the last time she'd done that, he'd pooped in her favorite boots — which had most definitely taken some time and effort on his part.

"Fine." She tossed up her hands. "I'll buy biscuits today, okay? And we'll go see Jake too."

At the name, Thor perked up. He knew that Jake kept dog cookies in his desk so he lifted his head, panting happily, one ear up and the other flopped over and into his eye.

She had to smile. "You're the cutest boot pooper I've ever seen. Now let's hit it. We're going to run first if it kills us."

Thor hefted out a sigh that was bigger than he was but got up. She clipped his Big Dog leash on him, and off they went.

They ran through Fort Mason, along the trail above the water. Not that they could see the water today. The early morning fog had slid in so that Pru felt like she had a huge ball of cotton around her head. They came out at the eastern waterfront of the Port of San Francisco, constructed on top of an engineered seawall on reclaimed land that gave one of the most gorgeous views of the bay.

It was here that Thor refused to go another step. He sat and then plopped over and lay right in front of her feet.

A guy running the opposite way stopped short. "Did you just kill your dog?"

"No, he doesn't like to run," she said.

Clearly not believing her, he started to bend down to Thor, who suddenly found a reserve of energy — or at least enough to lift his head and bare his teeth at the strange man who'd dared to get too close.

The guy jumped back, tripped over his own feet, and fell on his ass.

"Oh my God. Are you all right?" she asked.

He leapt back up, shot her a dirty look, and ran off.

"Sorry," she called after him and then glared down at Thor. "You do know that one of these days someone's going to call animal control on me and get you taken away, right?"

He closed his eyes.

"Come on, get up." She nudged him with her foot. "We've got a little bit more calorie annihilating to do."

Thor didn't budge an inch except to give *her* the low growl now.

"You know what? Fine. We'll risk not fitting into our bathing suits. I don't like swimming anyway," she said, happy enough for the excuse to stop. They walked the rest of the way to the Aquatic Park Pier, which curved out into the bay, giving the illusion of standing out on the water.

A wind kicked up and she was glad to not be out on the water. "Going to be choppy," she said. Which meant at least one person per tour would get seasick. Not that it was her problem. "No throw-up on my calendar today."

Thor, comfy in her lap, licked her chin. He didn't mind throw-up. Or poo. The grosser the better in his opinion. Setting the dog down, she craned her neck and took in the sight of Ghirardelli Square behind them. It wasn't out of her way to walk over there, but if she did she'd buy chocolate and then she'd have to run tomorrow too. She was debating that when Thor was approached by a pigeon who was nearly bigger than he was.

Thor went utterly still, not moving a single muscle, the whites of his eyes showing.

The pigeon stopped, cocked its head, and then made a faux lunge at Thor.

Thor turned tail and ran behind Pru's legs.

"Hey," she said to the pigeon. "Don't be a bully."

The pigeon gave her a one-eyed stare and waddled off.

Pru scooped up Thor. "I need to get you glasses because you just frightened a full-grown man and then cowered from a bird."

Thor blinked his big eyes at her. "Wuff."

At the sound, the pigeon stopped and turned back. In her arms, all tough guy now, Thor growled.

Pru laughed. "I'm setting you down now, Mr. Badass. We're going to run into work real quick to pick up another box of my stuff —"

Thor cuddled into her, setting his head on her shoulder, giving her the big puppy eyes.

"Oh no you don't with that look," she said. "I'm not carrying you all the way there."

He licked her chin again.

She totally carried him all the way there.

"Jake!" she yelled as she and Thor entered the warehouse on Pier 39 from which SF Bay Tours was run. "Jake?"

Nothing. Besides being her boss, Jake was her closest friend, and for one week awhile back, he'd also been her lover. They hadn't revisited that for many reasons, not the least of which was because Pru had a little problem. She tended to fall for the guys she slept with.

All two of them.

The first one, Paul, had been her boyfriend for two whole weeks when her parents had died. And since she'd fallen apart and he'd been eighteen and not equipped to deal with that, he'd bailed. Understandable.

Jake had been next. He'd loved her, still did in fact, but he wasn't, and never would be, *in* love with her. And the truth was, she hadn't fallen in love with him either. She actually wasn't sure she was made for that kind of love, receiving or giving. She wanted to be. She really did. But wanting and doing had proven to be two entirely different beasts. *"Jake!"*

"Don't need to yell, woman, I'm not deaf."

With a gasp, she whirled around and found him right there. She hadn't heard him come up behind her, but then again, she never did.

Jake had been in Special Forces, which had involved something with deep-sea diving and a whole lot of danger, and in spite of it nearly killing him, he hadn't lost much of his edge. He hadn't smiled when she'd nearly jumped out of her skin but he'd thought about it because his eyes were amused.

Thor was not. When Pru had jerked, he'd gone off, barking at a pitch that rivaled banshees in heat. "Thor, hush!" she said and turned to Jake, hand to her heart. "Seriously, you take five years off my life every time you do that. And you gave Thor epilepsy."

Jake didn't apologize, he never did. The man was a complete tyrant. But a softie tyrant, who held out his arms for Thor.

The poor dog was still barking like he couldn't stop himself, eyes wide.

"You're such a pussy," Jake told him.

"Excuse me," Pru said. "You know he can't see very well and you scared him half to death. And hello, he's a *dude.* Which means you two share the same plumbing. So he's not a pussy, he's a big, *male* baby."

"He doesn't have *my* plumbing, chica," Jake said. "I might not have my legs but at least I still have my balls." And with that, he pushed off on his wheelchair, coming closer as he pulled something from his pocket.

A dog cookie.

He held it up for the gone-gonzo dog to see and Thor stopped barking and leapt to him without looking back.

Jake whirled his chair around, and man

plus dog took off.

Pru rolled her eyes and followed them past the NO ONE BUT CREW PAST THIS DOOR sign, down a hall, then down another to a living area. "We're not staying," Pru said. "I'm just picking up one of the last boxes of my stuff."

"If you'd just use my truck, you could move all your stuff in one fell swoop instead of in a million stages," Jake said. "And I told you I'd help."

"I don't want your help."

He let out a rare sigh and rolled around to face her. "You're still mad that I kicked you out of the nest."

"No." *Yes.*

He caught her hand when she went to walk by him, looking up at her. "You remember why, right?"

"Because your sister's getting divorced and she needs the room you'd lent me here at the warehouse," she intoned.

"And . . . ?"

"And . . ." She blew out a breath. "You're tired of me."

"No," he said gently. "We agreed that I was a crutch for you. That you needed to get out and live your life."

"We?" she asked, her voice a little brittle. Because okay, she wasn't mad at him. She was . . . hurt.

Even as she knew he was right.

They'd been friends since her nineteenth birthday, when she'd applied for a job at SF Tours. He'd just recently left the military and had been through some painful recovery time, and was angry. She'd lost her parents and was equally angry. They'd bonded over that. He sent her for Maritime training and guided her way up the ranks. She couldn't have done it without him and was grateful, but she'd outgrown needing his help on every little thing. "Look," she said. "I'm doing what we both agreed needed to be done. I moved on, I'm getting back on the horse, blah blah."

Jake's mouth smiled but it didn't reach his eyes. "It's more than getting on the damn horse. I want you to want to get back into the game of life."

She sighed. "There's a reason no one plays Life anymore, Jake, the game's stupid. Important life decisions can't be made by a spin of a damn wheel. If it was that easy, I'd spin it right now and get my parents back. I'd make it so that they didn't kill someone else's dad and put all those others in the hospital, changing and ruining people's lives forever. I'd make it so that I could go back a few spaces on the damn board and stay

96

home that night so that no one had to go out and pick me up at a party I should never have sneaked out to in the first place." She let out a rough breath, a little surprised to find out just how much she'd been holding in. Sneaky little things, emotions.

"Pru," Jake said softly, pained.

She pulled her hand free. "No. I don't want to talk about it." She really didn't. It took a lot of time and effort to bury the feelings. Dredging them up again only drove her mad. She moved to leave but Jake wheeled around to stop her exit.

"Then how about we talk about the fact that you've now helped everyone involved that night?" he said. "You sold the Santa Cruz house you grew up in — the only home you ever knew — to be able to put college scholarships in the hands of the two boys of that woman who was hit crossing the street — even though she survived. You even became friends with them. Hell, I now employ Nick in maintenance and Tim said you were helping him find a place to live now that he's out of the dorm —"

"Okay now wait a minute," she said. "I'm not some damn martyr. I sold the house, yes, but I did it because I couldn't handle the memories. I was eighteen, Jake, it was just too much for me." She shook her head.

"I didn't give all of that money away. I went to school, I had expenses, I kept what I needed —"

"— Barely. And then there was Shelby, in one of the other cars, remember her? You gave her seed money she needed after her surgery to move to New York like she always wanted."

"I gave her some help, yes," she admitted. "Did you know she still limps?"

"You're still in touch with her?" he asked in disbelief.

She huffed out a breath. "Subject change, please."

"Sure. Let's move on to the O'Riley brothers. You made sure they got your parents' life insurance money, which they presumably used for education and to start their pub. So what now, Pru? It should finally be time to leave the past in the past, but it's not, so you tell me. What's really going on here?"

Yeah, Pru. What was going on? She drew in a breath of air, willing herself not to remember — and grieve — the home she'd sold, everything she'd given up. "He's not happy," she said.

"Who's not?"

"Finn. I want him to be happy."

Jake was shaking his head. "Not your deal."

"But it feels like my deal," she said. "Everyone else is happy, even his brother, Sean. I have to try and help him." Then she told him about the wish and he stared at her like she'd lost her marbles.

"He's going to fall for you," he said. "You know that, right? You have to tell him the truth before that happens, you have to tell him who you are first."

She snorted. "He's not going to fall for me."

Jake smiled, and this time it did reach his eyes. "Believe me, chica, you flash those eyes on him, that smile, some sass . . . he's as good as flat on the ground for you. And you know how I know?"

She shook her head.

"Because I've been there, done that."

"But you didn't stay flat on the ground."

Something flashed through his eyes at that. Regret. Remorse. "That's on me, Pru, not you. And you know it."

Jake didn't do love. He'd told her that going in and he'd never faltered, which wouldn't change the fact that he intended to keep her in his life. He'd proven that by being there for her through thick and thin, and there'd been a whole lot more thin than thick. She'd been there for him as well and always would be. But there were limits now, for both of them.

"Tell me about Finn," he said.

"You already know. He runs O'Riley's. He's loyal to his brother, he's protective and good to his friends, and . . ."

"And?" Jake asked.

And he kisses like sex on a stick . . . "And he works too hard."

"And you think what?" he asked dubiously. "That you're going to change that?"

"He needs a life," she said far more defensively than she'd meant to. "He was robbed of his."

"Not your fault, Pru," Jake said with firm gentleness.

"Well I know that."

"Do you?"

"Yes!" she said, *not* gently.

"Then why are you working your way into his life?"

A most excellent question.

"You didn't work your way into the life of any of the others," he said. "You did what you could and you stayed back, letting them move on without your presence. But not here, not with Finn. Which begs the question, chica — why?"

Again, a most excellent question. But she

had the answer for this one, she just didn't want to say it out loud.

Finn was different.

And he was different because she *wanted* him in her life in a way she hadn't wanted anyone for a very long time.

Maybe ever.

"You know what I think?" Jake asked.

"No, but I'm pretty sure you're going to tell me."

"I think, Smartass," he went on undeterred by her sarcasm, "that he's different because you have feelings for him."

No kidding. And she could have added that she was thrown off balance by that very thing. Confused too, because she'd never felt this way about anyone and she didn't want to hurt him. She didn't, but that left her digging a pretty damn big hole for herself. "I said I don't want to discuss this with you."

"Fine. Then discuss it with *him.*"

"I will. Soon. But I can't just spit it out, it's a lot to throw at someone. It's only been a few days, I'll get there."

Jake just looked at her for a long beat. "I was at the pub last night."

She froze. "What? I didn't see you."

"I don't see how you could have, since you didn't take your eyes off Finn."

Crap.

"I saw you with him. I saw the look on your face. And I saw the look on his. People are falling, Pru. Denying it is stupid, and one thing you aren't and never have been, is stupid."

"Okay, now you're just being ridiculous." But then she remembered Finn's unexpected kiss, that amazing, heart-stopping, gut-tightening, nipples-getting-happy kiss, and folded her arms over her chest. "*Seriously* ridiculous," she added and then paused. "You really think he could fall for me?"

Jake's eyes softened. "Any guy with a lick of sense would. But chica, you've got to —"

"— tell him, yeah, yeah, I know."

"Before it goes too far," he pressed. "Before you sleep with him."

"I'm not going to —"

Jake held up his hand. "Don't say something that you're going to have to take back, Pru. I was there." He gave her a grim smile. "Don't make me prove how much I love you by going behind your back to protect you by telling him myself."

She stared at him. "You wouldn't dare."

"Try me," he said. "And since I've got you all good and pissed off at me, you might as well remember something else as well. If you sleep with him before everything's square, I'll have to kill him for taking advantage of you when you're still messed up."

"I'm not messed up —" she started and then stopped. Because she was. She was *so* messed up. "Don't even think about interfering. This is my problem to handle." And with that, she strode into what had been her old room, grabbed one of her last boxes of stuff, and turned to go.

"Pru."

She stopped but didn't turn around. Instead she looked down at the box she held. It was labeled PICTURES, and she felt her heart clutch. She'd left this one for nearly last on purpose. Everything in it meant something to her and holding it all in her arms made her heart heavier than the box itself. It was almost more than she could bear, making her wish she'd grabbed one of the other few boxes left, like the one labeled KITCHEN CRAP I PRETEND TO USE BUT DON'T.

"You know I've got your back," Jake said.

She sighed and closed her eyes. "Even if I screw it all up?"

"*Especially* if."

CHAPTER 9
#REALWORLDPROBLEMS

In the end, Pru and Thor and Pru's big box of stuff took a cab back to the Pacific Pier building. They had to get out a block early because of traffic, which meant dragging Thor on his leash and carrying the box, which got heavier with each step.

In the courtyard she stopped by the fountain and set the box down for a minute to catch her breath.

Thor plopped down at her feet, panting like he was dying even though he'd barely had to walk at all and he certainly hadn't had to carry a heavy box.

"Hey," she said, "this adulting thing isn't for the faint of heart."

Thor gave the dog version of an eyeroll and huffed out a heavy sigh.

She took pity. "Look, I'm just trying to keep us in shape. Some of us are supposed to be in our prime."

Thor was unimpressed.

She was about to coax him up to her apartment with another bribe when her phone rang. Tim.

She'd met him and his brother Nick after the accident, in the hospital. They'd spent a few days there with their mom, who'd needed surgery to repair her badly broken leg. Michelle had been unable to work for months afterward, a huge strain on the family. They'd lost their apartment and had lived in their car until Pru had been able to sell her parents' house and help.

Michelle had easily accepted her friendship but not the money. In the end, Pru had made an anonymous donation through her attorney. All Michelle knew was that someone in the community had come up with funds to help her and her boys out.

At the time the boys had been in middle school and Pru had been so worried about them. But Nick was working for Jake now and Tim was in college studying to be an engineer.

She was so happy for them.

"Tim," she said when she answered. "Everything okay?"

"That lead you gave me on the apartment near campus, it might pan out," he said excitedly. "They're going to call you as my reference. If we get it, me and my friends will live there together."

"That would be great, Tim," she said.

"You know how hard it is to get a place here," he said. "Almost impossible."

She did know. It'd taken a hell of a long time for her to get into the Pacific Pier building.

"Anyway," he said. "Thanks for the lead. It means a lot." He laughed a little humorlessly. "We aren't looking forward to living in our cars. Been there, done that."

"No worries," Pru said, her stomach jangling unhappily at the memory. "How's school going?"

"Hard as fuck, but I'm in it," he said. "Gotta go. Talk to you soon."

Pru disconnected and looked at Thor. "We did good. They're going to be okay," she marveled. "All of them." And then she called her contact and put in a second good word for Tim, and was assured they were first in line for the place. It warmed her from the inside out to know it.

Now you need to get okay . . .

But she was working on that. "Come on, let's go."

Thor yawned.

"You know, I could have a cat. A big one who eats little dogs for snacks."

He blinked and she sighed. "Okay, I took

that too far. I'm sorry." She crouched down and hugged him in, which he graciously allowed, even giving her a sweet little lick on her cheek. "Love you too," she murmured, kissing the top of his head. "I'm not going to get a cat." She could barely afford to feed the two of them.

She'd never even meant to get a dog at all, but about a year ago, she'd been walking home late one night when she'd heard a funny rumbling sound coming from behind a Dumpster. She'd stopped to investigate, but the rumbling had stopped. It was only when she'd started walking again that the rumbling came back.

Pru had walked around the Dumpster. Crouching low, using the flashlight on her phone, she'd fallen back on her ass when two glowing orbs had locked in on her.

Scrambling up to run, she realized the rumbling had stopped again and she slowly turned back. Channeling her inner Super Girl, she'd moved closer and had peered down at a scrap of fur surrounding those two huge eyes.

Thor, underfed, filthy, and trembling in terror. It'd taken a bribe to get him out, and another before he'd let her pick him up. All she'd had on her was a granola bar but he'd not been picky. Or dainty. He'd nearly bitten her finger off in his haste to eat.

And Pru, who'd been known to snarl herself when hungry, had fallen in love.

Straightening now with Thor in her arms, her gaze caught on the window across the way.

Finn's office.

The pub wasn't open. The accordion doors were shut and locked, but the morning sun slanted inside. She could see Finn behind his desk, head down. He was either dead, or fast asleep.

Both she and Thor stared at him. "I know," she whispered to her dog. "He's something. But you can't get attached to him, because once I tell him everything, it's over."

Thor set his head on her shoulder. He loved her no matter how stupid she was being.

Leaving her box and Thor — his leash wrapped around a bench — to guard it, she quickly crossed the courtyard to the coffee shop.

Tina stood behind the counter. Tall, curvy, and gorgeous, she had skin the color of the mocha latte she was serving. When it was Pru's turn, Tina smiled. "Your usual?" she asked, her voice low and deep and hypnotic.

"No, this one's not for me," Pru said. "It's for a friend. Um, you don't happen to know how Finn O'Riley likes it, do you?"

Tina smiled wide. "Sugar, he likes it hot and black."

"Oh. Okay, um . . . one of those then."

Tina laughed her contagious laugh and got it ready. When she handed it over, there was a dog biscuit wrapped neatly in a napkin to go. "For Thor," she said. "And how about some advice that you didn't ask for?"

Pru bit her lower lip. Was she that obvious? "Yes, please."

"Two things. First, don't even try to speak to him before he's caffeinated. That man is hot as hell and a great guy, but he's also a bear before his coffee."

"And the second thing?"

"There's no doubt, he's a serious catch," Tina said. "But he's barricaded himself off behind work. So if you want him, you're going to have to show him what he's missing."

"I'm think I'm working on that."

Tina grinned at her. "Because you're the Fun Whisperer?"

Oh, God. "You heard that, huh?"

"Sugar, I hear everything." Tina winked at her, making Pru wonder if that meant that she'd also heard about Pru nearly killing him. Or their first kiss . . .

"Good luck," Tina said. "My money's on you."

Pru took the coffee and dog cookie and headed back through the courtyard. Finn was still asleep. She gave Thor his treat and put her finger to her lips. "Stay," she said and stepped into the planter that lined the building.

Thor ignored her and attacked his cookie.

Pru, draped on either side by two hydrangea bushes, knocked on Finn's window.

He shot straight up, a few papers stuck to his cheek. His hair was tousled, his eyes sleepy, although they quickly sharpened in on her. His five o'clock shadow was now twelve hours past civilized. And holy cow, he was a damn fine sight.

Before she even saw him coming, he'd crossed his office and opened the window, looking far more alert upon wakening than she'd ever managed.

"What the hell are you doing?" he asked, in the sexiest morning voice she'd ever heard.

"Got you something," she said. "It's not a waffle but . . ." She lifted the coffee and added a smile, trying to not look as if she hadn't just sweat her way through the courtyard with Thor and a heavy box of painful memories — impossible since her shirt was sticking to her and so was her hair. She didn't have to look in any mirror to know that she was beet red in the face, her usual after-exercise "glow."

Finn climbed out the window with easy agility. Pru backed up a step to give him room but he kept coming, stepping right into her space, reaching for the cup like a starved man might reach for a promised meal.

Clearly the man was serious about needing coffee. She stared up at him as he took the cup and drank deeply.

She might have also drooled a little bit.

"Thanks," he said after a long moment. "Most people won't come within two miles of me before I'm caffeinated."

Not wanting to tell him that Tina had already warned her because she didn't want to admit to soaking up info on him whenever and however she could, she just smiled. "How's the hole in your chest?"

He absently reached up and rubbed a hand over his pec, a completely unconscious but very male gesture. "Think I'm going to live," he said.

She eyeballed his hair and the crease on his cheek where papers had been stuck to him. "Living the wild life, huh?"

"The wildest." He looked past her. "So who's the fat cat?"

She turned and followed his line of sight to Thor, who'd curled up in a sunspot next to her box to doze. "I'll have you know that's my fierce, very protective guard dog."

"Dog?"

"Yes!"

He scratched his jaw while eyeing Thor speculatively. "If you say so."

"He protects me," she said. "In fact, he won't let anyone get near me. And don't even think about trying to touch him, he hates men."

"Not me," Finn said. "Dogs love me."

"No, really —" she started but Finn crossed the courtyard and crouched low, holding his hand out to Thor, who had opened his eyes and was watching Finn approach.

"Careful —" Pru warned. "He's like you without caffeine, only he's like that all the time. He might nip —"

To her utter shock, Thor actually moved toward Finn in a flutter of bravery, his little paws taking him a step closer, his tail wagging in a hopeful gesture that, as always, made Pru's heart hurt.

Then, unbelievably, Thor licked Finn's fist.

"Atta boy," Finn said approvingly in an easy voice full of warmth and affection. "She says you're a dog, what do you think?"

Thor panted happily and rolled over, exposing his very soft, slightly enlarged belly.

"What's his name?" Finn asked, head bent, loving up on her dog.

She glared at Thor. "Benedict Arnold."

Benedict Arnold ignored her completely and she sighed. "Thor."

Finn snorted. "A real killer, huh?"

"Yes, actually, he —"

And that's when Thor strained to reach up and lick Finn's chin. Pru couldn't exactly blame him, she wanted to do the same.

And then . . . her poor-sighted, man-hater of a dog climbed right into Finn's arms and melted like butter on a hot roll. Except minus the hot roll and add a hot guy.

"I can't believe it," she said to herself, watching as Thor settled against Finn's chest like he belonged there, setting his head on Finn's broad shoulder.

"You were saying?" he asked on a soft laugh.

She stared at him, a little dazzled by the laugh. And then there was that stubble and she wondered . . . if he kissed her now and then nuzzled her throat like he had the other night, would it leave a whisker burn?

She wouldn't mind that . . . "Do you have a dog?" she asked.

"No, but someday," he said, reminding her of what Willa had told her, that he wanted a house outside the city and a big dog.

"So what are you doing today?" he asked.

She pointed to the box. "Unpacking some more."

"And you say *I* need a fun whisperer," he teased.

"You were asleep at your desk," she said. "My statement stands. You most definitely need a fun whisperer."

"I'll put fun on my calendar, how's that sound?"

She laughed. "Planning the fun kinda takes the fun out of fun. And anyway, maybe it's also about adventure. Spontaneous adventure."

"I don't know," he murmured, watching her as he still stroked Thor into a pleasure coma. "I can think of a few things that if planned right, would be the epitome of fun *and* adventurous."

She lifted her gaze from her dog's contented face to Finn's and found his eyes warm and lit with something. Amusement? Challenge? "Like?"

He set Thor down, back in the sunspot, and rising to his full height, shifted toward Pru.

She backed up a step, a purely instinctual move because while her body knew how badly it wanted him, her mind was all too well aware that it was a colossally stupid move of the highest order.

He merely stepped forward again, backing her flush to the brick wall lining the courtyard.

Her breathing had gone ragged. Even more so when he leaned into her with his hands on either side of her head. "You're a contradiction," he murmured. "A push pull."

"Maybe it's because we're oil and water," she managed.

Hands still on her, blocking her escape — not that she wanted to escape those strong arms and that talented mouth — he flashed her a hot look. "Do you want this, Pru?"

She wasn't one hundred percent certain what "this" was, but she *was* one hundred percent certain that she wanted it. And God help her, she wanted it bad, too. When she gave a jerky nod, his hand came up and cupped her jaw, his fingers sliding into her hair, his thumb slowly, lazily, rasping over her lower lip. He watched the movement with a heat that made her legs wobble.

She swallowed hard. "We're in the center of the courtyard."

"What happened to adventurous?" he murmured, his thumb making another slow, intoxicating pass over her lip.

As always, her mouth worked independently of her brain and opened so she could sink her teeth lightly into the pad of his thumb.

He hissed in a breath. The sound egged her on and she sucked his thumb between her lips.

His eyes dilated to black.

Yeah. Suddenly she was feeling very . . . adventurous. Before she could stop herself, her arms encircled his broad shoulders, her fingers sinking into his hair.

This wrenched a low, sexy "mmmm" from him like he was a big, rumbling wildcat. A big, rumbly wildcat who clearly wanted more because he drew her up against him and lowered his lips to hers.

Meeting him halfway, she went up on her tiptoes. He slid a hand up her back to palm the back of her neck, holding her right where he wanted her. Then and only then did his mouth finally cover hers, his kiss slow and sweet.

After, he pulled back and looked into her eyes, smiling at whatever he saw — probably dazed lust. He kissed her again, *not* slow and most definitely *not* sweet this time. Again he ended it too soon but when he lifted his head, the rough pad of his thumb slid back and forth over her jaw while she struggled to turn her brain back on.

"Pru."

And oh, that deliciously rough morning voice. It slid over her like the morning sun, and made her eyes drift shut.

"You take the rugrat," he said. "I'll get your box."

Her eyes flew open. He was holding Thor again. "What?"

"I'll help you upstairs," he said.

Where her bed was. Oh God, had she made her bed? Wait — *was she wearing good panties*?

She mentally shook herself because none of that mattered. You're not going there with him, remember? She couldn't, wouldn't, because she hadn't yet told him who she was. She wasn't ready to do that. Because she knew that once she did, this would be over. He wouldn't want to be friends with the woman whose family had stolen his. He wouldn't want to make her fancy virgin cocktails or pet her silly dog.

Or kiss her stupid . . .

The truth was, he was the best thing to happen to her in a damn long time. And yes, it was selfish. And wrong.

And she hated herself for it.

But she couldn't tell him, not yet. "I've got it," she said. "Really. I'm good."

She just wished she meant it.

CHAPTER 10
#KARMAISABITCH

It was rare for Finn to find himself on unsure ground. Typically if he needed something, he handled it himself. If he wanted something, he went after it.

He both wanted and needed Pru. That was fact. The knowledge had been sitting in the frontal lobe of his brain and in the bottom of his gut, and also definitely decidedly south of both.

It'd been like that for him since the night she'd walked into his pub dripping wet and smiled that smile at him. And then she'd nailed him with that dart and he'd kissed her, and the problem had only compounded itself.

She drove him nuts, in the very best of ways.

And now she'd brought him a coffee and he'd kissed the daylights out of her again. But this time she didn't seem to want to climb him like a tree. She wanted to escape him.

Badly too, given the sudden panic in her eyes.

It should have been his clue to back off. Walk away.

But he found himself unable to do that.

"How about I just get you upstairs with your stuff," he said, going for as nonthreatening as possible. He bent to put Thor down so he could pick up the box but the dog had other ideas and clung like a monkey. He glanced down. "You sure he's a dog?"

Some of the stress left Pru at that and she laughed a little. "Yes, but whatever you do, don't tell him." She covered Thor's ears. "I think that he thinks he's a grizzly."

Finn met Thor's wary gaze. The little guy really was the most ridiculous looking thing he'd ever seen. Bedraggled, patchy, mud brown fur, he had one ear up and one ear down, a long nose, a small mouth that lifted only on one side like he was half smiling, half smirking, and the biggest, brownest eyes he'd ever seen. Hell, his ears and eyes alone were bigger than the rest of him, and the rest of him didn't weigh as much as a pair of boots. "Little Man Syndrome, huh?" he asked the dog sympathetically.

"He just likes to be carried," Pru said. "He

likes to be tall. And he can see better too. Once you pick him up, he won't let you put him down."

Finn tested this theory by once again starting to bend over.

Thor growled. Laughing, Finn tightened his grip on the little guy. "Don't worry, I've got ya," he said and reached to pick up Pru's box with his other hand.

Holy shit, it weighed a ton.

"What are you doing?" Pru asked, crouching at his side. Her voice was tight again. "I said I've got it."

"Pru, it weighs a ton. How far did you carry this thing?"

"Not far," she said, tug-o-warring with him. "Let go —"

"You're as stubborn as Thor, but I'm already here," he said. "Let me help —"

"No." She tried to wrench the box from him, her expression more than a little desperate now, which stopped him in his tracks. Whatever it was in the damn box, she didn't want him to see it, and he immediately backed off — just as she whirled from him. She lost her grip, and the box literally fell apart, the cardboard bottom giving way, the contents hitting the ground.

"Oh no," she breathed and hit her knees on the ground in front of a few old, beat-up photo albums, a few cheap plastic picture frames, and a glass one, which had shattered into a thousand pieces. "It broke," she whispered.

There was something in her voice, something as fragile as the now broken glass frame shattered in shards and pieces at their feet, and it made Finn's chest hurt. Even more so when he saw the picture free of its frame. A little girl standing between two adults, each holding one of her hands.

Pru, he thought, looking into those brown eyes. Pru . . . and her parents?

Her posture said it all as she reached right into the shards of glass for the picture, carefully brushing it clean to hug it against her chest like it meant the entire world to her.

Fuck. "Pru, here, let me —"

"No, it's fine. I'm fine," she protested, pushing his hands away when he began to gather up the photo albums. "I told you I've got this!"

Thor, soaking up Pru's anxiety, lifted his head and began to howl.

Pru looked close to tears.

Eddie, a.k.a. Old Guy, came out of the alley, presumably to help, took one look at the mess that Finn had found himself in, and did an about-face.

Finn gently squeezed Thor to him.

"Quiet," he said in a firm voice.

Thor went quiet.

Pru sucked in a breath, looking surprised right out of her impending tears, thank God. "Stop," he said as she reached into the glass for another picture with absolutely no regard for her own safety. Unable to put Thor down and risk him cutting his paws, he held the dog tight to his chest and reached for Pru's hand with his free one. Pulling her to her feet, he said, "Let's get Thor upstairs and then I'll come back and —"

"I'm not leaving it, any of it."

"Okay, babe, no worries." He whipped out his cell phone and called Archer. No way was Sean awake yet, much less up and moving, but Finn knew he could always count on Archer.

Archer answered with his customary wordy greeting. "Talk."

"Courtyard," Finn said and looked up. Sure enough Archer's face appeared in the second-story window of his office. "We need a box."

"Down in five," Archer said.

He made it in two. Archer set an empty box down on the bench and reached for Thor, presumably so Finn could handle Pru, but Thor bared his tiny little teeth and growled fiercely.

"Whoa, little dude," Archer said and raised his hands. "I come in peace."

Satisfied he'd protected his woman, Thor went back to cuddling into Finn.

Finn grabbed the box in his free hand and crouched in front of Pru, who had an armful of stuff. "Set everything in here," he said.

She hesitated and he leaned in. "It'll be safer," he said quietly, and she nodded and unloaded her full arms into the box.

Archer had sent a text and Elle showed up with a broom and dust pan, which seemed incongruous to her lacy tee, pencil skirt, and some very serious heels.

"You could've sent someone," Archer said to her.

Elle gave him a don't-be-stupid look and smiled at Pru. "Pretty photo albums. Shame about the frame." She swept up the glass, the line of thin silver hoops clanging on her wrist. "I've got some spare frames I'm not using that would love a home. I'd be glad to give them to you. Is that you and your parents?"

Pru nodded and rose. "Thanks for helping."

"Don't give it another thought," Elle said. "Oh, and it's girls' night out tonight. Karaoke. Doll yourself up, Finn promised nineties glam rock band music." Elle flashed a smile. "My specialty, so just ring if you need something to wear, I've got a closet full."

Archer snorted.

"Okay," Elle said, "so I have two closets full. Eightish work for you?"

Pru, looking a little bit dazzled and probably also more than a little railroaded by Elle's gentle but firm take-charge 'tude, shook her head. "I can't sing," she said.

"Nonsense," Elle said. "Everyone can sing. We'll duet, it'll be fun."

Pru didn't look convinced but she did look distracted instead of anguished, and for that Finn was grateful. He brushed a quick kiss on Elle's cheek. "Thanks."

She kissed him back and gave him a look that said *take care of her,* and he knew better than to not do what Elle wanted.

Besides, he wanted the same thing.

A few minutes later he got Pru and Thor upstairs.

"Thanks," she said quietly. "But I'm good from here."

Oh, he got that message loud and clear, but he was still holding both her dog and her box so he stepped into her apartment behind her.

He could see her small kitchen and living

room and the wall dividing them that had a square door right in the middle of it. It was a dumbwaiter, which cut through this whole side of the building, a long-ago leftover remnant from when the place had at one time been all one residence belonging to one of the wealthiest, most successful dairy families on the west coast.

Finn knew this only because he'd seen the dumbwaiter in Archer's office. Archer employed guys with major skills and they kept those skills sharp with company-wide training. Once a month that training came in the form of a serious scavenger hunt, and somehow Finn had once ended up one of the things on the list of items to gather.

Archer's idea of funny.

Team One had captured Finn in his sleep once. He'd escaped before they could win though, and he'd been lucky enough to use the dumbwaiter to make his hasty exit. He'd been unlucky enough to end up in the basement in nothing but his boxers, showing up at an illicit poker game between the building's janitor crew and maintenance crew.

He'd joined in and won two hundred bucks, which had kept him from trying to kill Archer.

Pru had the dumbwaiter door latched from her side. Smart girl. That didn't surprise him.

What *did* surprise him was that there was almost no furniture in the entire place.

"Where did you move from?" he asked.

"Not far. Fisherman's Wharf."

"You didn't move your furniture yet?"

"Uh . . ." She headed into her kitchen and was face first into her fridge now, leaving him a very nice view of her sweet ass in her snug yoga capris. "My place there was mostly furnished," she said. "But yeah I have a few things left to move over." Her tank gapped away from her front, affording him a quick flash of creamy, pale skin.

"You work out of Fisherman's Wharf too," he said. "At Jake's charter service, right?"

"Yes." She straightened and faced him. "He's got that huge old warehouse on Pier 39. I both work and lived there."

"With Jake." Wow, listen to him all casual, when his stomach had literally just hit his toes.

"He's got a lot of space. Not all of it is used for business. It's residential too."

Not, Finn couldn't help but notice, exactly an answer. He knew Jake. Knew too a little of the guy's reputation, which was that maybe his legs didn't work, but everything else most certainly did. That guy saw more action than Finn, Archer, Spence, and Sean all together.

Times ten.

"You and him . . . ?" he asked calmly, while feeling anything but.

"Not anymore."

Somehow this didn't make him feel better. He was still holding Thor and the box. Pru came back toward him and took Thor, setting him down, unhooking his leash. Then she turned back to Finn and reached for the new box.

Their hands brushed but he held firm, waiting until her eyes met his. He let his question stand. He had no idea why it mattered to him so much. Or maybe he did. In any case, he was usually good at letting things go, *real* good, but for some reason this wasn't going to be one of those things.

Finally, she blew out a sigh. "Did you think I'd kiss you if I was with someone else?"

"Do you always answer a question with a question?"

Making an annoyed sound, she tugged the box from his arms, her momentum taking her on a half spin from him but at the last minute she whirled back with something clearly on the tip of her tongue.

Problem was, he'd stepped in to follow right behind her. Which was how he ended up with the corner of the box slamming right into his crotch.

CHAPTER 11
#LOVEBITES

Pru felt the impact, took in where the box had hit Finn, and staggered back a step in horror. "Oh my God, I'm so sorry! Are you all right?"

He didn't answer. He did however let out a whoosh of air and bent over, hands on his knees, head down.

Good going, Pru. Since you didn't kill him the other night, you went for unmanning him and finishing the job. She quickly set the box down and hovered close, hands raised but not touching him, not sure *where* to touch him. Which was ridiculous. She'd had her tongue halfway down his throat. He'd seen her lose her collective shit over the photograph of her mom and dad . . . "Finn?" she asked tentatively. "Are you okay? *Say something.*"

Head still down, he lifted a finger, signaling he needed a moment.

Going gonzo with all the agitation in the

air, Thor was on a yipping spree, running in circles around them both, panting in exertion.

"Thor, hush!" she said, eyes on Finn.

Thor didn't hush, but she couldn't concentrate on the dog. "I'm so sorry," she said again, finally giving in to the urge to touch Finn, running her hand up and down his back, trying not to notice that under her fingers he was solid muscle. And thanks to his low-riding jeans having slid down his hips when he'd bent over, she could see an inch of smooth, sleek skin and it made her stupid. "I didn't mean to crush your . . . er, twig and berries."

He stilled and then lifted his head. He was pale. No, scratch that, he was green, and maybe sweating a little bit to boot. But he had a funny expression on his face.

Thor was still losing his mind, barking so hard that his upright ear bounced up and down and his floppy ear kept covering his eyes, freaking him out all the more.

"Shh," Finn said to him firmly but not unkindly.

Shockingly, Thor "shh'd."

Finn straightened up a little bit more, but not, Pru couldn't but notice, all the way.

"Twig and berries?" Finn repeated.

"Yeah, um . . ." Pru strained for another

reference so that she didn't have to spell it out. "You know, your . . . kibbles and bits."

The corners of his mouth quirked but she wasn't sure if he was mad or amused. "Frank and beans?" she tried.

At that, he out-and-out smiled. "I'm torn between giving you a break and stopping you, or making you go on."

Oh for God's sake. She crossed her arms. "I suppose you have better words."

"Hell yes," he said. "And when you're ready, I'll teach them to you."

Breaking eye contact, she — completely inadvertently, she'd swear it on a stack of waffles! — slid her gaze to where she'd hit him. Did it seem . . . *swollen*? "I've got an icepack if you —"

He choked. "Not necessary."

"Are you sure?" she asked. "Because I really am a good medic, I promise, and —"

He choked off another laugh. "And you're offering to do what, exactly?"

Uh . . . She bit her lower lip.

"Kiss it better?" he suggested in a voice that made her get a little overheated.

Note to self: *not quite ready for prime time with Finn O'Riley.*

He gave her a knowing smirk and moved to the door. Definitely with a slight limp. "You should take Elle up on her offer for a

132

new frame," he said. "That picture clearly means a lot to you and she's got some beautiful things in storage."

And then he was gone.

It was a matter of pride that Finn managed to walk across the courtyard without a limp. Or too much of one anyway. He'd thought about going up instead of down, heading to the roof, the only place in the building that he could go and probably be alone, but he didn't want or need alone time.

Or so he told himself.

"What's up with you, someone knee you in the 'nads?"

He turned his head and found Eddie in his usual place, sitting on a box in the alley. It was a good spot because from there the old man could see both the courtyard and the street.

"Isn't it early for you to be up?" Finn asked him.

"It's trash day."

Finn went through his pockets for extra change. Coming up with a five, he handed it over.

Eddie smiled his gratitude.

When a shadow joined theirs, Finn turned just as Archer appeared silently at his side.

Archer had some serious stealth skills,

earned mostly the hard way. He'd lost none of his sharp edges, which considering what he did for a living and the danger he still occasionally faced, was a good thing.

"What happened to your boys?" Archer asked.

Finn resisted the urge to cup his "boys" because they still ached like a son of a bitch from his collision with the corner of Pru's box. "Nothing."

"Maybe he finally got laid," Eddie said to Archer.

Archer's gaze cut to Finn's face. "Nah," he said. "He'd be more dazed. And happy."

Spence joined them. "What's going on?"

"The debate is whether or not Finn got laid," Archer said.

Spence took his turn studying Finn's expression. "He's not happy enough."

"That's what I said." Archer gave a rare smile. "Given how long it's been, I'd assume he'd be doing cartwheels and shit."

Finn took a deep breath as they both laughed at his expression. "How about I *assume* my foot up your ass?"

This only made them crack up harder.

Eddie got himself together first. "Gotta go," he said and headed for the alley. Trash day was his favorite day of the week because he loved nothing more than to go Dumpster diving for treasures.

Twice now, the entire building — all fond of Eddie and protective of him as well, had implemented a system where everyone bagged up anything that might be of interest to him separately so that he didn't have to go searching.

And then they discovered that Eddie was dumping out all the bags into the Dumpster regardless.

Turns out, Eddie liked the thrill of the find.

"You smell like a skunk," Archer said to Eddie.

Eddie blinked. "Is that right? Well, I'm sure we have skunks around here somewhere."

"You think?" Archer asked casually. "Because I'm thinking it smells like weed."

"Huh," Eddie said. "Good thing you're not a cop these days, huh?"

Oh boy, Finn thought. Even Old Man Eddie knew better than to remind Archer of his cop days, which in turn would remind him why he wasn't one anymore.

Archer's eyes went flat. "You growing?"

"Only exactly what I'm allowed," Eddie said and pulled out a laminated card on a ribbon from beneath his shirt.

"You selling?" Archer asked.

"Sir, no sir," Eddie responded, adding a smartass salute.

Finn and Spence both grimaced. "Man," Spence said. "What have we told you? Archer has *zero* sense of humor."

Eddie grinned. For reasons that Finn had never figured out, Eddie liked to fuck with Archer.

Archer gave a slight head shake, like he was talking himself out of making Eddie disappear. "You know the rec center on Union?" he finally asked.

Eddie nodded. "Past the porn shop but before the COME TO JESUS SIGN?"

"Yeah," Archer said. "They're having a free meal tonight. Pot roast and potatoes."

"I love pot roast and potatoes," Eddie said.

"You want a ride, come by my office at six," Archer told him.

Eddie grinned at him. "See, I knew you liked me. Though not as much as Finn. Finn gave me five bucks." Eddie looked hopefully at Archer.

Well versed in this game, Archer snorted. "I'll pay you ten if you tell me why lover boy here's limping like he was rode hard and put away wet. I know you know more than you're telling."

"You think he got his knob polished," Eddie said.

Archer flashed another grin. "Yeah."

Finn flipped Archer off, which only made Archer's grin widen.

"I don't know everything," Eddie said. "But I guess I do know some things."

"Such as?" Archer asked.

Eddie held out his hand.

Archer rolled his eyes, fished through his pockets and came up with the promised ten.

"Okay," Eddie said. "I know he went inside Trouble's apartment with her, but only stayed a few minutes. He came back out in this condition. It wasn't long enough for him to get laid . . ." He slid Finn a sideways look. "At least I hope it wasn't. You ain't a quick trigger, are you, boy?"

Spence about busted a gut and handed Eddie another ten. "Totally worth every penny."

Finn shook his head and walked away from those assholes, and he wasn't going back to the pub either. He needed a few hours horizontal on his bed — where he would absolutely not think about how he'd rather be getting his knob polished.

Nineties Karaoke Night cheered Finn up considerably. First Archer bet the gang that Spence couldn't rap "Baby Got Back."

Spence rapped "Baby Got Back." Perfectly. He was in a suit too, evidently fresh from some business meeting.

The ladies went nuts.

In penance, Archer had to sing "I'm Too Sexy" by Right Said Fred.

Shirtless.

The crowd went wild. But even better was what happened when the girls showed up. They walked in together, Elle, Willa, Haley . . . and Pru, all dressed in vintage nineties.

It was a cornucopia of hotness but Finn's gaze went straight to Pru. His heart about stopped. She wore a tight, short, high-waisted denim miniskirt that showed off her mile-long legs to mouth-watering perfection, a cropped white tee with an equally cropped leather jacket that kept giving sneak, tantalizing peeks of smooth, flat belly, and some serious platforms that told him Elle had been in charge. Her hair had been teased to within an inch of its life and she appeared to be wearing glitter as makeup.

Everyone had fun ordering nineties-style cocktails, so he made Pru a special one — a Chocolate Mock-tini. She raved over it so much that everyone else wanted one as well, and it became the night's special.

Eventually the ladies all got up to sing "Kiss" by Prince and brought down the house. Not because they were good. But because they were so bad.

Pru had been right. She couldn't sing. Couldn't dance either. Or keep rhythm. Not that this stopped her or the glitter floating around her in a cloud everywhere she moved.

Finn loved every second of it.

That was until she dragged his ass up on stage and made him do a duet with her. "The Boy Is Mine."

He was pretty sure not a single one of the guys would ever let him forget it either.

Sean bailed shortly after that, a woman on his arm, a smile on his face. Finn was happy for him, but when the night ended and the girls went to leave, he realized he was screwed because he didn't have the option of taking Pru home.

Even if that was only up two flights of stairs.

He had to stay until closing, add up the till, make sure everything got closed and locked up.

Which means he got to watch Pru, his Fun Whisperer, walk out.

She hugged him good-bye, and the feel of her up against him almost had him saying fuck it to the pub. But he couldn't. He showered and hit his bed two hours later. Alone.

And when he woke up the next morning he had glitter all over his pillow.

CHAPTER 12
#BITETHEBULLET

The next few days were busy at work, with Pru's shifts consisting of one cruise after another, but she still had plenty of time to think. A lot.

Karaoke night had been fun. Watching Finn laugh with Archer and Spence had been a highlight for her.

Fun looked good on him. It made her happy to see him happy, and she realized it'd been a good week for her, too. Willa, Elle, and Haley had been so welcoming, taking her in, adding her to their group without hesitation.

It meant a lot. It also meant that she wasn't entirely alone. She knew she had Jake, but he was like a brother at this point. An overprotective, obnoxious one.

You have Finn . . .

Even if she had no idea what to do with him. Although she'd had plenty of ideas the other night.

It turned out that dancing and singing karaoke in front of a crowd with Finn's eyes on her had been shockingly arousing.

Which apparently had been obvious. Haley had given her a knowing glance at the bar. "You look hungry," she'd said.

"Oh, no," Pru had told her. "I'm fine, I had a plate of chicken wings."

Haley and Willa had laughed.

Even Elle had smiled.

"You're not hungry for food," Elle had informed her, with Curly and Mo nodding their heads in agreement. "You're hungry for a good time. With our boy Finn."

"Well that's just . . . a bad idea," she'd finished weakly. She looked at Willa and Haley for confirmation of that fact.

"Hey, sometimes bad ideas turn out to be the best ideas of all," Willa had said. "Just do it. Have some magical sex. And whatever happens, happens."

What would happen is that Pru would screw up one of the only good things she had going for her right now. "Just do it? That's your big advice?"

"Or in this case, him. Just do him."

Pru snorted.

Willa had turned to Elle and asked, "Think she'll follow my sage advice?"

Elle studied Pru's face carefully. "Hard to

say. She's cute and sharp, but she's got some healthy survivor instincts. That might hold her up some."

"Stupid survivor instincts," Willa had said on a sigh.

And Pru agreed. She had some survivor instincts, and they often got in her own way.

"For days a cloud of glitter has been following you around," Jake said, startling Pru back into the here and now.

"I went to Karaoke the other night," she said. "Rocked it too."

"But you can't sing," Jake said.

"I can totally sing."

He snorted. "And the glitter?"

"It was Nineties Night. This required copious amounts of glitter, which apparently is like the STD of the craft supplies. Once you use it without protection, you can't get rid of it." Pru looked down at herself. "Ever."

"Even Thor's wearing glitter," he said. "You're messing with his manhood."

"Real men aren't afraid of glitter," she said.

"Real men are terrified of glitter."

At the end of the day, Pru collected her dog from Jake's office, where she found him asleep sprawled on top of the desk.

"Seriously?" she asked.

"He likes to see what's going on," Jake said.

And Jake liked the company. She'd almost felt bad about taking Thor away when she'd moved but oh yeah, it'd been Jake's idea for her to go. "I hope he got glitter all over you."

"Hell no," Jake said. "Glitter doesn't dare stick to me. But you've got some on your face."

She couldn't get rid of it. She'd already sent Elle an I-hate-you text. Twice.

"We're going to have to forfeit tonight's game," Jake said. "We're short a player. Trev's out with mono."

She and a group of Jake's other friends and employees played on a local rec center league softball team. Jake was their coach. Coach Tyrant. "Who gets mono at our age?" she asked.

Jake shrugged. "He's a ship captain, he sees a lot of action."

"I'm a ship captain," she said. "I see *no* action."

"And we both know why," Jake said.

Not going there. "Don't forfeit," she said. "I'll find us a player."

Jake raised a brow. "Who?"

"Hey, I have other people in my life besides you, you know."

"Since when?"

She rolled her eyes and ran out. Well, okay, she didn't run exactly. Thor refused to run. But they walked fast because she had an idea, one that would further her plan to bring Finn more fun.

Of course she'd deviated from the plan a couple of times now, starting with allowing her lips to fall onto his — not once but a holy-cow twice — but she'd decided to give herself a break because he was so . . . well, kissable.

And hey, now she knew that his mouth was a danger zone, she'd just steer clear. Her inner voice laughed hysterically at this, but whatever. She could do it.

Probably.

Hopefully.

In the courtyard, she tied Thor's leash to a bench, kissed him right between his adorable brown eyes and dashed through the open doors of the pub. Breathless, she scanned for Finn, but couldn't find him.

Sean flashed her a smile. "Hey, Trouble." He gestured to her face. "You've got some glitter —"

"I know!"

His smile widened. "Okay then, what can I get you?"

"Finn," she said, and then blushed when he just kept grinning. "I mean, I need to see

145

him. Is he in his office?"

"Nope, boss man isn't in."

She'd never been here when Finn hadn't. "But he's always here."

Sean laughed. "Almost always," he agreed. "But right now, he's . . . well, let's just say he's pissed off at me, so we decided he'd work from the house office so I could live to see another day."

He didn't seem all too worried by this. "I need a favor," she said.

He leaned over the bar, eyes warm. "Name it."

"I need his address."

Sean went brows up. "His address."

"Yes, please."

"You going to show him a good time?" he asked. "Because darlin', he sure could use it."

"I'm on it," she said and then realized what he'd meant, which was not what *she'd* meant. "Wait, that's not —"

"Oh, it's *way* too late," Sean said, laughing his ass off.

"I just need to *talk* to him," she said, trying to regain some dignity.

"Whatever you say." Grabbing a cocktail napkin, he pulled a pen from behind his ear, scrawled an address down, and handed it over to her. "We share a house in Pacific

Heights. Less than a mile from here. Go do your thing."

"Which is *talking*," she said.

"If that's what you kids are calling it these days," he said. "Good luck, Trouble."

Not sure why she'd need good luck, she grabbed Thor and headed back out.

Finn lived straight up Divisadero Street, a steep hill that had Thor sitting down and refusing to go another step about a hundred yards in.

Which was a hundred yards past when Pru had wanted to sit down as well. But she scooped the dog up and determinedly kept going, making a quick stop along the way for a spur-of-the-moment gag gift that she sincerely hoped Finn found funny.

By the time she arrived at his house near the top of the hill, she was huffing some serious air. She looked back at the view and was reminded of why she loved this city so much. She could see all of Cow Hollow and the marina, and beyond that, the gorgeous blue of the bay and the Golden Gate Bridge as well.

Worth every second of the walk. Almost. Finn's house was a Victorian-style, narrow row house. The garage was on the bottom floor, two stories above that, with steps leading up to the front door and down to a short driveway — on which sat a '66 Chevelle.

The sexy muscle car's hood was up and a very sexy jeans-covered tush was all Pru could see sticking out of it. She recognized the perfect glutes as Finn's — clearly a sign she'd been ogling said perfect glutes too much. Not that she was repentant in the slightest about this, mind you. In any case, his long denim-covered legs were spread for balance, his T-shirt stretching taut over his flexing shoulder and back muscles and riding up enough to expose a strip of navy boxers and a few inches of some skin.

She tried not to stare and failed. "Hi," she said.

Nothing. He just kept doing whatever it was he was doing under the hood, which involved some serious straining of those biceps.

She moved a little closer. "Finn?"

More nothing, but now she could hear the tinny sound of music and caught sight of the cord from his earbuds.

He was listening to something. Loudly. Classic rock by the sounds of it.

She stared at him, at the streaks of grease on his jeans and over one arm, at the damp spot at the small of his back making his shirt cling to him . . . It was the kind of thing that in the movies would be accompanied by a montage of him moving in slow motion to music, the camera moving in and focusing on that lean, hard body.

Giving herself a mental shake, Pru set Thor down, and holding his leash, shifted even closer to Finn before reaching out to tap him. But at the last minute she hesitated because once again she couldn't figure out where to touch him. Her first choice wasn't exactly appropriate. Neither was her second.

So she settled for his shoulder.

If he'd done the same to her, she probably would've jumped and banged her head on the hood. But Finn had better reflexes, and certainly better control over them. Still cranking on something with a wrench, he simply turned only his head to give her a level stare.

"Hi," she said again and bent over at the waist, hands to her knees to try to catch her breath. "That's quite a hill."

He reached up and pulled out one earbud. "Hi yourself. Need an oxygen tank?"

"You kid, but I totally do."

"You're still wearing glitter," he said with a smile.

"Five showers since that night," she said, tossing up her hands. "I've taken five showers and it's still everywhere. And Thor has been pooping glitter for days . . ."

Still smiling, he crouched and held out his hand for Thor. "You were quite the show the other night."

She chewed on her lip, not sure if he was teasing or complimenting her or not.

"I could watch you do that every night," he admitted.

"What, make a fool of myself?"

His smile turned into a full-fledged grin. "Sing and dance like no one's watching. *Live* like no one's watching."

And just like that, she melted a little.

Thor was sniffing Finn's hand carefully, cautiously, wanting to make sure this was his Finn, and finally he wagged his tail.

"Atta boy. It's just me." Finn opened his arms and Thor moved in for a hug.

Pru stared at the big, sexy guy so easily loving up on her silly dog and felt her throat go a little tight.

"I know Archer didn't tell you where I live," Finn said, eyes still on Thor. "Or Spence. I mean, Spence would if he thought it was funny but they're both pretty hard-core about having my back."

The hardcore part was undoubtedly true. She'd seen the three guys with each other. There were bonds there that seemed stronger than any relationship she'd ever had, a fact that played into her deepest, most secret insecurity — that she might be unlovable.

"Elle values privacy above everything else," Finn said, "which leaves the busybodies." He was watching her now. "Willa or Haley?" he asked.

"Neither." She hesitated, not wanting to get Sean in trouble.

"Shit." Finn rose, Thor happily tucked under one arm like he was a football. "Eddie?"

"Eddie?" Pru asked, confused. "Who's Eddie?"

"The old guy who enjoys Dumpster diving, eating dope brownies, and not minding his own business."

Pru gaped. "I've been feeding him for a month now and he's never told me his name. And I've asked a million times!"

"He likes to be mysterious. And also his brain might be fried from all those brownies. You going to tell me how you found me or not?"

She blew out a breath. "Sean. But he didn't tell me to mess with you or anything," she said hurriedly. "He did it because I have a favor to ask of you and needed to see you in person to do it."

"Sean was at the pub?"

"Yes," she said.

"Working?"

"I think so . . ."

"Huh," he said. "He must have fallen and bumped his head."

"He seemed to have all his faculties about him," she said. "Or at least as many as usual."

Finn snorted and set Thor down. The dog turned in a circle at Pru's feet and then plopped over with an utter lack of grace.

"I brought you a present," Pru said.

"What?" Finn lifted his gaze from Thor to her face. "Why?"

The question threw her. "Well, partly to butter you up for the favor," she admitted. "I figured if I made you laugh, you'd —"

"I don't need a present to do you a favor," he said, his voice different now. Definitely wary, and something else she couldn't place.

She cocked her head. "You know, presents are supposed to be a good thing."

When he just looked at her, she wondered . . . didn't anyone ever give him anything? And suddenly she wished it was a real present and not a gag gift. But it was too late now so she slipped her backpack off and pulled the bag from inside. Seriously second-guessing herself, not entirely certain of this, not even close, she hesitated.

He took the bag from her and peered

inside, face inscrutable.

Nothing. No reaction.

"It's a man's athletic cup," she finally said, stating the obvious.

"I can see that."

"I figured if we're going to hang out together, you might need it."

He stilled and then a low laugh escaped him. "What I need with you, Pru, is full body armor."

True statement.

He lifted his head. "And who says we're hanging out?" he asked, his gaze holding hers prisoner.

She hesitated briefly. "I do."

His eyes never left hers which was how she saw them warm. "Well, then," he said. "I guess it's true."

Their eyes stayed locked, holding for a long beat, and suddenly Pru had a hard time pulling in enough air for her lungs.

"So what's the favor?" he asked.

"I play on a coed softball league. We're short a player tonight and I was hoping —"

"No."

She blinked. "But I didn't even finish my sentence."

"You're short a player for tonight's game and you want me to fill in," he said.

"Well, yes, but —"

"Can't."

She took in his suddenly closed-off expression. "Because . . . you're against fun?"

He didn't react to her light teasing. He wasn't going to play. He clearly had a good reason, maybe many, but he didn't plan on sharing them.

"You should've called and saved yourself a trip," he said.

"I didn't want to make it easy for you to say no."

"I'm still saying no, Pru."

"What if I said I *need* you?" she asked softly.

He paused for the slightest of beats. "Then I'd say you have my full attention."

"I mean *we* need you. The team," she said. "We'll have to forfeit —"

"No."

She crossed her arms. "You said I had your attention."

"You have that and more," he said cryptically. "But I'm still not playing tonight. Or any night."

She knew he was living life carefully, always prepared for anything to go bad. But she knew that wasn't any way to live because the truth was that any minute life could be poof — gone. "Do you remember the other day when you caught me at my worst and

154

saw a few of my demons?" she asked quietly.

"You mean when the picture frame broke."

"Yes," she said, not surprised he knew exactly what she was talking about, that she hadn't been even slightly effective in hiding her painful memories from him.

"You didn't want to talk about it," he said.

"No," she agreed. "And you let me get away with that." She dropped her gaze a little and stared at his torso rather than let him see what she was feeling now. "Whether it was because it doesn't matter to you, or because you have your own demons, I don't know, but —"

"Pru."

Oh thank God, he'd shut her up. Sometimes she really needed help with that. She stared at his neck now, unable to help noticing even in her growing distress and sudden discomfort that he had a very masculine throat, one that made her want to press her face to it and maybe her lips too. And her tongue . . .

"Pru, look at me."

He said this in his usual low timbre, but there was a gentle demand to the tone now that had her lifting her gaze to his.

"It matters," he said. "*You* matter."

This caused that now familiar squishy

feeling in her belly, the one only he seemed to be able to evoke. But it also meant that it *was* his demons eating at him and this killed her. "Softball is a problem for you," she whispered.

"No." He closed his eyes for a beat. "Yeah. Maybe a little, by association." He blew out a sigh and turning his head, stared at the sweet car he'd been working on.

Which was when she remembered he'd had to quit playing baseball in college to raise Sean.

God, she was such an idiot.

"You'll have to forfeit?" he asked.

"Yes, but —"

"Shit." He shut the hood of the Chevelle and went hands on hips. "Tell me you guys are good."

She crossed her fingers. "You have to see us to believe it."

CHAPTER 13
#BADNEWSBEARS

Not ten minutes into the game, Finn stood behind home plate wearing all of the catcher's gear, staring at the team in complete disbelief.

He'd been recruited by a con artist.

He slid his con artist a look. She was playing first base, looking pretty fucking adorable in tight, hip-hugging jeans and a siren red tee with a ragged penny jersey over the top of it, heckling the other team.

She was without a doubt, the hottest con artist he'd ever seen.

"You suck," she yelled to the batter, her hands curved around her mouth.

The batter yelled back, "How about you suck *me*?" And then he blew her a kiss.

Finn straightened to kick the guy's ass but the ref pointed to the batter and then gestured he was out.

"On what grounds?" the guy demanded.

"Being an idiot."

This came from the coach of Pru's team. Jake. He sat at the edge of the dugout, baseball cap on backward, dark lenses, fierce frown . . . a badass in a wheelchair.

With Thor in his lap.

Finn waited for the ump to give Jake a T and kick him out of the game but it didn't happen. Instead, the hitter took one look at Jake, kicked the dirt, and walked back to his dugout.

The next two batters got base hits and both made it all the way home thanks to the fumbling on the field.

Pru's team was the Bad News Bears.

In the dugout between innings, Pru tried to keep morale up, clapping people on the backs, telling them "good job" and "you're looking great out there."

Her rose-colored glasses must also be blinders. Because no one had done a good job and no one had looked great out there either.

At the bottom of the next inning, Finn watched his teammates blow through two strikes in two batters.

The third person up to bat was a twenty-something who had her dark hair up in a high ponytail that fell nearly to her ass. She was teeny tiny and had a sweet, shy smile.

Finn did not have high hopes for her. He

might have muttered this under his breath. And Pru might have heard him.

She shot him a dark look. "Positive reinforcement only," she told him. "Or you'll have to go dark."

"Dark?"

"Yeah." She jabbed a thumb toward Jake, who was on the other side of her, watching the field, expression dialed to *irritated* as Thor snoozed on in his lap. "Like Coach Jake," Pru said and turned to her boss. "How are we doing tonight?"

Jake paused as if struggling with the right words. "Fuckin' great," he finally said.

He didn't look great, he looked like he was at stroke level, but Pru beamed at him and then patted his shoulder.

Jake blew out a heavy exhale. "I'll get you back, Prudence."

She gritted her teeth. "We talked about this. You only use my whole name if you want to die. Horribly and slowly."

"Prudence?" Finn repeated, amused by the death glare.

"I know, hard to believe, right?" Jake asked. "It's an oxymoron," Jake said. "She's anything *but* prudent."

Finn smiled. "And the 'they're doing great' part?" he asked *Prudence*. "Are we watching the same game?"

159

Jake did an impressive eyeroll, slid Pru a glare, and kept his silence, although it looked like it cost him.

"It's called encouragement," Pru said. "And Jake had to go dark, meaning he can't talk unless he's saying something positive, on account of how he used to lower our morale so badly we couldn't play worth anything."

Finn bit back the comment that they couldn't play worth anything now but as the girl at bat stood there letting two perfect strikes go by without swinging and Jake's expression got darker and darker, he nearly laughed.

Nearly.

Because he had no idea how Jake was doing it, keeping his mouth shut. Competition went to the bone with Finn and he was guessing Jake felt the same. "Is she going to swing?" he asked. "Or just keep the bat warm?"

A strangled snort came from Jake, which he turned into a cough when Pru glared at him.

"Abby is Jake's secretary," Pru said. "She's really great."

Finn looked at Jake.

Jake gave a slow head shake.

"What," Pru said, catching it. "She's

160

wonderful! She handles your entire office and she's always sweet, even when you're a total asshole."

"Yes," Jake said. "She's a sweetheart. She's great. In my office and also at handling me, even when I'm a total asshole. What she isn't great at is softball."

"She's learning," Pru insisted.

Abby struck out.

The next batter was a lean and lanky kid, late teens, early twenties maybe.

"Nick," Pru told Finn. "He works in maintenance."

"Pru got him the job," Jake said and Pru shushed him.

Nick strolled out of the dugout, winked at Pru and got a second base hit.

The next batter was a young kid who couldn't have been more than eighteen. She wore thick-rimmed glasses and squeaked at every pitch. She also swung at every ball that came her way and several that didn't. What she didn't do was connect with a single one. Probably because she kept her eyes closed, which meant that her glasses weren't doing jack shit for her.

Finn tried not to care. It was just a softball game, and a bad one at that, but come on. He looked over at Coach Jake and pointed to their batter. "Mind if I . . . ?"

Jake gestured for him to go ahead, his expression saying good luck.

"Kid," Finn called out.

The kid turned to face him.

"Finn," Pru said warningly but he didn't care. He didn't know how she'd gotten Jake to "go dark" but Finn hadn't made any such promise.

"What's your name?" Finn asked.

"Kasey," the girl said. "I work in accounts receivable."

"You know how to hit, Kasey?"

"Yeah." She paused. "No."

Shit. "Okay, it's easy," Finn said. "You just keep your eyes open, you got me?"

She bobbed her head.

"Make contact with the ball, Kasey. That's all you gotta do."

Kasey nodded again but failed to swing at the next pitch. She turned to nervously eye Finn.

"That's okay," Finn told her. "That was a sucky pitch, you didn't want a piece of that one anyway. The next one's yours." And he hoped that was true.

Pru watched Kasey swing at the next ball and connect.

Finn launched himself off the bench. "Yes!" he yelled, pumping his fist. "That's it, baby, that's it!"

He'd started off not wanting to be here, resenting the game, and yet now he was one hundred percent in it. Even, Pru suspected, having fun. Watching him gave her a whole bunch of feels, not the least of which was happy. She was really doing it, giving him something back.

After Kasey hit the ball, she dropped the bat like it was a hot potato and whipped around to flash a grin Finn's way, executing some sort of very white girl boogie while she was at it. "I did it! Did you see? I hit the ball!"

"Yeah, you did. Now *run,* Kasey!" Finn yelled, pointing to first base. "Run your little ass off!"

With a squeak, she turned and started running.

Finn laughed. He laughed and turned that laughing face Pru's way and she nearly threw herself at him.

"Having fun?" she asked, unable to keep her smile to herself.

"You tell me. *Prudence.*"

She was going to have to kill Jake in his sleep.

He grinned at the look on her face and leaned in close so only she could hear him. "You owe me."

163

"What for?"

"For neglecting to mention that you guys are The Bad News Bears." He glanced at the field and leapt back to his feet, throwing himself at the half wall. "Go, Kasey, go! Go, go, go!"

Pru turned in surprise to see that the shortstop had missed the ball and Kasey was rounding second.

The ball was still bouncing in right field.

"Keep going!" Finn yelled, hands curved around his mouth. "Run!"

Kasey headed toward third.

Finn was nearly apoplectic and Pru couldn't tear her eyes off him.

"That's right!" he yelled. "You run, baby! You run like the wind!"

His joy was the best thing she'd seen all day.

All week.

Hell, all month.

Scratch that, *he* was the best thing she'd seen.

Unbelievably, Kasey made it all the way home and the crowd went wild. Okay, so just their team went wild. Everyone piled out of the dugout to jump on Kasey.

Except Pru.

She jumped on Finn.

She didn't mean to, certainly didn't plan

it, her body just simply took over. She turned to him to say something, she has no idea what, but instead she literally took a few running steps and . . .

Threw herself at him.

Luckily he had quick reflexes, and just as luckily he chose to catch her instead of not. He caught her with a surprised grunt, and laughing, hauled her up into his arms. He slid one hand to her butt to hold her in place, the other fisting her ponytail to tug her face up to his.

"Did you see that?" she yelled, losing her ability to self-regulate her voice with the excitement. "It was beautiful, yeah?"

He looked right into her eyes and smiled back. "Yeah. Beautiful."

And then he kissed her, hard, hot, and quite thoroughly.

And far too short. She actually heard herself give a little mewl of protest when he pulled back and let her slide down his body to stand on her own two feet.

"We're still down by ten runs," he said.

She nodded, but she'd never felt less like a loser in her entire life.

CHAPTER 14
#THEWHOLENINEYARDS

In the end, they lost by five, which Pru actually considered a total win. In the very last inning, she'd dove for a ground ball and slid along the ground for a good ten feet, bouncing her chin a few times while she was at it, but hey, she got the ball.

She also got some road rash.

She hadn't felt it at the time, but by the end of the game when they'd all packed up and were going their separate ways, Pru's aches and pains made themselves known. She slowly shouldered her bag and turned, coming face to face with both Jake and Finn.

Jake — with Thor in his lap — gave her a chin nod. Since their venue was a middle school field only two blocks from his building, they usually walked back together.

Finn didn't give her a chin nod. He just stood there, watching her in that way he had that made her . . . want things, things she wasn't supposed to want from him.

Clearly she needed to work on that.

Jake grimaced. "You're a mess. Let's go, I'll patch you up at the office."

"I'm fine." A big fat lie, of course. Her road rashes were stinging like a sonofabitch. "I'm just going to head home."

Jake slid a look at Finn before letting his gaze come back to her. "You sure that's a good idea?"

Of course it wasn't a good idea. But she wasn't exactly known for her good ideas now was she? "Yep," she said, popping the *P* sound.

"You shouldn't go alone, you might need help."

"I've got her," Finn said.

The two men looked at each other for a long beat. Pru might have tried to mediate the landmine-filled silence between them but her brain was locked on Finn's words.

I've got her . . .

She had long fantasies where that was true . . . She reached to take Thor but Jake shook his head.

"He's coming home with me tonight for dinner. I've got steak."

"Steak?" Pru repeated, realizing she was starving. "But after our games, you usually make hotdogs."

Jake shrugged. "It's steak tonight. I've got enough for you to join, if it's okay with Thor."

Thor tipped his head back like a coyote and gave one sharp "yip!"

Pru spent a few seconds weighing a steak dinner cooked for her versus watching Finn in those sexy butt-hugging, relaxed-fit Levi's of his for a little bit longer. It was a tough decision, but in the end, she took the jeans. "No, thanks."

Jake just gave her a knowing head shake and rolled off.

"Did you just almost trade me in for a steak dinner?" Finn asked.

Pretending she hadn't heard that question, she started walking, but he stopped her.

"You okay?"

"Yeah," she said. "We lose all the time."

"I meant because you used your face as a slip-n-slide on that last play." Earlier, when she'd convinced him to come play, he'd gone inside his house for a duffle bag, from which he'd pulled out his mitt earlier. Now he pulled out a towel and gingerly dabbed it against her chin.

"Ow!" she said.

"But you're fine, right?" he asked dryly.

She removed the towel from her chin, saw

some blood and with a sigh put the towel back to her face.

Finn took her bag from her shoulder and transferred it to his, where it hung with his own. "I'll get an Uber."

"I don't need a ride." She started walking, and after a beat he kept pace with her. She worked on distracting herself. The temperature was a perfect seventy-five-ish. The sun had dipped low, leaving a golden glow tipped with orange flame in the west, the rest of the sky awash in mingled shades of blue.

"So what was that about?" Finn asked after a few minutes of silence.

"Nothing. Like I said, sometimes we lose, that's all." Or, you know, always.

"I mean the look Jake gave you."

"Nothing," she repeated.

"Didn't seem like nothing."

"He's got a condition," she said, huffing up the hill. Damn. Why had she said no to getting an Uber again? "You've got to ignore most of his looks."

"Uh huh," Finn said. "What kind of condition?"

"A can't-mind-his-own-business condition." Her aches and pains were burgeoning, blooming as they moved. It was taking most of her concentration to not whimper with each step.

"You sure you're okay?" he asked.

"One hundred percent."

He gave her a once-over, his dark gaze taking in the holes in her knees, and she amended. "Okay, ninety percent," she said and then paused. "Ten at the worst," she amended.

Finn stopped and pulled out his phone.

"We're over halfway there," she argued. "I'm not giving up now."

"Just out of curiosity — do you ever give up?"

She had to laugh. "No," she admitted.

He shook his head, but he didn't ask if she was sure, or try to tell her she wasn't fine. Clearly he was going off the assumption she was an adult.

Little did he know . . .

"Sean plays baseball too," Finn said out of the blue a few minutes later. "He sucks. Sucks bad."

"Yeah?" she asked. "As my team?"

"Well, let's not go overboard."

She took a mock swing at him and he ducked with a laugh. "In high school, he made it onto his freshman team," he said. "But only because they didn't have enough guys to cut anyone. The painful part was making sure he kept his grades high

170

enough."

Pru hadn't actually given a lot of thought to the day-to-day reality that a twenty-one-year-old Finn would have faced having to get a teenage Sean through high school. There would've been homework to do, dinners to prepare, food shopping needed, a million tiny things that parents would have handled.

But Finn had been left to handle all of it on his own.

Her stomach tightened painfully at all he'd been through, but he was over there smiling a little bit, remembering. "That year half of the JV and Varsity teams got the flu," he said, "and Sean got called up to the semifinals. He sat on the bench most of the game, but at the bottom of the eighth he had to play first base because our guy started puking his guts up."

"How did he do?"

Finn smiled, lost in the memory. "He allowed a hit to get by him with bases loaded."

Pru winced. "Ouch."

"Yeah. Coach went out there and told him if another hit got by him, he'd string him up by his balls from the flagpole."

Pru gasped. "He did not!"

"He did," Finn said. "So of course, the next hit came straight for Sean's knees, a low, fast hit."

"Did it get by him?"

"He dove for it, did a full body slide on his chin while he was at it." Finn gave her a sideways smile. "But he got the damn ball."

"Did he get road rash too?" Pru asked, starting to get the reason for story time.

"Left more skin on that field than you did." Finn grinned and shook his head. "He came through though. Somehow, he usually does."

She loved that the two of them had stuck together after all they'd been through. She didn't know anything of their mom, other than she'd not been in the picture for a long time. Whatever she knew about the O'Rileys was what she'd been able to piece together thanks to the Internet. She'd done her best to keep up by occasionally Googling every-one who'd been affected by her parents' ac-cident — needing to make sure they were all doing okay. When she'd discovered that Finn had opened O'Riley's only a mile or so from where she was living and working, she hadn't been able to resist getting in-volved.

And now here he was, a part of her life. An important part, and at the thought she got a pain in her heart, an actual pain, because she knew this was all short-lived.

She had to tell him the truth eventually. She also knew that as soon as she did, he wouldn't be a part of her life anymore.

"Tonight brought back a lot of memories," he said, something in his voice that had her looking at him.

Regret.

Grief.

"You miss baseball," she said softly.

He lifted a shoulder. "Didn't think so, but yeah, I do."

"Is that why you didn't want to come tonight?"

"I didn't think I was ready, even for softball." He shook his head. "I haven't played since my dad died."

"I'm so sorry." She sucked in a breath, knowing she couldn't let him tell her the story without her telling *him* some things first. "Finn —"

"At the time, Sean was still a minor. He'd have gone into the system, so I came home."

The familiar guilt stabbed at her, tearing off little chunks of her heart and soul. "What about your mom?"

He shrugged. "She took off when we were young. Haven't heard from her since."

Pru had to take a long beat to just breathe. "Sean was lucky to have you," she finally said. "So lucky. I hate that you had to give up college —"

"I actually hated school," he said on a low laugh. "But I really, *really* didn't want to go home. Home was full of shit memories."

Feeling land-locked by her misery, she had to run that through twice. "Finn, I —" She stopped. Stared at him. "What?"

He was eyeing a deli across the street. "You hungry?"

"I . . . a little."

"You ever eat anything from there? They make the most amazing steak sandwiches." He slid her a look. "Don't want you to miss out on steak on my account." He guided her inside where he ordered for them both.

Which was for the best because she couldn't think.

His memories of home were shit? What did that mean?

Finn paid and they continued walking. He was quiet, keeping an eye on her. But she didn't want quiet. "What do you mean home was full of shit memories?"

He took a moment to answer. "You grow up with siblings?" he asked. "Both parents?"

"No siblings but both parents," she said, and held her breath. "Until they died when I was nineteen."

He didn't make the connection, and why would he? Only a crazy person would guess that the two accidents — his dad's and her parents — were the same one.

"That sucks," he said. "Sucks bad."

It did, but she didn't deserve his sympathy. "Before that, it was a good life," she said. "Just the three of us."

"Well, trust me when I say, Sean and I didn't get the same experience."

His body language was loose and easy, relaxed as he walked. But though she couldn't see his eyes behind his dark sunglasses, she sensed there was nothing loose and easy in them. "Your dad wasn't a nice guy?"

"He was an asshole," he said. "I'm sorry he's dead, but neither I nor Sean was sorry to have to finish raising ourselves without him."

She stared at him in profile as she tried to put her thoughts together, but they'd just scattered like tumbleweeds in the wind. All this time she'd pictured his dad as . . . well, the perfect dad. The perfect dad who *her* dad had taken from him and Sean. She let out a shuddering breath of air, not sure how to feel.

"Hey." Finn stopped her with a hand to her arm and pulled her around to face him, pulling off his sunglasses, shoving them to the top of his head to get a better look at her. "You don't look so good. Your cuts and bruises, or too much sun?" he asked, gently pushing her hair from her face and pressing his palm to her forehead. "You're pale all of a sudden."

She shook her head and swallowed the lump of emotion in her throat. He'd hate her sympathy so she managed a smile. "I'm okay."

He didn't look like he believed her, proven when he switched the deli bag to his other hand and with his free one, grabbed hers in a firm grip. They were only a block from their building at this point, but before they could take another step, Finn stilled and laughed.

Pru looked up to see Spence coming toward them.

Tall and leanly muscled, with sun-kissed wavy hair that matched his smiling light brown eyes, he was definitely eye candy. He wore cargo shorts and an untucked button-down, sleeves shoved up his forearms. He was a genuinely sexy guy, not that he seemed to realize it.

He was walking two golden retrievers and a cat, all three on leashes advertising South Bark Mutt Shop, striding calm-as-you-please at Spence's side.

Spence himself was calm as well, and

completely oblivious to the two women craning their necks to stare at his ass as he passed them. He was too busy flipping Finn off for laughing at him.

"I didn't realize you worked for Willa," Pru said. *Or that one could actually walk a cat . . .*

"He doesn't exactly . . ." Finn said.

Spence didn't add anything to this as Finn looked at him. "You're walking a cat. They're going to take away your man card."

"Tell that to the owner of the cat," Spence said. "She asked me out for tonight."

"So now you're using these helpless animals to get laid?"

"Hell yes," Spence said. "And yuk it up now because later I'm going to let Professor PuddinPop here anoint your shoes. Fair warning, he had tuna for lunch and it's not agreeing with him."

"No cats allowed in the pub," Finn said.

"Professor PuddinPop is the smaller retriever," Spence said. "His brother Colonel Snazzypants is a specialist in evacuating his bowels over a wide area. Watch yourself. You've been warned."

"What's the cat's name?" Pru asked.

"Good King Snugglewumps," Spence said with a straight face. "He's actually an emotional support cat, which you look like you could use right now. What the hell happened to you?"

"I slid trying to catch a ball at my softball game," she said.

"With your pretty face?"

"No, that was collateral damage. But I did catch the ball."

"Nice job," he said with a smile and a high-five.

Finn had crouched down low to interact with the animals. The cat was perched on his bent leg, rubbing against him, and both dogs had slid to their backs so he could scratch their bellies.

"The Animal Whisperer," Spence said. "They always gravitate to him." He shook his head at Good King Snugglewumps. "Man 'ho."

Good King Snugglewumps pretended not to hear him.

Finn grinned. "I'm the Animal Whisperer, and Pru here is the Fun Whisperer."

Spence turned to Pru. "How's that going? He learning to have fun yet?"

"He's not much for cooperating."

"No shit." He looked at Finn. "Keep your shoes on, that's all I'm saying."

And then he strode off, two dogs and a cat in tow.

Finn pulled out his phone and snapped a

pic of Spence from behind.

Spence, without looking back, flipped him off again.

Still grinning, Finn shoved his phone back into his pocket and reached for Pru's hand. "Let's get you home."

Good idea. In just the minute that they'd stopped to talk, she'd gone stiff, but did her best to hide it. They entered the courtyard and she glanced at the fountain, which, she couldn't help but notice, had not been very busy fulfilling her wish for love for Finn. She sagged behind him just enough that she could point at the fountain and then at her eyes, putting it on notice that she was watching it.

The fountain didn't respond.

But apparently Finn had eyes in the back of his head because he laughed. "Babe, you just gave that thing a look that said you'd like to barbeque it and feed it in pieces to your mortal enemy."

She would. She absolutely would. Hoping for a subject change, she waved at Old Guy, sitting on a bench.

"Eddie," Finn said with a male greeting of a chin jut. "You look better than the other night."

Eddie nodded. "Yeah, it was either a twenty-four-hour flu thing or food poisoning," he said.

"You could stop eating everything everyone gives you," Finn suggested.

"No way! I get good shit, man. Cutie Pie here gives really good doggy bags. Chicken wings, pizza . . ." He looked at Pru. "You know what we haven't had lately? Sushi —" He broke off, narrowing his eyes. "What happened to you, darlin'? This guy get tough with you? If so, just say the word and I'll level him flat."

Eddie was maybe ninety-five pounds soaking wet and looked like a good wind could blow him over. Finn had at least six inches on him and God knew how many pounds of lean, tough muscle, not to mention a way of carrying all that lean, tough muscle that said he knew exactly what to do with it.

Pru caught him looking at her with a raised brow, like *are you really going to say the word?*

"I roughed myself up," she admitted. "Softball." She started to reach into her pocket for a few dollar bills to give Eddie but Finn put a hand on her arm to stop her. With his other hand he fished something out of his duffel bag.

The third sandwich he'd bought at the deli.

Eddie grinned and snatched it out of thin

air. "See? I get good stuff. And you know your way to a man's heart, boy. Mayo?"

"Would I forget? And extra pickles."

"Chips?"

Almost before the word was out, Finn was tossing Eddie a bag of salt and vinegar chips.

Eddie clasped a hand to his own heart. "Bless you. And tell Bossy Lady that I got the bag of clothes."

"Elle?"

Eddie nodded. "She said I was going to catch my death in my wife beaters and shorts, and insisted I take these clothes from her." He indicated his trousers and long-sleeved sweater. It was the surfer dude goes mobster look.

"How do they fit?" Finn asked, smiling, enjoying the old man's discomfort.

Eddie rolled his eyes. "Like a cheap castle — no ballroom."

Finn laughed and reached for Pru's hand again, tugging her toward the elevator.

That's when a whole new set of worries hit Pru. Was he going to come in?

Had she shaved?

No, she told herself firmly. *It doesn't matter if your legs aren't hairy, you are not going there with him.*

At her door, he held onto her hand while rummaging through her bag for her keys, and then opened her door like he owned the place.

But before they could get inside, the door across the way opened and Mrs. Winslow stepped out.

Pru's neighbor was as old as time, and that time hadn't exactly been particularly kind. Still, she was sharp as a tack, her faculties honed by staying up on everything and everyone in the building.

"Hello, dear," she said to Pru. "You're bleeding."

This was getting old. "Skiing accident," she said, trying something new.

Finn flashed her an appreciative grin.

Mrs. Winslow chortled. "Even an old lady knows her seasons," she said. "It's high summer, which means it was softball."

Pru sighed. "Yeah."

"Did you at least win this time?"

"No."

"I think the idea is to win at least some-times," Mrs. Winslow said.

Pru sighed again. "Yeah. We're working on that." She gestured to Finn at her side, steady as a rock, but looking a little hot and dusty. "I recruited a new player," she said.

"Good choice," Mrs. Winslow said. "He's put together right nice, isn't he."

Pru's gaze went on a tour of Finn from

head to toe and back again. Nice wasn't exactly the description she would use. Hot as hell, maybe. Devastatingly, disarmingly perfect . . .

At her close scrutiny, his mouth curved and something else came into his eyes.

Hunger.

"I got a little something delivered today," Mrs. Winslow said. "That's why I've been waiting for you."

"Me?" Pru asked.

"Yes, my package came via your dumbwaiter."

"Why?"

"Because, dear, the dumbwaiter is only on your side of the building."

Okaaay. Pru gestured to her open door. Mrs. Winslow let herself in, unlatched the dumbwaiter door and removed a . . . platter of brownies?

Pru's mouth watered as Mrs. Winslow smiled, gave a quick "thanks" and exited the apartment, heading for her own.

"Those look amazing," Pru said, hoping for an invite to take one.

Or two.

Or as many as she could stuff into her mouth.

"Oh, I'm sorry," Mrs. Winslow said with a negative head shake. "These are . . . special brownies."

Pru blinked and then looked at Finn, who appeared to be fighting a smile. "Special brownies?" she repeated, unable to believe that Mrs. Winslow really meant what she thought she meant.

"Yes," the older woman said. "And you're not of age, or I'd share."

"Mrs. Winslow, I'm twenty-six."

Mrs. Winslow smiled. "I meant over sixty-five."

And then she vanished into her own apartment.

Finn gently nudged Pru into hers, which answered the unspoken question. He was coming in. Into her apartment.

And, if her heart had any say at all, into her life.

Chapter 15

#DOH

Finn dropped both duffel bags and the deli bag on Pru's kitchen counter and then turned to her. "Okay, time to play doctor."

Her entire body quivered, sending "yes please" vibes to her brain. Luckily her mouth intercepted them. "Sure, if I can be the doctor."

His mouth curved. "I'm willing to take turns, but me first."

Oh boy. "Really, I'm fine. I think I just need a shower."

"Do you want something to drink? I could call down to the pub and —"

"No, thanks."

"I wasn't talking about alcohol," he said. "I already know you don't drink."

There weren't many who would so easily accept such a thing without some sort of question. People wanted and expected others to drink socially when they did. Usually whenever she politely declined, the interrogation inevitably started. *Not even one little drink?* Or *what's up with that, are you an alcoholic?*

Pru couldn't imagine actually being an alcoholic and facing that kind of inquisition with class and grace, but the truth was that she didn't drink because her parents had. A lot. They'd been heavy social drinkers. She didn't know if they'd had an actual problem or had just loved to party, but she did know it had killed them.

And that had quenched her thirst for alcohol at an early age.

But Finn didn't push. "How about something warm?" he asked. "Like a hot chocolate?"

She felt her heart squeeze in her chest for his easy acceptance. "Maybe after my shower."

He nodded and leaned back against the counter like he planned on waiting for her. Not knowing how to deal with that, she nodded back and headed for the bathroom. She shut and locked the door and then stared at that lock for a good sixty seconds, because did she really want to lock him out? No. She wanted him to join her, the steam drifting across their wet bodies as he picked her up, pressed her against the shower wall and buried himself deep.

Ignoring her wobbly knees, she left the lock in place, shaking her head at herself. Apparently it'd been too long since her last social orgasm and while she handled her own business just fine, her business was clearly getting bored with herself.

Stripping out of her clothes involved peeling her shirt from the torn skin of her elbows, not a super pleasurable experience. Same for her knees and her jeans. Naked, she took inventory. Two bloody knees, one bloody elbow and a bloody chin.

When she was little and got hurt, her mom would hug her tight and then blow on her cuts and bruises and whisper "see, not so bad . . ."

It'd been a long time, but there were moments like right now where she would've traded her entire world away for a hug like that again. She looked at her bruised, bloody self in the mirror and took a deep breath. "See, not so bad," she whispered and got into the shower.

She made it quick, partly because as she ran soap all over her body, she only ramped herself up, but mostly because her various road rashes burned like hell. But also because as she soaped up, she couldn't help but think of Finn standing in her kitchen, arms casually crossed, pose casual, his mood anything but.

Waiting for her.

Her good parts quivered so she turned the water off, going from overheated to chilled in a single heartbeat. With her bad parts stinging and her good parts throbbing, she stepped out of the shower.

At the knock at the door, she nearly had a stroke.

"How bad is it?" Finn asked through the wood.

She yanked her towel off the rack and wrapped it around herself, her hair dripping along her shoulders and down her back. "Not bad." Her voice sounded low and husky, and damn . . . inviting. She cleared her throat. "Not bad at all."

"I want to see." He tried the handle. "Let me in, Pru."

Her hand mutinied and unlocked the door, but didn't go as far as to actually open it for him. She couldn't because dammit, he was already in. In her head, her veins, *all* of her secret happy places, and, she suspected, her heart.

Finn pushed the door open and stood there, eyes scanning her slowly, his body stilling as he realized she was in just a towel.

He took what looked like a deep breath and stepped the rest of the way in, a first-aid kit in his hand. "Had this in my bag," he said and set it on the countertop to the left of the sink. Turning to her, he put his hands to her waist and lifted her, setting her on the right side of the sink.

Ignoring her squeak of surprise, he opened up his kit, fingered his way through, and came up with gauze and antiseptic. Turning toward her, he sprayed and then bandaged up her elbows, his brow furrowed in concentration as he worked. When he'd finished there, he crouched low.

With another surprised squeak, Pru pressed her legs together and tugged at the bottom of her towel, trying to make sure it covered the goods.

This got her an almost smile as he went about doctoring up both knees, using the spray again, keeping his eyes on his work, his big, strong, capable hands moving with quick, clinical efficiency.

Pru occupied herself and her nerves by watching the way his shirt stretched taut across his shoulders and back, every muscle rippling as he moved. His head was bent to her, his eyes narrowed in concentration, his long, dark lashes hiding his thoughts.

Fine with her, as she was having enough thoughts for the both of them, the number one being — if she relaxed her very tense thighs even a fraction, he'd be able to see straight up to the promised land.

The thought made her dizzy but she told herself it was the spray giving her a head rush.

Because actually, there was something incredibly erotic about that, her being nude beneath the towel and him being fully dressed. But she was all too aware that not only was she a wreck on the inside, she was looking the part.

His concentration shifted from what he was doing, his gaze cutting to hers. Reaching out he brushed his fingers over her cheek. "Why are you blushing?"

"I'm not."

He arched a brow.

"I'm a mess," she blurted out.

He rose at that, brushing his hands from her ankles up the backs of her calves, resting just behind her knees for a beat before giving a little tug, sliding her forward on the counter toward him.

Her legs parted of their own volition and he stepped between them, leaning in close at the same time, his body heat warming her up. His arms slid around her hips, snugging her closer as his lips gently brushed hers. Then those lips made their way along her jawline to just beneath her ear, trailing tiny kisses as he then worked his way down her throat.

"You're beautiful," he whispered. "A beautiful mess."

She choked out a laugh.

"You are," he said against her shoulder now. "So beautiful you take my breath away." Then he lifted his head to look into her eyes letting her see he meant it, entirely.

It'd been a long time since she'd felt beautiful, but she realized that she did. Very much so. She wanted to close her eyes and get lost in that, lost in him, but with one last nip at the sensitive spot where her neck met her shoulder, he shifted his attention to her chin.

She hissed in a breath when he pressed a gauze to it and then held her next breath as well when he leaned forward and kissed her there.

He'd shifted slightly to reach and the rough slide of denim brushed the skin of her bare thighs, making them tremble for more. "What are you doing?" she asked, sounding a little like Minnie Mouse on helium as his mouth and stubbled jaw gently abraded over her skin.

"Kissing your owies," he said innocently, his voice anything but as he continued with his ministrations.

Her traitorous body responded by arching and pressing closer, oscillating her hips to his for the sheer erotic pleasure of hearing him groan.

His mouth brushed her jaw one more time before he met her gaze. "Where else?"

Completely dazed, she shook her head. "Huh?"

"Where else do you hurt?"

She stared up at him. Where else did she hurt? Nowhere, because with his hands and mouth on her, all her pleasure receptors had overcome the pain. But not about to look a gift horse in the mouth, she pointed to her shoulder.

Finn gave it his utmost attention, running his finger over a growing bruise. Then he bent and kissed her there, letting his lips linger a little.

She looked at his mouth on her, those amazing lips pressed to her skin, and shivered.

With a wordless murmur, Finn shifted even closer, his warm, strong arms encircling her so that she could absorb some of the heat coming off him in waves. His long, dark lashes brushed his cheeks when his eyes were closed, like now. He hadn't shaved that morning and maybe not the morning before either. She could feel the prickles of his beard when he turned his head slightly and opened his eyes.

"Where else?" he asked, his voice pure sex.

And here's where she made her mistake. She needed to stay strong, that was all she had to do. But the problem was that she was tired of being strong. And she was having a hard time remembering why she needed to.

"Pru?"

She swallowed hard and pointed to her mouth.

He pulled back, gave her a hot look that melted her bones, and slowly worked his way up her throat with hot, wet kisses. When he got to her jaw, he fisted his hands in her hair and tilted her head right where he wanted her. She felt him open his mouth on her jawline, and with just the tip of his tongue made his way back to her mouth.

Wrapping her arms around his broad shoulders, she moaned and held on tight as he kissed her like maybe she was the best thing he'd ever tasted. And God, the feel of him against her, steady and solid. She didn't know how he did it but even after a long ball game he still smelled amazing. Something woodsy and pure male . . .

Then he pulled back.

Staring up at him, she ached. "Finn?"

"Yeah?"

"Remember how you said the ball was in my court?"

He pressed his forehead to hers for a beat, like he was working on control. She knew she should be as well but she didn't want him to leave, didn't want to be alone in this. "Don't go," she whispered softly.

He opened his eyes, the heat in them nearly sending her up in flames. Nope, she wasn't alone, thank God, because that would really suck. Out of words, she arched into him a little.

He groaned. "Pru."

Afraid the next words out of his mouth would be good-bye, she snuggled in and pressed her mouth to the underside of his jaw in a soft kiss. When he opened his mouth to say something, she took a nibble. At the feel of her teeth on him, he stilled and shuddered, and then his arms tightened on her.

Yes. *This.* It was just what she needed, because here, held by him like this, her guilt, her regret, her fears . . . all of it gave way to this heady, languid sensation of being desired and she didn't want it to stop.

Any of it.

His eyes were deep and intense as he shifted, nudging against the apex of her thighs. Keeping his gaze on hers, he kissed her again, sending licks of fiery desire right through her. Then those hands drifted down to her thighs, his fingers over the terry cloth, his thumbs beneath.

"Is this what you want?" he asked.

She gasped at the sensation of his callused thumbs grazing over her inner thighs, and he caught her mouth with his in a deep, hot, wet kiss as he slipped beneath her towel now, cupping her bare ass in his big hands.

When she was too breathless to hold the kiss, she broke it off, her head falling back as his mouth skimmed hot and wet down her throat, across her collarbone. Her entire body felt strung too tight, like her skin didn't fit. Impatient, she arched into him again, dragging a rough groan from him.

"Pru." His voice was thrillingly rough, but there was a warning there too. He wasn't going to let this get away from her. She was going to have to say how far they took things.

"I want this," she whispered, clutching at him. "I want . . ."

His mouth was at her ear, bringing her a delicious spine shiver. "Name it."

"You. Please, Finn, I want you."

Raising his head, he stared at her before kissing her again, stroking his tongue to hers in a rhythm that made her hips grind to his. The soft denim of his jeans rasped over the tender skin of her inner thighs and thrilling to it, she wrapped her legs even tighter around him, drawing him closer, the hottest, neediest part of her desperately seeking attention.

Finn said something low and inaudible, and then let out a quiet laugh as he nipped her lower lip, her throat, and then . . . her towel slipped from her breasts.

He'd loosened it with his teeth.

When he put his hot mouth to her nipple, she nearly went over the edge right then and there. He cupped her breasts in his big warm hands, shifting his attention from one to the other, his stubbled jaw gently scraping over her in the most bone-melting of ways, his movements sensual, so slow and erotic she could hardly stand it. *"Finn."*

He lifted his head and held her gaze while he spread the towel from her, letting it fall to her sides before he worked his way south, lazily exploring every inch of her like he had all the time in the world, humming in pleasure when he found the little compass on her hip. He spent a long moment there, learning her tattoo — with his tongue.

And all she could do was grip the counter on either side of her, head tipped back because it was too much effort to hold it up, her nerve endings sending high bolts of desire through her at his every touch.

She was completely naked to his fully dressed body now. Open, exposed . . . vulnerable in more ways than one. Certainly more than she'd allowed in far too long, although she didn't feel a single ounce of self-consciousness or anxiety about it.

She felt nothing but the sharp lick of hunger and need barreling down on her like a freight train in tune to his clever mouth and greedy hands. She was afraid if he so much as breathed on her special happy place, she'd go off like a bottle rocket.

And then he dropped to his knees.

His hands glided up her inner thighs, holding her open so his lips could make their way homeward bound. About thirty minutes ago she'd thought she needed steak more than anything but it turned out that wasn't true. She needed this, with Finn.

One of their phones buzzed, either hers on the floor in her pants pocket, or his from wherever he had it tucked away. She started to straighten but then his fingers stroked her wet flesh and she forgot about the phone. Hell, she forgot her own name. "Oh God, don't stop. Please, Finn, don't stop . . ."

"I've got you." And then he replaced his teasing fingers with his tongue, giving her a slow, purposeful lick. She whimpered as he continued to nuzzle her, luring her into relaxing again — and then his lips formed a hot suction.

And that was it, she'd become the bottle rocket and was gone, launched out of orbit. Hell, out of the stratosphere. When she came back to planet Earth, she realized she had Finn by the hair, her fingers curled tight against his head, her thighs squeezing his head like he was a walnut to be cracked. "I'm so sorry!" she gasped, forcing herself to let go of him. "I nearly ripped out your hair."

The words backed up in her throat when he turned his head and pressed a soft kiss to her inner thigh, sending her up a very male, very protective, possessive, smug smile. "Worth it," he said, and licked his lips.

She nearly came again. "Please come here."

He rose to his feet and her hands went to his stomach, sliding beneath his shirt to feel the heat of his hard abs. So much to touch, and the question became up or down . . .

His eyes were dark and heated, flickering with amusement as he read the indecision on her face.

"I'm not exactly sure what to do with you," she whispered.

"I could make a few suggestions."

She laughed a little nervously but let her hands glide up his torso, shoving his shirt up as she went. He was so beautifully made . . . "Off," she said softly.

He had the shirt gone in less than a heartbeat and she soaked up the sight of his broad shoulders and chest while her fingers played at the waistband of his jeans. They were loose enough that she could dip in and —

"Oh," she breathed, sucking in a breath as she encountered *much* more than she'd bargained for.

His hot — and amused — gaze held hers. On the surface, he was calm and steady and unflappable as always, but there was an underlying erotic tension in every line of his body, a sense that he was holding back, keeping his latent sexuality in check.

She popped the top button of his Levi's.

And then the second.

And then she'd freed him entirely, pushing his knit boxers aside and all his glory sprung into her hand — and there was a lot of glory. "Finn?"

His voice was rough and husky. "Yeah?"

"I think I figured out what I want to do with you."

It involved the condom that he luckily had in his wallet and her leaning back on the cold tile of her bathroom countertop, but they managed.

And when he slid deep and then grasped her ass in his two big hands and roughly pulled her closer so that he went even deeper, she arched her spine and let her head fall back and felt more alive than she'd felt in far too long. She got chills all over her body and with a wordless murmur, Finn brought her upright so that she was pressed tight to his warm chest. He wrapped his arms around her and she could feel her toes curl. She clenched tight, eliciting a groan from him, and held on. She knew she was digging her nails into his back but she couldn't stop, couldn't breathe . . . "Finn —"

"I know." His hands slid south, cupping her ass, protecting her from the tile. When he did something diabolically clever with those long fingers, she came in a giant, unexpected burst.

From somewhere outside of herself she felt Finn lose control as well. They ended up smashed up against one another, gripping each other hard, faces pressed together, breathing like lunatics.

They stayed like that for a few minutes and then slowly separated. She flopped back against the mirror, not caring that it was chilly against her overheated skin.

Finn sagged against the counter like he wasn't all that sturdy himself. He made quite the sight, shirtless, his jeans opened and dangerously low.

Sexy as hell. She'd do something about it but she felt like a boneless rag doll.

A very sated one. "I'm hoping it was the antiseptic spray," she managed.

"I'm hoping not," Finn said.

She needed to move but couldn't find her limbs to save her life. Finn didn't seem to have the same problem, he used his arms to lean over her and kiss her, eyes open like maybe he was taking her vitals.

She quivered for more. Good God. Since when was she addicted to sex?

Finn caught the look in her eyes and he laughed low in his throat. Sexy as hell. "Give me a minute," he said, voice husky.

She arched a brow, impressed. "Just one?"

"Maybe one and a half," he said, his gaze dropping to her mouth. "Tops."

Her good parts actually fluttered. *Seriously, what was wrong with her?*

"How's the road rash?" he asked, helping

her down off the counter and rewrapping her up in the towel.

It took her a moment to get her brain organized enough to even remember what he was talking about. "Good."

"Liar." His voice was quiet and very, very sexy. She wondered if he'd ever considered a side job as a phone sex operator. He'd be fantastic at it. Or maybe he could just read her a book, any book at all . . .

His phone buzzed once more and he blew out a sigh. "That's twice. I'm sorry, I have to look." He pulled his phone from his pocket and glanced at the screen.

A frown creased his brow as he accessed a text.

And then his easy demeanor vanished. He rose to his feet.

"What's the matter?" she asked.

He pulled her towel back around her, tucking it in between her breasts, stopping to brush a sweet kiss to her lips. "I'm sorry. I have to go. Sean's in trouble."

Her heart stopped. "Do you need help?"

"No, I've got it. We've been around this block before, more times than I can count."

"But . . ." She ran her gaze down his body, letting it catch on the unmistakable bulge behind his button fly. "Now?"

"Yeah." He ran the pad of his thumb along

her jaw and kissed her again. "Thanks for giving me a taste of you," he murmured against her mouth. "I already want another."

And then he was gone, leaving her sitting there, mouth open, blinking like a land-locked fish at the open doorway he'd just vanished through.

"I want a taste of you too," she said to the empty void he'd left behind. She looked around her at the steamy bathroom. "I don't even know what just happened," she told it.

But she totally did — she'd just compli-cated things even more. And in an irrevers-ible way, too.

Dammit, she was supposed to be fun whispering him. Instead, she'd fun whis-pered herself!

Chapter 16

#MYBAD

Finn took the stairs rather than wait for the elevator, and then jogged across the courtyard to the pub, his body practically vibrating with adrenaline.

He could still hear Pru's soft, breathy, whimpery pants in his ear. She'd stilled for his touch like she'd been afraid it would all stop too soon.

She'd even begged him. *Please, Finn, don't stop* . . .

If Sean hadn't called, they'd have moved to her bed by now and be in the throes of round two.

Not once in the past eight years since his life had changed so drastically had he'd had such a wildly hot, crazy sex-capade, but Pru brought it out in him. There was no denying that he felt more alive when he was with her than he'd felt in . . . well, shit.

A fucking long time.

There'd been few opportunities when he

was busy working 24/7 and trying to keep Sean on the straight and narrow.

But Pru had gotten under his skin, and like her, he wanted more. So much more. He wanted to know her secrets, the ones that sometimes put those shadows in her eyes. He wanted to know why she wanted to bring him fun and adventure, but didn't seem to feel like she deserved it as well. He wanted to know what made her tick. And more than anything, he wanted to taste her again.

Every inch of her.

He wanted to see more of her and he had no idea how she felt about that. For the first time in he had no idea how long, he was thinking about more than the bottom line of the pub.

He was thinking about a future, with an adventurous, frustrating, warm, sexy woman he couldn't seem to get enough of.

Skipping the crowded pub, he entered directly into his office, while thumbing through his email on his phone. "So what the hell's so important that —" He broke off as a sound permeated through his thick skull — the soft sigh of a woman experiencing pleasure.

Sexual pleasure.

Jerking his head up, he took in the sight

on his couch and whipped back to the door, which he slammed behind him. Grinding his back teeth into powder, he strode around the courtyard to the pub door and went directly to the bar.

Scott, the night's bartender, started toward him but Finn waved him off and grabbed a shot glass to serve himself.

He was trying to lose himself in the happy sounds of the crowd around him, pouring a double when Sean appeared, shirtless, shoeless, buttoning his Levi's.

Behind him was a tall, curvy blonde in a little sundress, her hair tousled, her high-heeled sandals dangling from her hand. Shooting Finn a wry smile, she turned to Sean, ran a hand up his chest and around his neck and leaned in to give him a lingering kiss. "Thanks for a good time, baby." With a last lingering look in Finn's direction, she padded out.

"Fuck," Finn said.

"Exactly," Sean said with a sated grin.

Finn shook his head and headed down the interior hallway to his office.

Sean followed.

"What the hell's the matter with you?" Finn asked.

"Absolutely nothing."

"I'm working real hard here at not chucking this shot glass at your head," Finn said. "You want to come up with better than that and you want to do it quick."

Sean blinked. "What the hell's your problem? Why are you raining on my parade?"

"What the hell's *my* problem?" Finn sucked in a breath for calm. It didn't work. "You texted me that you had an emergency. I dropped everything and race over here to find you fucking some girl on the couch in *my* office."

"I told you, you have the better office."

Finn stared at him, and some of his genuine temper and absolutely zero humor of the situation must have finally gotten through to Sean because he lifted his hands. "Look, you got back here faster than I thought you would, all right? And Ashley just happened to stop by and . . . well, one thing led to another."

Finn tossed back the smoothest Scotch in the place and barely felt the burn. "You told me there was an emergency. That you needed me. Exactly how long did you expect me to take getting here?"

"Longer than sixty seconds," Sean said. "I mean I'm good, but even I need at least five minutes." He flashed a grin.

Finn resisted the urge to strangle him. Barely. "Emergency implies death and destruction and mayhem," he said. "Like, say, our *last* emergency. When dad died."

The easy smile fell from Sean's face, replaced by surprise and then guilt, followed by shame. "Oh shit," he said. "Shit, I didn't think —"

"And there's our problem, Sean," Finn said. "You never do."

Sean's mouth tightened. "No, actually, that's not the real problem. Let's hear it again, shall we? You're the grown-up. I'm just the stupid problem child."

"You're hardly a child."

"But I'm still a problem," Sean said. "Always have been to you."

"Bullshit," Finn said. "Get your head out of your own ass and stop feeling sorry for yourself. Now what the hell's the emergency?"

Sean paused. "It was more of a pub thing," he said vaguely, no longer meeting Finn's gaze.

And a very bad feeling crept into Finn's gut. "What did you do?"

"It's more what I didn't do . . ."

"Spit it out, Sean."

"Okay, okay. But before you blow a gasket, you should know. It's not as bad as the time I nearly burnt the place down by accident. Let's keep it in perspective, all right?"

"Accident?" Finn asked. "You opened the place after hours to have a party with your idiot friends and were lighting Jell-O shots when you managed to catch the kitchen on fire. How exactly is that an *accident*?"

"Well, who knew that Jell-O was so flammable?"

Finn stared at him, at an utter loss. "This is a fucking joke to you, all of it."

"No, it's not."

"Yes, it is. You think I'm just the asshole making you toe the line. I'm trying to give you a life here, Sean, a way to make a living and take care of yourself in case something happens to me."

Sean laughed. *Laughed.* The sound harsh in the quiet room. "You're not dad, Finn. I don't need you to give me a life. I can do that for myself. Contrary to popular belief, I can take care of myself."

"Because you've done a great job of it so far?" Finn asked.

"Fuck you," Sean said and walked out.

"What's the damn emergency?" Finn yelled after him.

But Sean was gone.

This left Finn in charge of the place for the night instead of getting to go back up to 3B where he'd left his mind, and maybe a good chunk of his heart as well.

■ ■ ■ ■

The next morning was Sunday and despite it being a weekend, Finn was back at the pub. He was working his way through some of the never-ending paperwork that seemed to multiply daily when Sean appeared.

"Where have you been?" Finn asked, hating himself for sounding like a nagging grandma.

Sean ran his hand over his bedhead hair. "Slept on the roof."

Finn shook his head. "Bet you froze your nuts off."

"Just about." Sean paused. "I shouldn't have walked away last night. I'm sorry for that."

"Just tell me the damn emergency already," Finn said.

Sean's jaw went tight, a muscle ticking. A very unusual sight, and a tell that he was actually feeling stressed, something Finn hadn't known his brother could even feel.

Sean pulled two envelopes from his back pocket. "You know how I said I wanted to help you with the business side of things and you said I had to start at the bottom, and I said like the mail room? And you said we don't have a mail room, but yes a little bit like that?"

"It was a joke," Finn said. "Because you think you just jump in but there's a learning curve. So I suggested you start by handling our mail and our accounts payable. And you agreed as long as I didn't come along behind you to check up on you."

"Didn't need dad in the house looking over my shoulder," Sean said.

"Actually, if I'd been dad, I'd have used my fists, or whatever else was handy and just beat the shit out of you," Finn said. "Or have you forgotten?"

Temper flashed in Sean's eyes. Temper, and something else that he got a hold of before Finn could. He didn't speak for a moment, which was rare for Sean. He just stood there, fists clenched at his side, working his jaw muscles. "Fuck it. Fuck this," he finally said and started to turn away but stopped. "No, you know what? Fuck you. Sideways."

"Mature."

But Sean wasn't playing. He shoved a finger in Finn's face. "You think I've forgotten which one of us dad got off on beating up? You think I don't remember at night when I close my eyes that you took it for me, every single time? That I don't know you made sure you were between him and me so I'd be safe? That I survived only because of you? That I'm *still* surviving because of you? You think I don't know that I'm a fuckup who's only here with a semblance of a normal life because you gave it to me?"

Okay, so the something else in Sean's gaze had been grief and remembered horror. And Finn shouldn't have tried to be glib about it, there was nothing glib about how they'd grown up. "I didn't mean to take this there," he said quietly. "You're not a —"

"I forgot to pay our liquor license." Sean's face was hard. Blank. "I forgot and it was due today."

Finn stared at him. "That was the one thing I reminded you of two months ago when you took on the bills."

"The envelope fell behind my desk and got lost. And it wasn't alone. The property tax on the house was back there too and that one's now past due."

"Are you kidding me?"

"Do I look like I'm kidding?" Sean inhaled a deep breath, spread out his arms and shook his head. "See? You were right. I really am just a fuckup. You should demote me back to —"

"What? Sweep boy?" Finn found his own temper. And hell if he was going to let Sean default to his favorite thing — self-destruction, just because it was easier than growing up. "You wanted to do this, Sean. You wanted in. And now you're telling me what, things are too hard, you're too busy having fun that you can't get your head out of your ass and grow up?"

Sean's eyes narrowed. "Guess so."

Finn stared at him waiting for regret, for an apology, for any-fucking-thing, but nothing came. Just Sean's hooded gaze, body braced for a fight, all sullen 'tude. Finn shook his head. "Fine. You win."

"What does that mean?"

"It means I need some air," Finn said and walked out the door to the courtyard.

It was late morning and unusually warm. Summer was in full swing, which in San Francisco usually meant a sweatshirt sixty-five-ish and fingers crossed for a hope to get into the seventies.

But now, in direct opposition to his mood, it was sunny and warm, and it didn't suit him in the least.

He had no idea where he'd intended to go, only knowing he was going somewhere, needing to vent the ugly inside him, the ugly his dad had bequeathed him.

The gym maybe. He'd go punch the shit out of a bag at the gym.

But to do that, he'd have to walk past Pru standing there watching him, a look on her face that told him she'd heard everything.

CHAPTER 17
#THEREAREN'TENOUGHCOOKIESFORTHIS

Pru stared into Finn's face, wishing like hell she could go back and vanish before he caught sight of her, or barring that, at least do something to ease the pain and anger in his eyes.

"Did you get all of that or do you need me to repeat some of it?" he asked.

"I didn't mean to get any of it," she said. "It was an accidental eavesdrop."

He blew out a sigh, shook his head, and stared over her head at the fountain.

Regret slashed through her. She'd been caught eavesdropping many times, all of them accidental. Once when she'd been young, she'd caught her parents going at it on the dining room table with gusto. It'd been ten o'clock at night and she'd been fast asleep only to wake up thirsty. Not wanting to disturb her parents, she'd made her own way to the kitchen.

At first glance she'd smiled because she'd

thought that her dad was tickling her mom. Her mom had loved it when he'd done that, and they'd touched often.

But she'd never seen naked tickling before . . .

Later when Pru had been a teenager, she'd come home from school to find her parents at the table with their neighbor, Mr. Snyder, who was also their accountant, talking about something called bankruptcy. Her mom had been crying, her dad looking shell-shocked.

And then there'd been the night her grandpa had shown up where she'd been spending the night at a friend's. Weird, since she'd called her mom and dad for a ride, not her grandpa. She'd wanted to go home because her friends had decided to sneak in some boys and she hadn't felt comfortable with the attention she'd been getting from one of them. He'd been in her math class, and was always leaning over her shoulder pretending to stare at her work when he was really just staring at her breasts.

The other reason it'd been weird for her grandpa to show up was because she hadn't seen him in years. Not since he and her dad had been estranged for reasons she'd never known. And her dad and her grandpa being estranged meant that Pru was estranged by default.

So why was he at her friend's house?

The night had gone on to become a real-life nightmare, the kind you never woke up from because she'd listened to her grandpa explain to her friend's mom that he'd come to tell his granddaughter that her parents were dead, that her father had been past the legal drinking limit. He'd crossed the center median in the road and had hit another car head on, clipping a second along with the people on the sidewalk.

Pru did her best not to think about that moment, but it crept in at the most unexpected times. Like when she was in the mall and passed by a department store in front of the perfume aisle and caught a whiff of the scent her mom had always worn. Or when sometimes late at night if there was a storm and she got unnerved, she'd wish for her dad to come into her room like he always had, sit on the bed and pull her into his arms and sing silly made-up songs at the top of his lungs to drown out the wind.

Nope . . . eavesdropping had never worked out for her. And when she'd heard Sean and Finn yelling at each other through Finn's open office window, she honestly hadn't meant to listen in. Now she couldn't unhear what she'd heard. What she *could* do was be there for them. Because this whole thing, their fight, their being parentless, Finn having to raise Sean, all of it, was *her* family's doing. She swallowed hard. "I'm sorry, Finn."

He just shook his head, clearly still pissed off. "Not your fault."

Maybe not directly but she felt guilty all the same. But telling him the truth now when he was already lit up with temper wouldn't help him. It would hurt him.

And that's the last thing she'd ever do.

At her silence, he focused in on her. "How are you doing, are you —"

"Totally fine," she said. "The road rash is healing up already."

Something in his eyes lit with amusement. "Good, but this time I actually meant from when we —"

"That's fine too," she said quickly and huffed out a sigh when he laughed. She looked around for a distraction and saw a couple of women talking about throwing some coins into the fountain. Pru nodded her head over there. "You know about the legend?"

"Of course. That myth brings us more foot traffic than our daily specials."

"You ever . . . ?"

"Hell no," he said emphatically.

She managed a smile. "What's the matter,

you don't believe in true love?"

His gaze held hers for a beat. "I try not to mess with stuff that isn't for me."

She couldn't imagine what his growing-up years had been like or the hell he'd been through but she managed a small smile. "Maybe you shouldn't knock something unless you've tried it."

"And you've tried it?" he challenged.

"Oh . . ." She let out a little laugh. "Not exactly. I'm pretty sure that stuff isn't for me either."

His gaze went serious again and before he began a conversation she didn't want to have, she spoke quickly. "I really didn't mean to overhear your fight with Sean. I was just wondering if I could help with whatever was wrong before I went to work."

"What's wrong is that he's an idiot."

"If it helps, I think he feels really bad," she said.

"He always does."

Her heart ached for him as she took in the tension in every line of his body. "You guys do that a lot?" she asked. "Fight like that?"

He slid his hands into his pockets. "Sometimes. We're not all that good with holding back. We sure as hell never did master the art of the silent treatment."

"My family never did either," she said. "Silence in my house meant someone had stopped breathing — thanks to a pillow being held over their face."

Finn gave her a barely there smile, definitely devoid of its usual wattage. "Was there a lot of fighting?" he asked.

"My parents were high school sweethearts. They were together twenty years, most of them spent in a very tiny but homey Santa Cruz bungalow house, where we were practically on top of each other all the time." She sighed wistfully, missing that house so much. "Great house. But seriously, half the time my mom and dad were like siblings, at each other over every little thing. And the other half of the time, they were more in love with each other every day." The ache of losing them had faded but it still could stab at her with a white hot poker of pain out of the blue when she least expected it, like now.

"Sounds pretty good," he said.

"It was." *He'd beaten the shit out of you . . .* The words were haunting her and her gaze ran over Finn's tough, rugged features. It hurt to picture him as a helpless kid standing between a grown man and his little brother, taking whatever punishment had been meant for Sean to spare him the pain of it, and she had to close her eyes against the images that brought.

A hand closed around hers. She opened her eyes as Finn tugged her into him. He stroked the hair from her face and looked down into her eyes. "You sure you're okay?"

He'd just had a huge blowout with Sean and he was asking about her. She swallowed hard and nodded. It's you —"

He set a finger to her lips. "I'm fine."

The two women at the fountain were laughing and chatting. "Think it's really true?" one of them asked. "If we wish for true love, it'll happen?"

"Well, not with a penny," the other one said, eyeing the change her friend was about to toss in. "How many times have I told you, you can't be cheap about the important stuff."

Her friend rolled her eyes and fished through her purse. "I've got a quarter. Is that better?"

"This is for love, Izzy. Love! Would you buy a guy on the clearance rack? No, you would not."

"Um, I wouldn't buy a guy at all."

"It's a metaphor! You want him new and shiny and *expensive.*"

Izzy went back into her purse. "A buck fifty in change," she muttered. "That's all I've got. It's going to have to be enough."

She closed her eyes, her brow furrowed in concentration, then she opened her eyes and tossed in the money.

Both women held still a beat.

"Nothing," Izzy said in disappointment. "Told you." She turned away from her friend to stalk off and ran smack into Sean, who'd come out of the pub.

His hands went to her arms to catch from falling to her ass. He looked down into her face with concern. "You all right, darlin'?"

Izzy blinked up at him looking dazed. "Um . . ."

Her friend stuck her head in between them. "Yes," she told Sean. "She's okay. She just can't talk in the presence of a hot guy. Especially one she wished for."

He smiled, though it was muted. "You work at the flower shop, right?" he asked Izzy.

She nodded emphatically.

"Well come into the pub and have a drink any time," he said.

Izzy gave another emphatic nod.

"That means yes. And thank you," her friend translated and dragged Izzy away. "Oh-em-gee, the fountain totally works!"

Pru watched them go and had to laugh. Luck was where you made it for yourself and she knew that. She'd wished for love for Finn, and she still wanted that for him but she was realizing that would mean letting him go.

She had to let him go.

Sean looked at Finn. "Need to talk to you," he said.

Finn, face blank, nodded.

"I'll meet you inside," Sean said.

Finn nodded again.

When Sean walked way, Finn turned to Pru.

"Work calls," she said with a small smile.

"Story of my life," he said. "About last night."

Her heart skipped a beat.

"We were onto something."

Her nipples went hard. "Were we?"

"Yeah. And you liked it too."

She felt herself blush a little. "Maybe a little."

"Just a little, huh? Because I still have your fingernail imprints in my scalp." He was out-and-out smiling now, a naughty sort of smile that made her thighs quiver. "I wasn't finished with you, Pru," he said softly. "I had plans."

Oh boy. "Maybe I had plans, too."

"Yeah?" Closing the gap between them, one of his hands went to her hip, the other slid up her back to anchor her to him. "Tell me. Tell me slowly and in great detail."

She laughed and fisted her hands in his shirt, but just before her lips touched his, someone cleared their throat behind them.

"Dammit," she whispered, her lips ghosting against Finn's. "Why do we keep getting interrupted?"

"That is the question," he murmured.

With a sigh she pulled free and turned. "Jake," she said in surprise. "What are you doing here?"

In Jake's lap was a box and on top of that box sat Thor, one ear up, one ear down, his scruffy hair looking even more thin and scruffy than usual, sticking up in tufts on his head.

"Brought you the last box," Jake said. "Never seen anyone stretch a move out so long."

"Yes, well, hiring movers was cut from the budget." Pru scooped up her Thor, kissing him right on the snout. He panted happily, wriggling to get closer, bicycling his front paws in the air, making her laugh and hug him.

"I'm taking him for a grooming at South Bark," Jake said. "He's past due."

"Also cut from the budget," Pru said. But she traded Thor for the box. "Thanks."

"I'll bring him to work when he's finished," Jake said.

And then he didn't roll away.

Pru gave him a long look, but Jake's picture was in the dictionary under *pig-headed* so he didn't budge. "You're going to be late," he told Pru in his boss voice.

With a sigh, she turned to Finn. "I picked up an extra Sunday shift today. I've got to go. Hope you have a good day."

"In case it's our last you mean?"

"You don't think Sean will get the license paid tomorrow?" she asked.

"If he wants to live, he will." But Finn's attention was on Jake.

Pru forced a smile. "Okay, so we're all going off to our own corners now, yes?"

"Go to work, Pru," Jake said.

"Um —"

"It's okay." Finn gave her hand a squeeze. "Knock 'em dead today," he said.

Right. Dammit. With nothing else she could do, she lifted the box of her stuff and walked away from the only two men to have ever earned a spot in her heart. She just hoped they didn't kill one another.

CHAPTER 18

#BEAMMEUPSCOTTY

Finn watched Pru make her way toward the elevator with her box before he turned back to Jake.

Both he and Thor were watching him watch Pru.

Jake was brows up, the picture of nonchalance. "What's going on?"

"Nothing much," Finn said.

Jake took that in and nodded. "You've got an arm on you. The other night at the game you nearly saved our asses — not that anyone could've actually saved our asses."

Finn shrugged. "I played some in college."

"You going to keep playing for us?"

"Depends."

"On what?" Jake asked.

"On if this sudden interest in my ball-playing abilities is in any way related to the woman we both just watched walk away," he said.

"About ninety-nine percent of it, yeah,"

Jake said.

Okay, so the guy got brownie points for honesty. "Why don't you tell me what you really want to know," Finn suggested.

"I don't want to know anything," Jake said. "I want *you* to know that if you make her so much as shed a single tear, I'll break every bone in your body and then feed your organs to the pigeons. I mean, sure, I'd have to hire it out to do it, but I'm connected so don't think I won't."

Finn stared at him. "You forget your meds or something?"

"Nope."

"Okay, then, thanks for letting me know," he said and turned to go.

Jake rolled into his path. "I'm not shittin' you."

"Also good to know." Finn cocked his head. "I'm going to go out on a limb here and guess that you already had a shot at her and you blew it."

"Why would you think that?"

"Because you just threatened me with death and dismemberment. Only one reason to do that — you fucked up somehow."

Jake stared him down for a minute. He might be in a chair but Finn got the sense he could more than handle himself.

"That might be partially true," the guy

finally said.

Finn wrestled with his conscience a moment. "I'd say something helpful here, like it's 'never too late' or 'you can fix any mistake,' because truthfully, I like you. But —"

"— But you like *her* too," Jake said.

"But I like her too," Finn agreed firmly, not willing to back down, feeling a little bit like Thor did about his prized dog cookies. "Much more than I like you."

"It's a bad idea," Jake said. "You and her."

"That's for me and Pru to decide."

Thor jumped down from Jake's lap, walked over to Finn and put his paws on his shins to be picked up — which Finn did.

Then it was apparently Jake's turn to wrestle with his conscience. "What the hell. The damn dog likes you?"

Finn shrugged and gave Thor a quick cuddle before setting him back down on Jake's lap.

Jake muttered something to himself that sounded like "she bit off more than she can chew this time" and turned his chair to roll off.

"Yeah," Finn said to his back.

"Yeah what?"

"Yeah I'm going to keep playing on your team. But I want to buy new jerseys."

Jake rolled back around to face him. "Why?"

Because it would make Pru happy. "You got a problem with SF Tours splashed across everyone's backs in bold letters?"

"Not in the least." Jake paused. "I suppose you also want O'Riley's on there somewhere."

"It'd be nice."

Jake stared at Finn for a beat before nodding. "Our next game's tomorrow night," he said and again he made to leave but didn't. "About Pru and me. We didn't work out for one simple reason."

"What's that?"

Jake looked behind him to make sure Pru wasn't standing there, which normally would've made Finn smile but he wanted to know the answer to this question shockingly bad.

"I made a mistake with her," Jake said, and then grimaced. "Okay, more than one, but the only one you need to know is that she's strong and resilient and smart, so much so that I believed she didn't need anyone, and certainly not me. It must have showed since she called me out on it. She said we couldn't be intimate anymore because I wasn't in love with her and she didn't love me either, at least not in that way. To my shame, I didn't realize that I hurt her by so readily agreeing, by not giving much thought to how she felt about splitting." He paused. "Pru doesn't do casual. She can't. Her heart's too damn big."

"Are you trying to scare me off?"

"Yes," Jake said bluntly. "I hurt her," he said again. "Don't you do the same, don't you even fucking think about it."

"Or the aforementioned death and dismemberment?" Finn asked, only half kidding.

Jake didn't even crack a smile.

Monday morning Pru was waiting outside the county courthouse building, hoping she was in the right place at the right time. When she saw Sean heading for the steps, she pushed away from the wall with relief.

He stopped in surprise at the sight of her. "Hey, Trouble," he said. "What are you doing here?"

"Helping you fix your mess." She smiled at his confusion. "You here to get the liquor license all square, right?" she asked.

He blew out a sigh, looking disgusted. "Finn told you I screwed up."

"No," Pru said quietly. "He wouldn't. I . . . overheard you arguing."

"Yeah." Sean grimaced and scrubbed a hand down his face. "Sorry. I just hate disappointing him."

"If that's the case, why do you give him such a hard time?"

Sean shrugged. "It's how we show affection."

Pru shook her head with a low laugh. "Boys are weird."

"Hey, at least we don't kick and scratch and pull hair when we fight."

"If that's how you think girls fight, you're with the wrong girls."

He grinned. "You know, I like you, Pru. I like you for Finn. You've got his back. He'd say he doesn't need that but he's wrong. We all need that. He know you're here?"

"No, and he doesn't have to know," she said. "Especially since I'm going to save your ass."

"What do you mean?"

"Follow me." She led him inside the offices, bypassed the public sign-in area and waved through the glass partition to a guy at a desk.

The guy was Kyle, Jake's brother.

Kyle gave her a chin nod and hit a button that had the door buzzing open to them.

"Hey, cutie," he said and took a look at Sean. "What's up?"

"I've got a friend who didn't pay their liquor license bill in time," she said. "What can you do for me?"

"First, tell your friend he's an idiot."

She looked into Sean's tight face. "I think he's aware," she said with a small smile.

"Second, have a seat. You're going to owe me," he told Pru. "Caramel chocolates from Ghirardelli. You know the ones."

"Consider it done," she said and ten minutes later they were back on the front steps of the building.

"You're a lifesaver," Sean marveled. "And a super hero."

"I'll add both to my résumé. Maybe it'll get me a raise."

Sean laughed and hugged her. "Dump my brother and marry me."

She laughed because they both knew he wasn't the marrying type, at least not yet.

There'd been a time where she would've said the same thing about herself, but she knew now that she was changing. A part of her *did* want to let love into her life again. Maybe even have a family someday.

How terrifying was that?

Finn made sure to get to the softball field well before the start of their game.

He had no idea why he was looking forward to it, there were a million things he should be doing instead. But he lowered his sunglasses and scanned the area for Pru.

"She's not here yet," Jake said, rolling up to his side.

"Who?" Finn asked casually.

But not casually enough because Jake snorted.

Giving up on pride, Finn asked, "Is she coming?"

"I'm not privy to her schedule."

"Bullshit."

Jake smiled. "Jealous of me, O'Riley?"

"Do I need to be?"

Jake's smile spread.

Shit.

"Got the new jerseys," Jake said. "You work fast."

Finn shrugged like no big deal. It'd only cost an arm and a leg and a huge favor to get them done in one day.

"I like the SF Tours across the backs," Jake said.

"Good."

"Could've done without the O'Rileys on the breast."

Finn smiled and didn't respond. He was looking forward to seeing his name on Pru's breast.

"What's going on with you two?" Jake

wanted to know.

"You ask her?"

"Hell no. I like living."

This gave Finn some satisfaction — that she'd kept what was between them to herself. But then again, that could be because she didn't think there was anything between them.

"I meant what I said yesterday," Jake said.

"About the death and dismemberment?"

"About you and her not becoming a thing."

That's when Finn felt it, a low level of electro-current hummed through him. Turning, he leveled his eyes on Pru and watched as she found him from across the field and tripped over her own feet.

He read her lips and smiled because she was swearing to herself as she picked up speed.

"Sorry I'm late!" she exclaimed breathlessly, like maybe once she'd seen them talking, she'd run over as fast as she could. Hand to her chest, the other holding onto Thor's leash, she divided a look between them. "So . . . what's going on?"

Finn opened his mouth but Jake beat him to the punch. "Game's about to start. Head or tails for home advantage."

Pru slid him a long look and then leveled

that same look on Finn, who tried his best to look innocent. And he was actually pretty sure he *was* innocent since he had no idea what was going on any more than she did.

"Tails," she finally said. "It's always tails."

It was heads.

And . . . they had their asses handed to them like last time. But Kasey got a two base hit, and Abby caught a fly ball, and Pru got two base hits.

And once again, Finn had the time of his life.

Afterward, they all made their way back to O'Riley's. Sean immediately pulled him aside.

"Your girlfriend's wearing your name on her breast. Nicely done. You're faster than I gave you credit for, Grandpa."

"The entire team is wearing our logo, not just Pru," Finn said.

"Interesting."

"What?"

"You didn't deny the girlfriend thing," Sean noted.

Finn didn't take the bait and Sean sighed. "Yeah, yeah, you're still pissed off at me. Newsflash, I'm pissed off too."

"I didn't do shit to you."

"I know," Sean said. "I meant I was pissed off at me. For disappointing you."

Finn stilled and then shook his head. "I know you didn't mean to disappoint me."

"But I did. And not only that, I let you down. I let *us* down." Sean paused. "Earlier today, I handled the liquor license problem with Pru's help."

And then Sean told him the entire story of how Pru had been waiting for him and had smoothed the way with ease.

While Finn was still processing that, marveling over the lengths that she'd gone to help without mentioning it or wanting any credit for it, Sean went on.

"After that I went to pay the property taxes. I was there at their offices when they opened at ten."

"Wow," Finn said. "I didn't know you've even seen ten a.m."

Sean shoved his hands into his pocket and looked a little sheepish. "Yeah, I know. It was a first, and believe me it wasn't pretty. And it was worse than having to go to the damn DMV office, too. Got there right on time and had to take a number. Sixty-nine." He flashed a small smile. "I held up my ticket but no one else in the place was amused. The old lady who had number seventy flipped me the bird. She looked like this sweet little old granny and there she was, telling me I'm number one, can you believe it?"

In spite of himself, Finn laughed. "It's true. You are number one."

Sean's smile faded. "I know."

Regret slashed through Finn. "I didn't mean it like that."

"Yeah, you did," Sean said. "And I deserve it. I'm a fuckup, right?"

"Okay, I'm officially taking that back."

For a beat, Sean's expression went unguarded and filled with relief, making Finn feel even worse. There were times, lots of them, when he wanted nothing more than to wrap his hands around Sean's neck and squeeze.

But more than that, he wanted to never be like his dad. Ever. "So . . . how much were the late fees and penalties on the tax bill?"

Sean grimaced. "You remember Jacklyn?"

"The stripper you dated for a whole weekend last year?" Finn asked.

"Exotic dancer. And she doesn't do that anymore."

Oh shit. "Sean, tell me she doesn't now work at the property tax office."

Another grimace. "Well I could tell you that, but it'd be a lie."

Sean had done his charm-the-panties-off-the-girl and then pulled his also usual I'm-moving-to-Iceland. Or maybe it'd been it's-not-you-it's-me. Either way, he'd dumped her. The only reason Finn even remembered was because Jacklyn had then pulled the crazy card.

She'd stalked Sean. It hadn't been all that hard either, Sean had no sense of secret and always put himself out there, one hundred percent. It probably hadn't taken any effort at all for her to find out about the pub.

She'd come in and had climbed on top of one of the tables, stripping and crying at the same time, telling everyone what a scumbag Sean was.

It'd been a spectacle of massive proportions.

"What happened?" Finn asked. "She refused to let you pay up?"

"Not exactly," Sean said.

"Then what exactly?"

Sean looked . . . embarrassed? Impossible, he never got embarrassed. "She said I could renew on one condition," he said. "If I got up on her counter and did a striptease like she'd done at *my* place of work."

"Well, you gotta hand it to her," Finn said. "It's ingenious."

"Diabolical, you mean," Sean said.

"Whatever, but your next sentence better be 'so I totally got up on that counter and did a striptease for her.' ”

"Did I mention the place was full?" Sean asked. "And that there were old ladies in there? *Old ladies,* Finn. I took one look at them and things . . . shriveled."

"And?" Finn asked.

"And . . . I didn't want to take my clothes off with shrinkage going on!"

Finn pressed the heels of his hands into his eye sockets, but it didn't work. His brain was still leaking out. Slowly and painfully. "Fine, I'll go down there and talk to her and straighten things out."

"Because that's what you do," Sean said. "You straighten things out. I fuck it all and you come along and clean it back up again, right?"

"Sean —"

"No. I'm done with that shit, Finn," Sean said. "I'm done being the idiot baby brother who needs saving. For once, for fucking once, I want to do the right thing. I want to save you." He shook his head. "No, I didn't get up on the counter. But I apologized to her for being a dick. And then I paid the penalties and late fees, all from my personal account. Our property taxes are current and will stay that way, and it won't happen again."

"Wow," Finn said. "That's great. And

thanks." He paused. "From your personal account, huh?"

"Yeah and that hurt, man." Sean rubbed his chest like he was physically pained. "It hurt bad."

Finn smiled. "Also good."

"Now about your girlfriend," Sean said.

Finn raised a brow. He knew Sean was fishing. He had baited the hook and was going to keep saying "girlfriend" until he got a rise out of Finn.

Not going to happen.

"I like her," Sean said quietly.

Again, not what Finn had expected. He'd do just about anything for Sean, and had. But he didn't think he could walk away from Pru.

Not even for his brother.

Sean shook his head. "No, man, I mean I like her for *you.*"

The scary part was that they'd finally agreed on something because Finn liked Pru for him too. So much so that at the end of the night — which was really three in the morning, he found himself outside her front door. Not wanting to scare her to death with the late hour, he texted her.

You up?

It took her less than a minute to respond.

Is this a booty call?

He stared down at the words and felt like the biggest kind of asshole on the planet. He was in the middle of texting back an apology when she texted him again.

Cuz I want it to be . . .

He was still smiling when her next text came in:

There's a key hidden on the top of the doorjamb.

He let himself in, crawled into bed with her and pulled her warm, sleeping form in close.

"Finn?" she murmured sleepily, not opening her eyes.

Well, who the hell else? "Shh," he said, brushing his mouth over her temple. "Go back to sleep."

"But there's a man in my bed." She still hadn't opened her eyes, but she did wind her arms around him tight, pressing her deliciously soft curves up against his body, sliding one of her legs in between his.

"Mmm," she said. "A *hard* man . . ."

And quickly getting harder. "I didn't mean for this to be a booty call —"

"Finn?"

"Yeah?"

"Shut up." And she rocked against him so that his thigh rasped over the damp heat between hers, taking what she wanted from him.

He loved that she'd figured out that her confidence and belief in herself was as sexy to him as her gorgeous body.

"Mm," she hummed in pleasure, rocking against him, making him even harder. "I wonder what to do about this . . ." she mused.

He rolled, tucking her beneath him, and buried himself deep. "Let me show you."

CHAPTER 19
#JUSTLIKETHAT

Typically as summer progressed and more tourists poured into San Francisco, Pru got buried in work. This summer was no different. She worked long days, during which time she dedicated most of her daydreams to one certain sexy Finn O'Riley and what he looked like in her bed.

And what he did to her in it . . .

"What are you thinking about?" Jake asked her at the end of a shift while she was doing paperwork. "You keep sighing."

"Um . . ." She struggled to come up with something not X-rated. "I'm thinking about how much of a slave driver you are."

"Uh huh," he said, not fooled. "You tell Finn yet?"

"I'm getting there," she said, her stomach tightening in panic and anxiety at the thought.

"Pru —"

"I know, I know!" She blew out a breath.

"You don't have to say it. I'm stalling. Big time."

His voice was quiet, almost gentle. "You're really into him."

She closed her eyes and nodded.

His hand slipped into hers and he squeezed her fingers. "You want a chance with him."

She nodded again.

"Chica, to have that chance, you've got to tell him before your window of opportunity closes and things go too far." He waited until she looked at him. "Before you sleep with him or —"

Oh boy.

"— I've got this," she said. "I know what I'm doing."

But they both knew she had *no* idea what she was doing.

That night, Elle and Willa dragged Pru out for "ladies' " night.

They surprised her when they ended up at a lovely spa, snacking on cute little sandwiches and tea before deciding on their individual treatments.

Pru stared at the spa's menu, a little panicked over the luxury that she couldn't really afford.

"It's my treat," Elle said, covering the

244

prices with her hand. "This was my idea. I owe Willa a birthday present."

Willa smiled. "Cuz I can't afford it either."

"But it's not my birthday," Pru said.

"Pretend," Elle said. "I want a mani/pedi and a Brazilian, and I don't like to primp alone."

Which is how Pru ended up with a mani/pedi and her very first Brazilian.

The next day it rained all day long. Pru joked to Jake that after eight long hours on the water — in the rain — she felt like Noah.

Jake felt no mercy at all. "Make the money now, chica. Come wintertime you'll be whining like Thor does for that mini chow across the street, the one who's got fifty pounds on him and would squash him like a grape if given the chance."

So she worked.

At the end of another crazy day, she changed out of her uniform into a sundress and left Pier 39. She was Thor-less. After a stunt where he'd rolled in pigeon poo for some mysterious reason that only made sense to himself, Jake had once again taken him to the South Bark Mutt Shop for grooming.

All Pru wanted to do was to go home and crawl into her bed. For once she was too tired to even dream about having Finn in that bed with her. She wouldn't be able to lift a finger. Or a tongue.

Not that she'd mind if he insisted on doing all the work . . .

But that fantasy would have to wait. She had an errand to run before getting home, hence the sundress. She wanted to look nice for her weekly visit.

She walked up the steps to the home where her grandpa lived and signed in to see him.

Michelle, the front desk receptionist waved at her. Michelle had worked there forever, so they were old friends.

"How is he today?" Pru asked her.

Michelle's easy smile faded. "Not gonna lie, it's a rough one, honey. He's agitated. He didn't like his lunch, he didn't like the weather, he didn't like wearing pants, the list goes on. He's feeling mean as a snake. You want to come back another day?"

But they both knew that the bad days far outweighed the good ones now, so there was no use in waiting or she might never see him. "I'll be fine."

Michelle nodded, eyes warm, mouth a little worried. "Holler if you need anything."

Pru took a deep breath, waved at Paul the orderly in the hallway, and entered her grandpa's room.

He was watching *Jeopardy!* and yelling at the TV. "Who is Queen Victoria, you jack-ass!" He picked up his cane and waved that too. "Who is Queen Victoria!"

"Hi, grandpa," Pru said.

"No one ever listens to me," he went on, dropping his cane to shake his fist at the TV. "No one ever listens."

Pru moved into his line of sight and picked up the cane for him, wondering if he would know her today. "It's me, Pru —"

"You," he snapped, narrowing his eyes on her, snatching the cane from her hands. "You've got some nerve coming here, Missy, into my home."

"It's good to see you, Grandpa. You sound good, your cold's gone from last week, huh? How are you feeling?"

"I'm not telling you shit. You were a terrible influence on my son. You encouraged him to be a good time, to party, when you knew —" He jabbed the cane at her for emphasis. "It's your fault he's dead. You should be ashamed of yourself."

This hit her hard but she did her best to ignore the hurtful words. "Grandpa, it's Prudence." She purposely kept her voice low and calm so that maybe he would do the same.

No go.

"Oh I know who you are. I knew you for what you were the first day I saw you," he said, "when Steven first brought you home. He said 'this is Vicky and I love her,' and I took one look into your laughing eyes and I knew. All you wanted to do was have fun and you didn't care what fell by the wayside. Well, I'll tell you what, our business fell by the wayside because he wanted to spend time with you, not that you even noticed. Our business went into the ground because of you, because you didn't care if he had to work —"

"Dad worked," Pru said. "He worked a lot. Mom just tried to get him to enjoy life when she could because he did work so hard —"

"You were trouble with a capital T, that's what you were," he snapped out. "And you still are. Told you that then and I'll tell you again. You're Trouble to the very bone."

She'd frozen to the spot. She'd had no idea that her grandpa had called her mom Trouble, that he thought she'd been a bad influence on her dad simply because she'd wanted him to have a life outside of work.

The irony of this was not lost on her.

What *was* lost on her was how long she must have stood there, mouth open, gaping, letting old wounds reopen and fester because her grandpa grabbed something from the tray by his bed and chucked it at her.

She ducked and a fork skidded across the floor.

"Okay," she said, raising her hands. "That wasn't nice. Grandpa, I'm not my mom. I'm not Vicky. I'm your granddaughter Pru —"

"I don't have a granddaughter!" A piece of toast came hurtling her way, which she also dodged. "You killed him, Vicky. You killed him dead, so go rot in hell."

The words spilled from him, cruel and harsh and this stopped her cold so that she didn't duck quickly enough the next time.

His mug caught her on the cheek.

"Ouch, dammit!" she said straightening, holding her face. "You've got to listen to me — I'm not Vicky!" She went hands on hips. "Grandpa, you are not two years old, you need to stop with the temper tantrums!"

"That's right," he yelled. "I'm not two, I'm a *million* and two. I'm old and alone, and it's all your fault!"

Up until that very moment she'd somehow managed to separate herself from what he was saying, but suddenly she couldn't. Suddenly she wasn't feeling strong and in charge and on top of her life. She was just a girl who'd lost her parents, who had a grandpa whose elevator didn't go to the top floor. She was doing the best she could with what she had, but it wasn't adequate.

She wasn't adequate, as proven by her track record of no one loving her enough to stay with her, and the terrifying thing was, she didn't know how to be more.

"Get out!" he bellowed at her.

Paul appeared in the doorway, looking startled. "What's going on, Marvin?"

"What's going on is you let her in!" And in case there was any doubt of the "her" in question, her grandpa stabbed a spoon in Pru's direction.

"Okay, now let's just take it down a notch," Paul said, doing his orderly thing, moving between Pru and her grandpa. "Put that utensil down, Marvin. We don't throw stuff here, remember?"

But Marvin couldn't be deterred. "It's her fault! Get out," he yelled at Pru. "Get out and don't come back, you tramp! You son-stealer! You *good for nothing free-loading hussy!*"

Michelle poked her head in, her eyes wide. "Paul, you need help?"

"We're good," Paul said evenly. "Aren't we, Marvin?"

"No, I'm not good! Can't you see her? She's standing right behind you like a coward. Get out!" he bellowed at Pru. *"Get out and stay out!"*

Michelle slipped into the room and put her hand in Pru's. "Come on, honey. Let's give him some alone time."

Pru let herself be led out of the room, heart aching, feeling more alone than she ever had. Her grandpa had never been the best of company but he'd at least been someone who shared her blood, her history . . . and now he wasn't remembering any of that and all she did by visiting him was upset him. She might have to stop coming entirely and then she'd be completely alone.

You already are . . .

She walked home slowly even though it was misting and she was wearing just the sundress and sandals. Her heart hurt. Rubbing it didn't assuage the deep ache that went behind the bone to her wounded soul. She missed her mom. She missed her dad. And dammit, she'd missed feeling whole.

She missed feeling needed. Wanted. Like she was crucial, critical to someone's life. A piece of their puzzle.

Instead she was a tumbleweed in the wind, never anchored. Never belonging to anyone.

With her head down and her thoughts even lower, she nearly ran right into someone on the street. Two someone's, locked in an embrace, kissing as if they were never going to see each other again. The man's arms were locked around the woman, an expression of love and longing on his face as he pulled back, still holding the woman's hands.

Had anyone ever looked at Pru like that? If so, she'd forgotten it, and she didn't think one could ever forget true love. All she wanted, all she'd ever wanted since the day she'd lost her parents, was for someone to care enough to come into her life and stay there.

Her chest tightened and her throat burned, but she refused to give into that. Crying wouldn't help. Crying never helped. All crying did was make the day a waste of mascara. And since she'd splurged on an expensive one this time in a useless effort to give her lashes some volume, she wasn't about to waste it. *Get it together,* she ordered herself. *Get it together and keep it together. You're okay. You're always okay . . .*

But the pep talk didn't work. The lonely still crawled up her throat and choked her.

The man smiled down at the woman in front of him, his gaze full of the love that Pru secretly dreamed of. He took his girl's hand and off they went into the rain, shoulders bumping, bodies in sync.

252

It broke her heart more than it should have. They were complete strangers, for God's sake. But watching them made her feel a little cold. Empty.

A crack of lightning lit the sky. She startled and then jumped again at the nearly immediate boom of thunder, sharp and way too close. Skipping the wrought-iron entrance to the courtyard, she instead ran directly into the pub.

She stood just inside, her eyes immediately straying to the bar.

Finn stood behind it with Sean, who was addressing everyone in the place, and all eyes were on him.

Except for Pru, who was watching Finn. He stood at Sean's side, his blank face on. Though Pru knew him now, or was coming to anyway, and she could tell by his tight mouth and hooded eyes that he wasn't feeling blank at all.

"So raise your glasses," Sean concluded, lifting his. "Because today's the day, folks, our first anniversary of O'Riley's, which we modeled after our dear departed Da's own pub, the original O'Riley's. He'd have loved this place." Sean clasped a hand to his heart. "If he were still with us — God bless his soul — he'd be sitting right here at the bar with us every night."

The mention of this loss would normally have made Pru's heart clutch because of her family's part in their loss, and there was certainly some of that, but she hadn't taken her eyes off Finn. He wasn't sad. He was pissed. And she thought maybe she knew why.

His dad hadn't been anything like hers. He hadn't cuddled his sons when they'd skinned a knee. He hadn't shown them love and adoration. He hadn't carried them around on his shoulders, showing them off every chance he had.

But for whatever reason, Sean was telling a different story. She had no idea why, but Finn's feelings on the matter were clear.

He hated this toast.

"We miss him every single day," Sean went on and finished up with a *"Slainte!"*

"Slainte!" everyone in the place repeated and tossed back their drinks.

Sean grinned and turned toward Finn. He said something to him but Finn didn't respond because he'd turned his head, and as if he'd felt Pru come in, he'd leveled his gaze right on her.

If she'd thought the oncoming storm outside was crazy, it was nothing compared to what happened between her and Finn every time they so much as looked at each other.

You're trouble with a capital T.

Her grandpa's words floated around in her brain, messing with her head, her heart.

One look into your laughing eyes and I knew. All you wanted to do was have fun and you didn't care what fell by the wayside.

She couldn't do this. She'd thought she was doing the right thing by helping Finn find some fun and adventure in his life but now she knew she wasn't. Worse, she felt too fragile, way too close to a complete meltdown to be here. And yet at the same time, she was drawn, so terribly, achingly drawn to the strength in Finn's gaze, the warmth in his eyes. She knew if he so much as touched her right now, she'd lose the tenuous grip she had on her emotions.

Go. Leave.

It was the only clear thought in her head as she whirled to do just that but Finn's warm, strong arms slid around her, turning her to face him.

He'd caught her.

"I'm all wet," she whispered inanely.

His eyes never left her face. "I see that."

"I'm —" *A mess,* she nearly said but the ball of emotion blocked her throat, preventing her from talking. Horrified to feel her eyes well up, she shook her head and tried to pull free.

"Pru," he said softly, his hand at the nape of her neck, threading through her drenched hair. There were tangles in it but he was apparently undeterred by the rat's nest. Pulling her in slowly but inexorably, his lips brushed her forehead. She could feel his mouth at her hairline as he whispered soothing words she couldn't quite make out.

She melted against him. No other words for it really. He was real. He was solid and whole. He was everything she wanted and couldn't have, no matter how badly she ached for him. She'd already wandered way off the track she'd set for herself, a fact that was now coming back to bite her hard because . . .

Because she was falling for him.

And what made it even worse; her day, her life, this situation . . . was that she not only wanted him in her life, she was desperately afraid and increasingly certain that she *needed* him as well.

She almost cracked at that. Almost but not quite.

But God, she couldn't seem to let him go.

Finn tightened his arms on her, pressing his cheek to the top of her head. "It's okay," he whispered. "Whatever it is, it's going to be okay."

But it wasn't. And she didn't know if she'd ever feel okay again so she pressed her face into his throat and let herself take another minute. Or two.

Or whatever he'd give.

CHAPTER 20

#HOWYOUDOIN

Finn cuddled Pru into him, alarmed by her pallor, by the way she trembled in his arms, the tiny little quivers that said she was fighting her emotions and losing. Her dress had plastered itself to her delicious curves, her long damp hair was clinging to her face and shoulders.

Pulling back, he took her hand and led her to the bar so he could grab a fresh towel. He started to dry off her wet face and realized it was tears, not rain. "Pru."

"No, it's nothing, really," she said quietly, head down, his fearless fun whisperer . . .

"It's not nothing," he said.

"I just . . . I need to go."

Yeah, not going to happen. At least not alone. Finn turned and jerked his chin at Sean, wordlessly telling him he was in charge of the bar.

Sean nodded and Fin took Pru's hand, leading her down the hallway, not in the least bit sorry for leaving Sean in the lurch. After that stunt toast Sean had just given, Finn was saving his brother's life by leaving now.

"Finn, really," Pru said. "Really, I'm fine. Really."

"And maybe if you say really one more time, I'll believe you."

She sighed. "But I am fine."

She wasn't but she would be. He'd damn well see to it. He took her to his office.

Thor leapt off the couch where he'd been snoozing, immediately launching into his imitation of a bunny. Bounce, bounce, bounce while bark, bark, barking at a pitch designed to shatter eardrums. "Thor," he said. "Shut it."

Thor promptly shut it and sat on his little butt, which shook back and forth with every tail wag that was faster than the speed of light. The result was that he looked like a battery-operated toy dog.

On steroids.

Pru choked out a laugh and scooped him up. "Why are you here, baby?"

"He got done at the beauty salon and Willa had to go before Jake could pick him up, so I said I'd take him for you."

"It's not a beauty salon," she said, face pressed into Thor's fur, doing a bang-up job at keeping up the pretense of being fine.

"Babe, it's totally a beauty salon," he said. "When I walked in to pick him up, Willa was presiding over a wedding between two giant poodles, one white, one black. The black one was wearing a wedding dress made of silk and crystals."

She slid him a look. No more tears, thank God, but her eyes were haunted even though she did her best to smile. "Wow," she said.

"Impressed by the lengths Willa's shop goes to make money?" he asked.

"No, I'm impressed that you can recognize silk and crystals."

"Hey, I'm secure in my manhood." He took Thor from her and tucked the dog under an arm. The other he slipped around her waist. "Let's go."

"Where?"

"I'm taking you home. You look about done in."

"I passed done in about an hour ago," she admitted.

They didn't speak again as they crossed the courtyard. But Thor did. He started barking at a pair of pigeons and when Finn gave him a long look, the dog switched to a low-in-the-throat growl.

"They outweigh you," Finn told him. "Pick your battles, man."

The dog was silent in the elevator but that was only because Max, who worked on the second floor in Archer's office, was in it. With his Doberman pinscher Carl.

When Max and Carl got off the elevator, Thor let out a long sigh that sounded like relief, which under better circumstances would've made Finn laugh. "You know your particular breed of mutt was bred to kill Dobermans, right?" he asked the dog.

Thor blinked up at him.

"It's true," Finn said. "They get stuck right here —" He pointed to his throat.

Pru choked out a laugh. "Finn, that's a horrible story!"

He smiled and tugged lightly on a strand of her hair. "But you laughed," he said.

"I laughed because it was a *horrible* story," she said, but was still smiling.

And because she was, he leaned in and kissed her. Softly. "Hey," he said.

"Hey," she whispered back.

He wasn't sure what was going on with her, but it'd only taken one look at her open, expressive face to know she'd somehow been devastated today.

And, given the cut on her cheekbone, also hurt.

Both infuriated him.

The elevator opened and he took Thor's

leash in one hand and used the other to guide Pru off. They were in the hallway in front of her door when Mrs. Winslow's door opened.

"Another special delivery?" Pru asked her.

"Not for me," Mrs. Winslow answered. "It's for you."

"Um, I don't eat a lot of special brownies," she said. "No offense."

Mrs. Winslow smiled. "Oh, none taken, honey. I'm just passing the word that there's a little something in the dumbwaiter for you."

"For me? Why?"

"For your bad day," Mrs. Winslow said.

Pru blinked. "How do you know I had a bad day?"

"Let's just say a little birdie looks after all of us," Mrs. Winslow said. "And he let me know to let you know that you're not alone."

"He who?" Pru asked.

But Mrs. Winslow had vanished back into her apartment.

Finn and Pru walked into hers. Finn crouched down and freed Thor from his leash and the dog immediately trotted to his food bowl.

Pru dumped a cup of dry food into it, patted the dog on his head and then went straight to the dumbwaiter.

Finn went to her freezer. He didn't see an ice pack but she did have a small bag of frozen corn. Good enough.

At her gasp, Finn turned to her. She'd pulled out a basket of muffins from the coffee shop. Tina's muffins, the best on the planet.

Finn wrapped the bag of corn in a kitchen towel and gently set the makeshift ice pack to her cheek and then brought her hand up to it. "Hold it here a few minutes," he said.

While she did that, he carried the basket to the kitchen table and they dove into the muffins right then and there.

"Good to have friends in high places," he said instead of asking her about her face, and when she visibly relaxed he knew he'd done the right thing.

Didn't mean he didn't want to kick someone's ass, because he did. Badly.

"It'd be better to know who those friends are," she said, clearly not reading his murderous thoughts. She met his gaze. "Do you know?"

He had an idea but didn't know for certain so he shook his head.

She took another muffin, chocolate chip by the looks of it. "Sean's toast at the pub upset you," she said.

Sitting across from her at her table, with

Thor in his lap while he worked his way through a most excellent blueberry/banana muffin, he didn't want to get into Sean's toast. He much preferred to get into whatever had happened to *her.* But he knew that she wasn't going to open up.

Unless he did.

Problem was, he hated opening up. To anyone.

"I'm sorry your dad never got to see the bar and what a success you made of it," she said quietly.

He put his muffin down. "My dad couldn't have cared less what we did with ourselves when we were kids. He wouldn't care what we do now either."

"But Sean said —"

"Sean's so full of shit that his eyes are brown," he said. "My dad never had a pub. Hell, he never even acknowledged he was Irish. My brother perpetuates the lie because he thinks Irish pubs do well and he isn't wrong. We *have* done well but it isn't because we're Irish, it's because we work our asses off."

"You mean you work *your* ass off," she said.

He met her knowing gaze. "I just hate the fraud."

"It's not a fraud if it's true, even a little

264

bit." Reaching across the table, she covered her hand with his. "Stop feeling guilty about something that isn't your fault and isn't hurting anyone. Let it go and enjoy the success you've made of the place, in spite of your father."

He stared at her. "How is it that you're cute, sexy as hell, *and* smarter than anyone I know?"

She gave him a small smile. "It's a gift."

Leaning over the table, he wrapped his fingers around her wrist and pulled the bag of corn from her face. Gently he touched her cheekbone. "You okay?"

"I will be."

Her resilience made him smile. "Yeah?" he asked. "And how's that?"

She shrugged a shoulder. "Well, it's raining, and I love the rain. Someone sent me a basket of muffins, and I love muffins. Thor is actually clean and going to stay that way for at least the next few minutes. I don't have to work until midday tomorrow. And I have company." She smiled. "The good kind." She lifted a shoulder. "It's all good."

She was aiming for light and she'd succeeded. It was how she dealt, he got that. And he was getting something else too — that he could learn a hell of a lot from her.

She rose from her chair and came around

the table. She lifted Thor from his lap and set the dog down. Then she climbed into Finn's lap herself and cupped his face.

His arms closed around her and one thought settled into his brain. This feels right.

She feels right.

CHAPTER 21
#UPSHITCREEKWITHOUTAPADDLE

Pru lifted her gaze to Finn's, startled by the sudden intensity in his gaze. It said she wasn't alone, that she mattered, a lot.

At least you're not the only one falling . . .

This thought was a cool tall drink of relief immediately followed by a chaser of anxiety.

Because she hadn't meant for this to happen. She hadn't meant for *any* of it; his attention, his affection, his emotional bond . . . and all of it was a secret dream come true for her.

Just as all of it was now a nightmare as well, because how was she supposed to give it up? Give *him* up?

Although the tough truth was, she wouldn't have to. Telling him the truth would accomplish that because *he* would give *her* up once she did.

She'd known they'd be getting to this. She hadn't missed him looking at her cheek, or the temper that flashed in his eyes whenever he did. "It's —"

"Not nothing. Don't even think about saying it's nothing." His voice was gentle but inexorable steel.

"My grandfather's in a senior home," she said. "Has been for years. I visit him every week but he doesn't always recognize me."

"He hit you?" he asked, his voice still calm, his gaze anything but.

"No." She shook her head. "Well, not exactly."

"Then what exactly?"

"He was trying to get me to leave," she said. "He threw the stuff on his lunch tray at me."

His brow furrowed. "What the fuck?"

"It's that sometimes he thinks I'm my mom," she said. "He didn't like her."

Finn's fingers slid into her hair, soothing, protective, and she felt herself relax a little into his touch.

"Why not?" he asked quietly.

"She . . ." Pru closed her eyes and pressed her face to his throat. "She was a good-time girl. She loved to have fun. My dad loved to give her that fun. We spent a lot of time out on the water and at Giants games, his two favorite things."

He smiled. "And you're still out on the water."

She nodded. "It makes me feel close to them. I used to tell my dad I was going to captain a ship someday, which must have sounded ridiculous but he told me I could do anything I wanted." She paused. "I loved them, very much, but in some ways my grandpa was right. My mom encouraged my dad. The truth is they were partyers, and big social drinkers . . ."

"Is that why you never drink?"

"A big part of it," she admitted for the first time in her life. "Is that weird for you, being with someone who doesn't drink?"

He palmed her neck and waited until she looked at him. "Not even a little bit," he said.

She smiled. "My dad used to say my mom was the light to his dark. He loved that about her. He loved her," she said, her chest tight at the memory of her mom making him laugh. "They loved each other."

There was empathy in Finn's eyes and in his touch. Empathy, and affection, and a grim understanding. He'd had losses too. Far too many.

"I'm glad you have those memories of your mom and dad together," he said. "I know it sucks having them gone, but at least when you think of them, you smile."

Mostly. But not always. Not, for instance,

when she thought of how they'd died.

And who'd they'd taken with them . . .

"I'm sorry you don't have those memories," she said quietly.

"Don't be. Because I don't know what I'm missing." He met her gaze. "You had it worse. Your life was a complete one-eighty from mine. You know exactly what you're missing."

And there went the stab to her gut again. "Finn —"

"It's not your fault, Pru. Any of it. Forget it."

As if she could.

He tightened his grip on her. "No more going into your grandfather's room alone. You take an orderly with you, or anyone. Me," he said. "I'll go with you. Or whoever you want, but I don't want you in there with him alone again."

"He's not always that bad —"

"Promise me," he said, cupping her face, taking care with her cheek. "There's only honesty between us, right? We have no reason for anything but. So look me in the eyes and promise me, Pru."

She inhaled deeply, feeling like the biggest fraud on the planet. "I promise," she whispered, hating herself a little bit. "Finn?"

"Yeah?"

Eyes on his, she leaned in close. "Do you remember when you kissed away my hurts?"

"After the first softball game," he said and smiled. "Yeah, I remember. It was a highlight for me." His eyes went smoldering. "Want me to do it again?"

"No, it's your turn," she said. "I'm going to kiss away *your* hurts."

He stilled. "You are?"

"Yes." *Please want me to, please need me to . . .*

A rough sound escaped him then, regret and empathy, making her realize she'd spoken out loud. Closing her eyes, she tried to turn away but his arms tightened around her, his voice low and rough. "I do," he said fiercely. "I'm going to show you just how much I need you. All night long, in fact."

She stared into his eyes, letting the strength in the words, in his body, in his gaze convince her he meant every single word. "The whole night," she repeated, needing the clarification.

"For as long as you need."

Since that was too much to think about, she had to set it aside in her head. Instead she slid her fingers into his hair as his hands caught her, rocking her against her very favorite body part of his. She oscillated her hips, thrilling to the way he groaned at the contact.

No slouch, Finn stroked up her arms, encouraging the spaghetti straps of her sundress to slip from her shoulders. The bodice was stretchy and lightweight and still damp from the rain, which meant it took very little effort for him to tug it to her waist so that her breasts spilled out.

A rough, very male sound of appreciation rumbled up from deep in his throat and his hands went under her dress to cup her ass, pulling her in tighter to him, putting his mouth right at tease-her-nipples level.

He captured one in his mouth and her brain ceased working. Just completely stopped. Probably for the best since she was about to do things with him that she'd told herself she wouldn't do again. "Finn —"

Finn groaned again, a near growl. "Love the sound of my name on your lips," he said and sucked hard, his hands pushing her dress up her thighs as he did.

"Oh no," she said, and right then, with his teeth gently biting down on her nipple and his hands up her dress, he froze.

"No?" he repeated.

"No, as in I'm not going to be the first one naked this time," she clarified. "Why am I always the first one naked?"

"Because you look amazing naked. Here,

let me show you —"

"Now just hold on," she said with a low laugh, feeling dizzy with lust. "Good God, you're potent." She shoved his shirt up his chest and hummed in thrilled delight at the sight of his exposed torso. "Off," she demanded.

He took a hand off her thigh, fisted it in his shirt between his shoulder blades and yanked it over his head, never taking his eyes from hers, immediately going back to the business of driving her right out of her everloving mind.

Her hands slid down his bare chest over his abs, which were rigid and taut enough that even though he was sitting, there was no fat ripple. If she didn't want him so badly, she'd hate him for it. She popped open his button-fly jeans and a most impressive erection sprang free into her hands.

He was commando.

"Laundry day," he said.

She stared at him and then laughed. She had him full and hard in her hands, and she was hot and achy and already wet for him, and she was laughing.

"It's not nice to laugh at a naked man," he said, smiling at her, not insulted in the least, the cocky bastard, and it only made her laugh harder.

"I'm sorry," she managed on a snort.

Straightening up, causing those delicious ab muscles to crunch, he nipped her jaw. "You don't look sorry."

She stroked his hard length and her body practically vibrated for him. "I'll work on that," she managed as he pushed up the hem of her sundress.

Her amusement backed up in her throat.

Air brushed over her upper thighs now. Her panties were tiny, enough that when Finn reached his hands around to her ass, there was bare cheek groping.

"Mmm," rumbled approvingly from his throat. His fingers dug in a little, cupping, squeezing, and then slipped beneath the lace, making her quiver.

"Hold this," he said.

She automatically took hold of her own dress at her waist. She felt hot. Achy. *Desperate.* She was already straddling him but his big hands adjusted her legs so that the two of them fit together like two pieces of a puzzle.

"Yeah," he said. "Like that." And then he scraped aside her little scrap of panties and stilled as he got a good look at what he'd exposed.

And that's when she remembered the Brazilian. "It's Elle's fault," she blurted out.

"Oh Christ, Pru." He stroked a reverent finger across her exposed flesh.

Her exposed, *bare* flesh. "She took me and Willa to the spa and —"

The pad of Finn's finger came away wet and he groaned.

"— the next thing I knew . . ." she trailed off when, holding her gaze, he sucked his finger into his mouth. "So . . . you like?" she whispered.

"Love." His hands went to her hips and he lifted her up to the table, plopping her on the wood surface. Then, calm as you please, he scooted his chair in close, draped her legs over his shoulders, lowered his head and . . .

Oh. *Oh.* Her last coherent thought was that maybe Elle had been onto something . . .

"Missed the taste of you," Finn murmured a few minutes later, when he'd rendered her boneless. And not very many minutes either. He shifted back, and afraid he was going away, she made a small whisper of protest and clutched at him.

Flashing her a smile, he reached behind him, pulling his wallet from his back pocket.

"It's a little late to exchange business cards, isn't it?" she asked, trying to make light of their compromising situation because as was already established, her mouth never knew when to stay zipped.

He pulled out a condom.

"Right," she said. Damn, she should have thought of that. Problem was, at the moment, with her dress basically a belt around her waist, exposing all her goodies, she was incapable of thought.

"You take my breath," he said, eyes on her as he tore the packet open with his teeth and then rolled the condom down his length.

She'd never seen anything so sexy in her entire life.

With what looked like effortless strength, he scooped her from the table and lowered her over the top of him, in total control of how fast she sank onto him — which was to say not fast at all. Seemed Finn liked the slow, drive-her-insane grind, and she let out a sound of impatience that made him flash her another smile.

"You think this is funny?" she managed.

"You panting my name, whimpering for more, and trembling for me?" He brushed his stubbled jaw very gently across her nipple and gave her an entire body shiver. "Try sexy as hell."

She was no longer surprised to realize that she felt it. Sexy as hell. It was an utterly new experience for her and she didn't quite know how to rein herself in. So she didn't even try. Instead she went after every inch of him that she could reach, following each touch of her fingers with her mouth. His shoulders, collarbone, his throat . . . God, she loved his throat. But what she loved even more? The rough, extremely erotic sounds she coaxed from him.

"Lift up," he whispered hotly in her ear, and then rather than wait for her to comply, he guided her with his hands on her hips, showing her how to raise up on her knees until he nearly slipped out of her, and then to sink back down, once again taking him fully inside her.

They both gasped as she began to move like that, urged on by his hands, all while their mouths remained fused, kissing hot and deep. When they ran out of air, he wound his fist in her hair and forced her head back, sucking on her exposed throat, his other hand possessive on her ass.

Then that hand shifted to the groove between her hip and thigh, his fingers spread wide so that his thumb could rasp over the current center of her universe. She gripped his wrist and held his hand in place.

"You like?" he asked hotly against her ear.

"Just don't stop." Ever . . .

He didn't. He swirled that roughly callused thumb in a very purposeful circle that was exactly the rhythm she needed, making her cry out his name as she came hard.

When she opened her eyes, his were hot and triumphant, and she wrapped her arms tight around his neck. "It was your turn to go first."

"Always you first," he said and melted her heart.

"I'm not sure that's fair."

He smiled. "Hell yeah, it is. I love watching you come for me." He nipped her chin. "You say my name all breathy and you dig your nails into me. So fucking sexy, Pru."

With a low laugh, she buried her face in his neck.

"That shouldn't embarrass you," he said. "Watching you come makes my world go around."

At the thought, her body clenched around him and he groaned.

"Your turn now," she whispered, and did it again.

"Yeah?"

"Yeah." Empowered, she gave him a little push until he leaned back in the chair. "You just sit there and look pretty," she said. "Let me do the work now."

He flashed her a sexy grin that almost

made her come again before he leaned back, clearly one hundred percent good with giving her the reins and letting her have her wicked way with him.

She gave him everything she had, and in the end when he banded his arms around her, his head back, his face a mask of stark pleasure as he shuddered up into her, she felt herself go over again. With him. Into him . . .

It shocked her. A co-orgasm. An *effortless* co-orgasm. She didn't realize it was a real thing. She'd honestly thought it was a myth, like unicorns and good credit ratings.

When she caught her breath and her world stopped spinning out of control she looked at him. Sprawled beneath her, head back, eyes closed, he had a smile on his face.

"Damn," he said. "That just gets better and better."

Dazed, she stood on shaky legs and began to rearrange her dress. "This isn't anything like what I expected."

He gave a sexy laugh. "Liar."

She froze and looked at him.

"Admit it," he said. "You've wanted me since day one. I sure as hell have wanted you since then."

Laughing at her expression, he pulled her back onto his lap, cuddling her, kissing the top of her head. "You think too much, Pru."

That was definitely also true. She rested her head against his chest and listened to his heartbeat, strong and steady.

"I've got something to say," he murmured, his hands sliding down to palm and then squeeze her ass.

She wriggled a little bit, just to hear that low growl and feel his fingers tighten on her. But while his body was giving her one message, his words gave another.

"You helped Sean out and that means a lot to me," he said.

She froze and lifted her head to look at him. "He told you? He didn't have to do that."

"I'm glad he did. I already knew you're warm and sexy, funny and smart, but what you did, Pru, having his back like that — and by extension, my back as well — that told me everything I need to know about you."

She shook her head. "Anyone would have —"

"No," he said. "They wouldn't. I've got my brother and a select core group of friends that would do anything for me, and that's been it. But now I've got you too. Means a lot to me, Pru. You mean a lot to me."

Oh God. "I feel the same," she whispered. "But Finn, you don't know everything about me."

"I know what I need to."

If only that was true. "Finn —" But before she could finish that statement, the one where she told him the truth, the one that would surely change everything and erase their friendship and trust and . . . *everything,* someone knocked on her door.

"Ignore it," Finn said.

"Pru," came a deep male voice from the other side of her door.

Jake.

Oh, God. *Jake.*

This was bad. Very, very bad. If Jake found Finn here with *that* look on his face, there'd be no holding back the storm. Jake had told her to tell Finn before things went too far, and when Jake told someone to do something, they did it.

But she hadn't.

And things had gone far with Finn. Just about as *far* as a man and a woman could get . . .

She was in trouble. Big trouble. One of the problems with having a wounded warrior as a BFF is that he saw everything as a conflict to fix. She had no doubt he'd take one glimpse at them and very possibly butt his big nosy nose in and enlighten Finn himself.

And that would be bad. Very, very bad. She jumped up and straightened her dress before whirling to Finn. He'd pulled up his jeans, but hadn't fastened them. Nor had he put on his shirt, which meant he sat there in nothing but Levi's, literally, his hair completely tousled from her fingers — bad fingers! — an unmistakable just-got-laid sated expression all over his face.

Not moving.

She waved her hands at him. "What are you doing? Get dressed!"

"Working on it." He stretched lazily, slowly, like he had all the fricking time in the fracking world.

Jake knocked again, annoyance reverberating through the wood. Jake had many good qualities but patience wasn't one of them. "Pru, what the hell are you doing in there — and it'd better not be Finn," he said.

She'd just sent her hands on Finn's chest to give him a little hurry-up nudge, so she had a front-row view of his brows shooting up.

Well, crap.

Then, from outside her door, came the unmistakable sounds of keys rattling, which reminded her of the unfortunate time on moving day when she'd given Jake her damn key. *What had she been thinking?* "You've got to hide!" she whispered frantically to Finn.

"What the hell for?"

With a sound of exasperation she whirled around and eyeballed potential hiding places.

She had little to no furniture.

"Dammit!" Then she focused on the dumbwaiter. Perfect. "Here," she said, opening it and then pushing him toward it. "I need you to get in here for just a minute —"

Finn, solid and steady, didn't move when she'd pushed him. What was it with her and big, badass alphas who only could be budged when they wanted to be budged?

He looked down into her face and seemed to take in her clear panic because he gave a slight head shake. "You've lost it."

"Yes, now you fully understand! I've completely lost it, but to be honest, I lost it a long time ago!"

"I meant me, babe," he said. "I've lost it to even be melted by those eyes of yours, enough that I'll do just about anything for you."

"Good," she said quickly. "Go with that. Please, I can't explain right now, but I need you to hide, for just a minute, I promise."

He shook his head again, muttered some more, something that sounded like "you're a complete dumbass, O'Riley," but then God bless him, he folded up his rangy form in the dumbwaiter.

"Just for a minute," she repeated and slammed the door shut on his gorgeous but annoyed face and turned back to the kitchen — where Finn's shirt and shoes were lying scattered on the floor. *Shit!* She snagged everything up, ran back to the dumbwaiter, opened the door and shoved them at Finn and then slammed the door.

Just as Jake rolled into her kitchen.

Finn sat there in the dumbwaiter, somewhere between pissed off and bemused. And maybe a little turned on, which showed just how messed up in the head he really was.

No one handled him. Ever. And yet Pru just had, like a pro.

Which meant he sat here squished into the dumbwaiter in only his unbuttoned jeans, his shirt in one hand, his shoes in his other, wondering — What. The. Fuck.

He tried to come up with a single reason why, if Pru and Jake were not a thing, that he had to be a dirty little secret. But he couldn't.

And his amusement faded.

Because that's exactly what he was at the moment. Pru's dirty little secret, and while the thought of that might have appealed in fantasy, it absolutely did not hold up in reality.

Not even close.

Leaning in, he tried to catch whatever was going on in Pru's kitchen.

"Why are you breathing like a lunatic?" Jake asked. "And you're all flushed. You sick?"

Try as he might, Finn couldn't catch Pru's response.

But he had no problem catching Jake's next line. "Why is there a pair of men's socks on your floor?"

And that's when the dumbwaiter jerked and went on the move, taking Finn southward.

Chapter 22

#SILLYRABBIT

"Shit!" Finn had no choice but to hold on as the dumbwaiter began to move, taking him past the second floor, and then the first . . . all the way to the basement. It was a bad flashback to the last time this had happened.

Before he could catch his breath, the dumbwaiter door opened, and yep, he was in the basement. He had an audience too. Luis the janitor, Trudy the head of building cleaning services, Old Guy Eddie, Elle, Spence, and Spence's two buddies Joe and Caleb all sat around a poker table smoking cigars and playing what looked like five-card stud.

They stared at Finn — still in only his jeans, still holding his shirt and shoes — with various degrees of surprise and shock.

Luis didn't even blink, but then again the guy had lost a leg in Vietnam so not much rattled him. He just shook his head. "Some people never learn."

Trudy had been married to Luis — three times. They'd recently celebrated their third divorce, which meant they were already sleeping together again and probably thinking about their fourth wedding. Trudy took in Finn's state of dress — or in this case undress — and her cigar fell out of her mouth.

"Hot damn," she said in a been-smoking-for-three-decades voice. "I didn't even know they made real men that look like that!"

Joe, the youngest one here at twenty-four, who'd MMA-ed his way through college for cash, lifted up his shirt to look down at his eight-pack. "Hey, I'm made like that too."

Spence snorted.

"You're drooling," Elle told Trudy and tossed some money into the pot without giving Finn a second glance.

Finn didn't take this personally. Everyone knew Elle had a thing for Archer. Well, except for Elle herself. And also Archer . . .

Eddie looked at Finn and then pulled the cigar out of his mouth. "You got your wallet on ya somewhere, kid?"

"Yeah," Finn said. Minus his emergency condom . . .

"Well then get over here," Eddie said. "We'll deal ya in on the next round."

Finn looked down at himself. He thought about the night he'd had, how it had started out about as amazing as a night could get, how it'd ended up going south.

Literally.

"I'm raising thirty," Elle said, mind on the game. Not much distracted Elle from her poker game.

"You sure?" Spence asked her.

She narrowed her eyes. "Why wouldn't I be sure?"

Spence just looked at her. He didn't like to waste words but as one of the smartest guys Finn had ever met, he didn't often need them.

Caleb didn't mind using *his* words. "Do you remember the last time we played?"

Elle sighed. "Yeah, yeah, the last time I raised, I ended up signing over my firstborn to Spence. Good thing I'm not planning on having kids." She blew out a breath and folded. "You're right."

"What?" Spence asked, a hand curved around his ear.

"I said you're right!" Elle snapped.

Spence gave a slow smile. "I heard you. I just wanted to hear it again. Can I get it in writing for posterity?"

Elle flipped him off.

This only made Spence grin. "Sticks and

stones . . ."

"How about a big, fat loss," Elle griped. "Will that hurt you?" She looked around. "What the hell does a girl have to do to get a drink refill and to keep the game moving?"

Joe scrambled to pour her a drink, infatuation in his gaze. Elle absently patted him on the head and went back to her cards. "You coming or not?" she demanded of Finn.

That was Elle, always on a schedule. With a shrug, he tossed aside his shirt and shoes. What the hell. "Deal me in."

It was three in the morning before Finn staggered home and into bed, where he lay staring at the ceiling.

He'd lost his ass in poker — damn Elle, she had balls of steel — and afterward he'd dragged himself to the pub to check in and help close. It'd been a busy night, too busy to keep one eye on the door for a certain brown-eyed beauty.

Not that she'd shown up.

Neither had Jake.

Which meant that Finn had ground his back teeth into powder wondering if he'd been played. Or if he was overreacting. Or if he was a complete idiot . . .

It's just that he couldn't stop thinking about how he'd felt buried deep inside Pru, so deep that he couldn't feel regret or pain. Could feel nothing but her soft body wrapped around him, her wet heat milking him dry, her mouth clinging to his like she'd never had anyone like him, ever.

"Shit," he muttered and flopped over, forcing his eyes closed. So she'd wanted to hide what they'd done. So what. He'd had a hell of an incredible time with her and that had been all he'd needed.

Now it was back to the real world.

He'd halfway convinced himself that he believed it when someone knocked on his door.

In Finn's experience, a middle-of-the-night knock on the door never equaled anything good. In the past, it'd meant his dad was dead. Or Sean needed bail money. Or there was a kitchen fire at the pub.

Kicking off his covers, he shoved himself into the jeans he'd left on the floor. As he padded to the door, he shrugged into a shirt, looking out the peephole to brace himself.

It wasn't what he expected.

Instead of a cop, it was a woman. The one woman who had the ability to turn him upside down and inside out. She was in jeans and a tee now, looking unsettled and anxious. Dammit. He pulled back and stared at the door.

"Don't make me beg," Pru said through the wood.

Resisting the urge to thunk his head against the door, he unlocked and opened up.

Pru stared up at him, squinting through the long bangs that hadn't been contained and were in her face. "You left," she said.

"You shoved me in the dumbwaiter."

"You left," she repeated.

He crossed his arms over his chest and refused to repeat himself. She'd stuffed him into the dumbwaiter so she didn't have to reveal to Jake what they'd been up to on her kitchen table. He'd talked himself into filing that away in his head, in a file drawer labeled STUFF THAT SUCKS. He'd thrown away the key.

But apparently he'd forgotten to lock it.

She closed her eyes. "Can I come in?"

"For?"

She opened her eyes and leveled him with those warm brown eyes. "I wanted to apologize."

"Okay. Anything else?"

"Yes." She sighed. "I know this looks bad, Finn, but it's not what you think."

He leaned against the doorjamb. "And what do I think, Pru?"

She put her hands to his chest and gave a little push. A complete sucker, he let her squeeze in past him, taking some sick delight in the fact that she smelled like him.

She strode straight into his bedroom and he followed because he was Pavlov's dog at this point.

She checked out his room, the unmade bed, the moonlight slanting in through his window, casting his mattress in grays and blues. When he came in behind her, she turned to face him and kicked off her shoes.

"We both know what you thought," she said. "But Jake and I aren't a thing. I wasn't hiding you, at least not like that."

"Then like what?"

She held his gaze for a long beat. "I don't always act with my brain. Sometimes I act with my heart, without thinking about the consequences. Jake is my boss and my friend, and he looks out for me."

"He thinks I'd hurt you?"

"No," she said and looked away. "Actually, he thinks *I'll* hurt *you*. And he's probably right."

"You going to break my heart, Pru?" he asked softly, only half joking because what he knew — and she didn't — was that she could absolutely do it if she wanted. She could slay him.

"Actually," she said very quietly. "I'm pretty sure it's going to be the other way around." She reached for him and pushed his still unbuttoned shirt off his shoulders, assisting it back to the floor.

"What are you doing?" he asked.

"What does it look like?" Her fingers drifted down his chest and abs to play with the top button on his jeans.

"You're trying to get me naked."

"Yes," she said. "You going to help?"

Good question. First things first though. He gathered her hands in one of his and cupped her face with the other, tilting it up to his. "You and Jake are —"

"No," she said without hesitation, eyes clear.

He might regret this later but he believed her. "No more hiding, Pru. I won't be anyone's dirty secret, not even yours."

"I know," she said and freed her hands to caress his chest. "We weren't done with each other."

"No?"

She gave a small head shake and let her fingers drift southbound. "Unless . . . you were done with me?"

Not by a long shot. "You're wearing too

many clothes," he said and then proceeded to get her out of them. He tugged her T-shirt from the waistband of her jeans and yanked it over her head. Her bra followed the same path and her breasts spilled into his hand, warm and soft, tugging a groan from the back of his throat.

Her hands and mouth were just as busy, landing on whatever they could reach, which at the moment meant she was nibbling at his collarbone, her fingers unbuttoning his Levi's.

Quickly losing control, he crouched in front of her, taking her jeans and panties down with one hard tug. With his face level with one of his favorite parts of hers, he clasped her hips in his hands and tugged her a step closer.

"Oh," she gasped, off balance, sliding her fingers into his hair to steady herself.

But he had her. He had her and he wasn't going to let her fall. He'd had no such luck for himself. He'd already fallen and hard. And feeling his heart squeeze at the thought, he leaned in and put his mouth on her.

Another gasp escaped her lips and his fingers tightened on his hair. "Finn —"

He licked. He nuzzled. He sucked. All while her soft pants and helpless moans and wordless entreaties wormed their way in his ears and through his veins until he didn't know where he ended and she began.

When she came, she came hard and with his name on her tongue. Satisfaction and triumph surged through him at that. When her knees buckled, he rose and scooped her up at the same time, feeling like a superhero as he tossed her down to his bed.

She bounced once and then he was on her. Maybe a little rougher than she expected because she blinked up at him in surprise as he pinned her to the mattress.

"What are you doing?" she asked, her voice a little hoarse, for which he took full credit.

"Giving you what you showed up here for."

"What if *I* wanted to be in the driver's seat?" she asked.

"Dumbwaiter," he said.

"So . . . this is payback?"

He gathered both of her wandering hands and pinned them to the pillow on either side of her head. "Yes." He nudged her thighs open with one of his and made himself at home between them. "But you can do whatever you want to me in return. Later." He bowed his head and licked his way down her neck. Christ, she tasted good. "Much later."

He'd planned on going slow and savoring all the naked skin against him but as she softened beneath him, wrapping her legs around his waist, he suddenly wasn't interested in slow. He could feel her, hot and wet and ready, and when he slid in deep, they both gasped and instantly combusted with his first hard thrust.

CHAPTER 23
#CAFFEINEREQUIRED

That day at work, Pru was going over the schedule for the day when Nick poked his head in from the docks. "Hey," he said. "Got a minute?"

She'd gotten him the job here working for Jake, but they were both always so busy, they didn't often get a chance to talk. "I've got exactly a minute," she said, glancing at the clock and then smiling at Nick. "What's up? How's your mom? How's Tim? I talked to him about a week or so ago."

"Mom's fine," Nick said. "And Tim got that apartment." He smiled. "Thanks to you. Does Jake know he has a saint working for him?"

"Believe me," she said on an uncomfortable laugh. "I'm no saint. And Jake doesn't need to be told otherwise."

"Why? Maybe he'd give you a raise."

"For being a saint? No. Now if I figured out how to clone myself," she said. "He might be so inclined."

Nick gave her a quick, hard hug.

"What's that for?" she asked.

"Everything."

When he'd left, she got a text from Elle that had her staring at her phone, mouth open.

> I don't know how or why, but thanks for sending last night's comic relief to poker night.

She stared at the text, horrified. She still couldn't believe she'd done that to Finn.

And that's not the only thing you've done to him . . .

She'd let her emotions get the better of her. That was a mistake, but oh God, what a delicious, sexy, heart-stopping wonderful mistake.

She responded back to Elle with a ? on the off chance she was jumping to conclusions, and Elle was all too happy to explain in her next text:

> Biweekly poker night in the basement turned into a peep show when Finn showed up in the dumbwaiter half nekkid. Lucy, you've got some 'splainin' to do.

Her stomach hurt. Her plan to bring Finn

a little fun, a little adventure while waiting on the fountain to bring him love, had seemed so simple. Fun and adventure, and maybe even a little walk on the wild side. She honestly hadn't meant to do that in bed.

Or on her kitchen table.

Or in her shower . . .

Oh, God. This whole thing was bad. Very, very bad. And yet it'd all been so heart-stopping good at the same time that she found herself just standing in place at odd moments, her brain glazed over as it ran through erotic, sensual memories like a slide show behind her eyelids. Finn bending her over the end of the bed, his mouth at her ear whispering hot little sexy nothings as he'd teased and cajoled her right out of her inhibitions, his body hard against her.

In her . . .

She blew out a shaky breath. Dangerous thoughts. Because it was her being selfish, and she wasn't going to do that again.

Absolutely not.

Or, you know, as much as she could.

Ugh. She slapped herself in the forehead. *Go back to your plan,* she ordered herself, not giving her inner smart-ass a chance to chime in. No more sexy times, no matter how deliciously demanding he was in bed. And this time, she meant it. One hundred percent. Or at the very least, seventy-five percent.

Certainly no less than fifty percent . . .

Luckily, work was crazy busy and helped keep her mind off all things Finn-related. The weather was warm, which meant that everyone and their mama wanted to get outside. They wanted to be on the water, see Alcatraz, Treasure Island, the Pier 39 sea lions . . .

She was on her second tour of the day when a guy tried to propose to his girlfriend. Unfortunately for him, he apparently hadn't checked out her Pinterest page where she'd pinned pictures of acceptable rings. The proposal went fine until she opened the little black box. It didn't end well, especially since he'd done it in the first five minutes of the two-hour tour, and then had to endure the rest of the ride in frosty silence.

On her last tour, Pru had a bunch of frat boys who kept making jokes, wanting to know if she'd be their captain below deck as well, nudge, nudge, wink, wink, if she'd ever played pirates with her passengers, because they wouldn't mind pillaging and plundering. At that she'd pulled out the baseball bat she kept beneath her captain's chair and asked if anyone needed their balls rearranged or if they wanted to sit down and shut up for the rest of the tour.

They'd gone with sitting down and shutting up.

She'd gotten a call from Jake the second the last of her passengers debarked.

"You have problems with passengers, you let me kick their ass, you don't need to do it," he said. "You're not alone out there, I'm always in your ear."

Literally. They were in constant communication when she was on the water via comms. "Maybe sometimes I want to do my own ass kicking," she said.

"My point is that you don't have to."

"It's a good stress reliever," she said.

"Uh huh. As good as sleeping with the guy you haven't been honest with and then shoving him bare-ass naked into your dumbwaiter to avoid your ex, your boss, and your best friend?"

The air left her lungs in one big whoosh. "Who told you?"

"Eddie would snitch on his mama for food or cash, you know that."

"And how did Eddie know?" she demanded. "I didn't tell anyone!"

"Didn't have to. Eddie was in the basement at a very intense poker game with a select few when the dumbwaiter opened and out stumbled your boy, pants in hand."

"Shirt!" she yelled. "He had his *shirt* in hand. He was *wearing* his pants!"

"Just tell me you told him."

"I'm working on that."

"Dammit, Pru, it's like you *want* to self-implode your own happiness. Promise me you won't do anything that stupid again until you tell him."

She closed her eyes, knowing he was right. Hating that he was right.

"Pru —"

"— I hear you," she said.

"Promise me. I know you would never break a promise, so right here and now, promise me that —"

"I promise," she said. "I've always intended to tell him and I will. I get that it's been two weeks but I'm working up to it, okay? I'm going to tell him soon as the time is right."

"Just don't miss your window of opportunity, chica, that's all I'm saying."

"I hear you."

They disconnected and Pru closed her eyes. Hard to pretend something hadn't happened when everyone in the free world knew.

She didn't linger after work like she usually did. Instead she hightailed it out of there. Needing to clear her head, she and

Thor walked. Well, *she* walked. Thor got tired about halfway and stopped. He planted his little butt on the sidewalk and steadfastly refused to walk another step.

"You're going to get fat," she told him.

Thor turned his head away from her.

"Come on," she cajoled. "I want to walk out the Aquatic Park Pier and watch the sky change colors as the sun sets."

Thor sneezed and she could have sworn she heard "bullshit" in the sound. And the sad thing was that her dog had more brain cells than she did because he was right.

She was stalling going home. It was just that she'd come to count on Finn's company so much. Too much. He made her smile. He made her ache. He made her want things, things she'd been afraid to want. He made her feel . . . way too much.

Thor hadn't budged so she scooped him up and carried him out to the end of the long, curved pier. She watched the water and thought maybe this wasn't so bad. Yes, she'd made a mistake. She'd been with Finn a few times.

So what.

Other people, normal people, slept with people all the time and she didn't see anyone else angsting over it. For all she knew Finn hadn't given it a second thought, and in fact would laugh off her worries.

But you've slept with him now, as in actually *slept,* snuggled in his arms all night long . . . And that was more intimate than anything else and it changed things for her. "Maybe I'm just being silly," she said hopefully to Thor.

Thor, lazy but utterly loyal, licked her chin.

She hugged him close. "I always have you," she murmured. "You'll never leave me —"

But he was squirming to get down so desperately she did just that. "What's gotten into you?" She stopped when he bounced over to a fellow dog a few feet away.

A small, dainty, perfectly groomed Shih Tzu. The dog stilled at Thor's approach and allowed him to sniff her butt, and then returned the favor while Pru glanced apologetically at the dog's owner.

The woman was in her thirties, wearing running tights and a tiny little running bra, the brand of which Pru couldn't even afford to look through their catalogue.

"Baby," the woman said. "What have I told you? You're a purebred not a disgusting mutt."

"Hey, he's not disgusting, he's just —"

But Pru broke off when Thor lifted his leg and peed on Baby.

By the time Pru got to her building, Thor had fallen asleep in her arms, which were nearly dead. Seemed nothing stopped him from catching his beauty sleep, not snooty little dogs with snooty little owners, and certainly not the squealing of said snooty little dogs' owners about the cost of dog grooming and how Pru had let her heathen ruin her "baby."

A low-lying fog rolled in to join dusk as she entered through the courtyard, staying close to the back wall, not wanting to be seen by anyone.

The temps had dropped so she wasn't surprised to see the wood fire pit lit. She was surprised to see Eddie manning the pit. He waved her over.

Halfway there she realized the entire courtyard smelled like skunk. When she got to Eddie, she pulled the uneaten half of her sushi lunch pack from her bag and gave it to him.

"Thanks, dudette." Pocketing the sushi in his sweatshirt, he poked at the fire with a long stick.

"It's going out," she said.

"I know. I burned it hot on purpose, I had

some stuff to get rid of."

"Stuff? Stuff related to the skunk smell?"

He just smiled.

A few minutes went by and Pru realized she was still standing there, now with a wide grin on her face. "I'm starving."

"Me too," Willa said from right next to Pru.

Pru blinked. "When did you get here?"

"A while ago." Willa looked into her face and grinned too. "You're high as a kite."

"What? Of course I'm not," Pru said.

"It's a contact high." Willa looked at Eddie, who had the decency to look sheepish.

"I had some dead seedlings I had to get rid of," Eddie said. "It's fastest to just burn them."

"You can't just burn them out here!" Willa said. "Right, Pru?"

But Pru was feeling distracted. "I need food," she said. "Chips, cookies, cakes, and pies."

"And pizza," Willa said. "And chips."

"I already said chips."

"Double the chips!" Willa yelled to the courtyard like she was placing an order with an invisible waitress.

Pru laughed at her. "I'm not high as a kite. *You* are."

"No, *you* are."

"No," Pru said, poking Willa in the arm. "*You* are."

"You both are." This was from Archer, who'd appeared in front of them.

"Whoa," Willa said. "The police are here. Run!"

Archer reached out and snagged her hand to keep her at his side. Frowning down at her, he then turned and eyeballed Pru.

She did her best to look innocent even though she felt very guilty. Why, she had no idea.

"Shit," he said in disgust to Eddie. "You got them both stoned out of their minds. What the hell did I tell you an hour ago?"

"You said you'd arrest me if I didn't put out the fire. I'm working on it. It's almost out, dude."

A muscle in Archer's jaw bunched. Willa set her head on his shoulder and looked up at him with a dreamy smile. "Elle's right," she murmured, batting her lashes. "You do look really hot when you're all worked up."

"I'm not worked up —" He broke off and slid her a speculative look. "Elle thinks I'm hot?"

"When you're worked up. When you're not, she thinks you're a stick in the mud."

Archer shook his head and pulled out his phone. "Elle, your girls need you in the courtyard. Now." He slid both Pru and Willa a long look and added, "You're going to want to feed them. Oh, and Elle? Remind me that we have something to discuss."

Willa smacked him. "You can't tell her that I told you that she thinks you're hot!" she hissed.

Archer lifted a finger in her direction and listened to something Elle said. He let out a rare smile. "Yes, that was Willa."

Willa smacked her own forehead. "She's gonna kill me."

Archer disconnected with Elle and pointed at them. "Don't either of you move until she comes and gets you. You hear me?"

"Hear you," Pru said, eyes locked on the pub. The doors were open to the street and the courtyard. The place was full and spilling out sounds of music and laughter.

Behind the bar, Sean and Finn were elbow to elbow, working hard. Finn was shaking a mixer and laughing at something a woman at the bar was saying to him.

Elle appeared in a siren red sheath dress that screamed serious business. Her black heels echoed the statement. "What's going on?" she demanded, hands on hips. "Archer pulled me out of a meeting with the building's board —"

"Was the owner there?" Willa asked. She

looked at Pru. "None of us have ever met the owner. He's exclusive."

"Elusive," Elle corrected, narrowing her eyes on each of them, and then Eddie.

Who unlike when he'd been dealing with Archer, actually sunk in on himself a little, seemingly sheepish. "I didn't realize," he said.

"Oh for God's sake." Elle took a deep breath and looked a little less uptight. She took another and sighed. "I need pizza."

"Right?" Willa said, grinning.

"Count me in." This was Haley, who arrived from the elevator in her white doctor's coat, looking quite official.

"You're still doctoring," Willa said.

"Nope," Haley said, pulling off her lab coat. "The smoke and commotion drew me down here but I'm done for the day, thankfully. It was a busy one."

"Spence come in for glasses yet?" Elle asked.

Haley bit her lower lip. "I saw him, yes."

"And?" Elle asked. "His eyesight is bad, right?"

"I'm sorry, I can't say," Haley said. "Or HIPAA would drag me away in chains. He'll have to tell you himself."

Elle stared into her eyes and then smiled. "Yeah, he got glasses."

"Damn," Haley said. "I hate when you do that."

"She reads minds," Willa told Pru.

"Like magic?" Pru asked, awed.

"Not magic," Elle said. "You all just wear your every single thought on your sleeves."

"Oh, look at you, dear," Mrs. Winslow said to Pru, coming up to her with a wide smile. "You look amazing."

"Uh . . ." Pru looked down at herself. She was still in her usual work uniform of a stretchy white button-down and navy trousers and boots. "Thanks?"

"Must be all the sexual activity with Finn," the older woman said. "Intercourse does wonders for your skin."

Looking shocked, Willa nearly swallowed her tongue. She turned to Elle, who shrugged.

"You *knew*?" Willa asked.

"When are you going to get it? I *always* know," Elle said.

Pru admired a woman who always had the answers. She really hoped Elle shared some of them because she could really use a few right about now.

"Burgers and hot dogs!" a guy yelled walking through the courtyard. It was Jay. He owned the food truck that usually sat out front, but now he had a tray strapped on him and was making sales left and right like he was going up and down the rows at a baseball stadium. "I've got beef burgers and six inches of prime sausages here! Get 'em while they're hot!"

"Six inches would do me just right," Mrs. Winslow said wistfully. "I wouldn't know what to do with seven or eight."

Try nine, Pru thought and clapped a hand over her mouth to keep from saying it out loud.

"Something you want to share with the class?" Haley asked.

Most definitely not, but the vultures had the scent of roadkill and were circling.

"Oh, she'll talk," Elle said, staring into Pru's eyes. "She'll talk over a loaded pie and a bottle of wine. Girls, let's hit it."

And she walked off.

"She's so badass," Willa whispered, staring after her. "I mean look at that dress. She's badass, kickass, *and* she has a great ass. It's really not fair."

"I can hear you," Elle called out over her shoulder without looking back. She snapped her fingers. "Put it in gear."

And Pru, Haley, and Willa followed after her like puppies on a leash.

Chapter 24

Pru had no idea how Elle did it, but by the time they got to the street, there was an Uber ride waiting on them.

"Lefty's Pizza," Elle said to the driver.

"I thought you were on a diet," Haley said, climbing into the car.

"Some days you eat salads and go to the gym," Elle said. "And some days you eat pizza and wear yoga pants. It's called balance."

"I always eat pizza and wear yoga pants," Willa said. She gasped. "Does that make me unbalanced?"

"No, actually, it makes you smarter than me," Elle said with a small smile.

Willa sighed. "Or maybe I've just given up on men."

"That's only because you dated a few frogs," Elle said.

"That's an extremely nice way of saying that I'm a loser magnet. And I couldn't get rid of that one frog either. I still owe Archer for stepping in and pretending to be my boyfriend so he'd back off."

"That's not why he backed off," Elle said. "He backed off because Archer threatened to castrate him if he contacted you again."

Willa gaped. "He did? I was wondering at how easy he made it look."

"And you can make it look easy too," Elle told her. "Next time you want to lose a guy, just tell them 'I love you, I want to marry you, and I want children right away.' They'll run so fast they'll leave skid marks."

Willa snorted. "I'll keep that in mind."

Thirty minutes later they were in a booth, one bottle of wine down, another ready to go, and a large pizza on its way to being demolished. Pru's stomach hurt, but that hadn't slowed her down any.

Willa pulled a book from her purse. "Have either of you been to that new used bookstore down the street from our building?"

"I download my books right to my phone," Elle said. "That way I can read while pretending to listen in on meetings."

"Your boss doesn't mind?" Pru asked.

"My boss knows everything," Elle said. "And one of the things he also knows is that me doing my thing allows him to do his thing."

Made sense.

"Plus, I know where the bodies are hidden," she said.

Probably she was kidding.

"Well, I like the feel of a book in my hand," Willa said and looked at Pru.

"I go both ways," Pru said and then blushed when they all laughed. "You know what I mean."

"I do," Willa said and handed her the book. "Which is why I bought this for you."

Pru eyed the title and choked on a bite of pizza. Willa had to pound her on the back while Pru sucked a bunch of wine down to try and appease her burning throat. No go. "*Orgasms For One?*" she finally managed.

Willa nodded.

"Um . . . thank you?"

"I bought it after you told us that you hadn't dated in a while but before I heard about the dumbwaiter, so . . ."

Pru sighed. "So everyone knows about the dumbwaiter."

"Little bit," Haley said. "What we don't know are the deets."

Elle pointed at Pru. "You. Finn. Go."

"It's . . . a long story."

"I love long stories," Willa said.

Elle just arched a brow. She didn't like to be kept waiting.

"Might as well start talking," Haley told Pru. "She'll get her way eventually, she always does. I've found it's best to give in earlier than later. Besides, I'm tired." She accompanied this statement with a wide yawn.

Pru rubbed her aching stomach. She was starting to feel sick. "Maybe we should postpone this for another day. When I haven't eaten my weight in pizza."

Elle didn't break eye contact with her. She didn't budge a muscle, not even to blink.

Pru sighed. "Fine. Maybe something's happened between me and Finn, but it's not going to keep happening."

Willa grinned. "So you *did* sleep with him."

"Past tense," Pru said, her gaze still held prisoner by Elle's. "Even if I wish it wasn't." Dammit. "Where did you get this super power?" she demanded. "I need it."

Elle smiled. "I'd tell you but —"

"— But she'd have to kill you," Willa finished on a laugh. "Love it when you say that."

"Except you never let me say it," Elle pointed out.

Pru's stomach turned over yet again and she put a hand on it. "I really don't feel so good."

"Because you're holding back on your new BFFs," Willa said.

"I like you for Finn," Elle said to Pru. "He hasn't chosen anyone in a long time. I'm glad it's you."

"Oh, no. That's the thing," she said. "It's not me. I mean, it was great. He was great. And when I was with him, I felt . . ." She closed her eyes, the memories washing over her. "*Really* great." She could still hear his low, sexy voice in her ear telling her what he was going to do to her, and then his even sexier body doing it, taking hers to places it hadn't been in so long she'd nearly forgotten what it was like to be in a man's arms and lose herself.

"So why is it over then?" Haley asked. "Do you realize how rare 'really great' is? I haven't had 'really great' in so long I don't even know if I'll recognize it."

"You'll recognize it," Elle said, looking at Pru, waiting on her answer.

But Pru didn't answer. Couldn't. Because she hated the reason why. "It's . . . complicated."

"Honey," Elle said with surprising vulnerability and wistfulness in her voice. "The best things always are." She paused. "You'd be really good for him."

Elle wasn't a woman to say such a thing

unless she meant it so Pru felt herself warm a little at that. Even if it wasn't true. She wasn't good for Finn. And when he found out the truth about her and who she was, she'd in fact be very bad for him.

"He hasn't dated since Mellie," Willa said thoughtfully. "And she turned out to be —"

"Willa," Elle said quietly. Warningly.

"I'm sorry," she said, not sounding sorry at all. "But I hated her for what she did to him. To him *and* Sean."

"It was a long time ago," Elle said firmly.

"A year. He liked her, a lot. And he got hurt," Willa said. "And you hated her for it too, admit it."

Elle gave a slight head nod. "I would have liked to kill her," she said casually in the way most people would comment on the weather.

"And it changed him," Willa said. She turned to Pru. "Mellie had the dressy boutique here in the building for a while before she sold it. She was wild and fun and gregarious, and she was good for Finn. At first. Until —"

"Willa." Elle gave her a long look. "You're telling tales. He's going to kill you."

"Only if you tattle," Willa said. "Pru needs to know what she's up against."

"What am I up against?" Pru whispered

in spite of herself, needing to know.

"Mellie and Sean got drunk one night. And they . . ." She grimaced.

Pru gasped. "No," she breathed. "She slept with his brother?"

"Well, apparently when Finn walked in on them they hadn't quite gotten to home plate but it was close enough."

"Finn walked in on them?" Pru asked, horrified, trying to imagine. She didn't have a sibling, but in her fantasies, if she'd had a sister or brother, they would stand at her back, always. "How awful."

Willa nodded. "It caused a big fight, but they've always fought. Sean had had way too much to drink that night, he was really out of it, and later he kept saying he'd never have made a move on her if he'd been in his right mind. But Mellie wasn't drunk. She knew exactly what she was doing."

"But why would she do that to Finn?" Pru asked.

"Because she'd been after him for a commitment. At that time, he was still finishing up his business degree. She hated that he went to classes early in the morning, studied after that, then handled the business side of O'Riley's, and then often had to work the pub all night on top of that. When he wasn't working his ass off on any of those things, he was dead asleep. He was giving everything one hundred percent, even her, but it wasn't enough. She was bored and lonely, two things that didn't agree with her."

Elle slid Willa a look. "You think he's going to thank you for airing his dirty laundry when he finds out?"

"No, I think he'll put out a hit on me," Willa said. "But he's not going to find out. I'm doing our girl a service here, explaining some things about her man that he's certainly not going to explain to her."

"He's not my man," Pru said.

"He's not going to explain," Willa said to Elle as if Pru hadn't spoken, "because he thinks the past should stay in the past."

"He's not my man," Pru repeated, holding her stomach, which was killing her now.

"The past should *absolutely* stay in the past," Elle said to Willa, something in her voice saying she believed that to the depths of her very soul.

Willa closed her eyes briefly and covered Elle's hand with her own, the two of them sharing a moment that Pru didn't understood. They had history. She got that. They were close friends, and clearly there was a lot about them that she didn't know. Such as what had happened to Elle to make her want her past to stay buried.

Pru didn't have many people in her life. Her own fault. She didn't let many in. It didn't take a shrink to get why. She'd lost her parents early. Her only other living relative often mistook her for devil spawn. There were some school friends she kept in occasional contact with, and she had her coworkers. And Jake.

But it would be really nice to have Willa and Elle as well.

Her stomach cramped painfully again, which she ignored when Willa took her hand.

"I'm trusting you with this, Pru," she said. "Do you know why?"

Unable to imagine, Pru shook her head.

"Because you're one of us now," she said and looked at Elle. "Right?"

Elle turned her head and met Pru's gaze, studying her solemnly for a long beat before slowly nodding.

Willa smiled. "Look at that." She looked at Pru again. "Here's something you might not know. Elle doesn't like very many people."

Elle snorted.

"It's because she's scary as shit," Haley said, drinking the last of her wine.

"Sitting right here," Elle said calmly, glancing at her nails.

Which were, of course, perfect.

Not appearing scared in the slightest, Willa just smiled. "But one thing about her, she never says anything she doesn't mean. And once you're a friend, you're a friend for life." She paused and glanced at Elle, brow raised.

Elle shrugged.

Willa gave her a long look.

Elle rolled her eyes but she did smile. "Friends for life," she said. "Or until you piss me off. Don't piss me off."

A new warmth filled Pru and her throat tightened. "Thanks," she whispered.

Elle narrowed her eyes. "You're not going to cry, are you? There's no crying on pizza night."

"Just got something in my eye," Pru said with a sniff and swiped under her eyes.

Elle sighed and handed her a napkin. "Look, I know I'm a cold-hearted bitch, but Willa's right, you're one of ours now. And we're yours. This is why we're trusting you with Finn. Because he's also one of ours and he means a lot to us."

"Oh no, you can't trust me with him," she said. "I mean —" She shook her head. "It's just that I'm not — we're not a real thing."

"It's cute you think that." Willa patted her hand. "But I've seen you two together."

Pru opened her mouth to protest but the dessert they'd ordered arrived — a pan-size homemade cookie topped with ice cream, and then there was no speaking as they stuffed their faces.

When Pru was done, it came up on her suddenly. Her stomach rolled again and this time a queasiness rose up her throat with it.

Uh oh.

The good news was that she recognized the problem. The bad news was that she was about to be sick. She searched her brain for what she might have eaten and gasped.

Sushi for lunch.

Which meant she'd made Eddie sick too. "I've got to go," she said abruptly. The last time she'd had food poisoning she'd laid on her bathroom floor for two straight days. Privacy was required for such things, serious privacy. Standing on wobbly legs, she pulled some money from her purse and dropped it on the table. "I'm sorry —" She clapped a hand to her gurgling stomach and shook her head. "Later."

She got a cab, but the traffic and the ensuing stop/start of navigating said traffic just about killed her. She bailed a block early and moved as fast as she could. When she cut through the courtyard of her building, she slid a quick, anxious look at the pub.

Please don't be there, please don't be there . . .

But fate or destiny or karma, whoever was in charge of such things as looking out for her humility, had taken a break because all the pub doors were still open to the night. Finn stood near the courtyard entrance talking to some customers. And like a beacon in the night, he turned right to her.

She kept moving, her hand over her mouth, as if that would keep her from throwing up in public. If she could have sold her soul to the devil right then to ensure it, she totally would have.

But not even the devil himself had enough power to alter her course in history. She was dying at this point, sharp, shooting pains through her gut combined with an all-over body ache that had her whimpering to herself with each step. Holding back from losing her dinner had her sweating in rivulets.

"Pru," came Finn's unbearably familiar voice — from right behind her.

"I'm sorry," she managed, not slowing down. "I can't —"

"We need to talk."

Yep, the only four words in the English language destined to spark terror within her heart. Talk? He wanted to talk? Maybe when she died. And given the pain stabbing through her with the force of a thousand needles, it wouldn't be long now. Still, just in case, she moved faster.

"Pru."

She wanted to say *look, I'm about to throw up half a loaded pizza and possibly my intestines, and I like you, I like you enough that if you see me throw up that half a loaded pizza, I'll have to kill myself.*

Which, actually, wouldn't be necessary seeing as she was about to die anyway.

"Pru, slow down." He caught her hand.

But the more she put off the now inevitable, the worse it would be. "Not feeling good," she said, twisting free. "I've gotta go."

"What's wrong?" His voice immediately changed from playful to serious. "What do you need?"

What she needed was the privacy of her own bathroom. She opened her mouth to say so but the only thing that came out was a miserable moan.

"Do you need a doctor?" he asked.

Yes, she needed a doctor. For a lobotomy.

With sweat slicking her skin, she ran directly for the elevator, praying that it would be on the ground floor and no one else would want to get on it with her.

Of course it wasn't on the ground floor.

With another miserable moan she headed for the stairwell, taking them as fast as she could with her stomach sending fireballs to her brain and her legs weakened by the need to upchuck.

And oh lucky her, Finn kept pace with her, right at her side.

Which made her panic all the more because seriously, she was on a countdown at this point, T minus sixty seconds tops, and there would be no stopping or averting liftoff. "I'm fine!" she said weakly. "Please, just leave me alone!" She threw her hand out at him to push him away so she could have room in case she spontaneously imploded.

A very real possibility.

But the man who was more tuned into her body than she was had apparently not yet mastered mind reading. "I'm not leaving you alone like this," he said.

She pushed him again from a well of reserved strength born of sheer terror because she was about to become her own horror show and didn't want witnesses. "You have to go!" she said, maybe yelled, as they *finally* got to the third floor.

Mrs. Winslow stuck her head out her door and gave Pru a disapproving look. "You might be getting some but you're not going to keep getting some if you talk to your man like that. Especially after shoving him into the dumbwaiter the other night."

Oh for God's sake!

How did everyone know about that?

Not that she could ask.

Hell, no. Instead, she stopped and pawed through her purse for her keys before dropping it to scratch and claw at the door like she was being kidnapped and tortured.

Finn crouched down at her feet to pick up her purse and scoop the contests back in. He had a tampon in one hand and Willa's book — *Orgasms For One* — in the other. He should've looked utterly ridiculous. Instead he looked utterly perfect.

"Pru, can you tell me what's wrong?"

"I think she's having a seizure," Mrs. Winslow said helpfully. "Honey, you look a little bit constipated. I suggest a good fart. That always works for me."

Pru didn't know how to tell her she was about to let loose but it wouldn't be nearly as neat as a fart. By some miracle, she made it inside. She was sweating through her clothes by the time she stumbled along without even taking her keys out of the lock, racing to the bathroom, slamming the door behind her.

She had barely hit her knees before she got sick.

From what felt like a narrow, long tunnel, through the thick fog in her head and her own misery, she heard him.

"Pru," he said, his voice low with worry.

From right.

Outside.

Her.

Bathroom.

Door.

"I'm coming in," he said and she couldn't stop throwing up to tell him to run, to save himself.

CHAPTER 25

#BADDAYATTHEOFFICE

Pru felt one of Finn's hands pull her hair back and hold it for her, the other encircling her, fingers spread wide on her stomach. He was kneeling behind her, his big body supporting hers.

"I've got you," he said.

No one had ever said such a thing to her before and she would have loved to absorb that and maybe obsess over why it meant so much, but her stomach had other ideas. So she closed her eyes and pretended she was alone on a deserted island with her charged Kindle. And maybe Netflix. When she could catch her breath, she brought a shaky hand to her head, which was pounding like the devil himself was in there operating a jackhammer, whittling away at what was left of her brains.

Finn kept her from sliding to the floor by wrapping both arms around her and bringing her gently back, propping her up against him.

"I'm sorry," she managed, horrified that she'd thrown up in front of the hottest man she'd ever had the privilege of sleeping with by accident.

"Breathe, Pru. It's going to be okay."

"Please just leave me here to die," she croaked out when she could, pulling free. "Just walk out of this room and pretend it never happened. We'll never speak of it again."

And then, giving up trying to be strong, she slid bonelessly to the bathroom floor. Her body was hot and she was slick with perspiration. Unable to garner the energy to hold herself up anymore, she pressed her hot cheek to the cool tile and closed her eyes.

She heard water running and squeezed her eyes tight, but that only made her all the dizzier. A deliciously cool, wet washcloth was pressed to her forehead. She cracked an eye and found Finn. "Dammit, you never listen."

"I always listen," he said. "I just don't always agree."

His hand was rubbing her back in soothing circles and she thought she might never move again if he kept on doing that until the end of time. "Why won't you go away?"

When he didn't say anything, she again opened an eye. He was still looking at her with concern but not like she was at death's door. Except if she wasn't dying, that meant she was going to have to live with this, with him seeing her flat on the floor looking like roadkill.

"Do you think you can move?" he asked.

"Negative." She wasn't moving. *Ever.* She heard him on his phone, telling someone he needed something liquid with electrolytes in it.

"Not drinking anything either," she warned him, her stomach turning over at the thought.

He got up and left her, and she was grateful. When he came back in a moment later, she was back to worshipping the porcelain god, trying to catch her breath.

"Any better?" he asked when she was done.

She couldn't speak. She couldn't anything.

He peeled her away from the seat and gathered her in his lap. He laid her head against his shoulder and wrapped his arms around her. "Take a few deep breaths. Slowly."

She tried but she was shaking so hard she thought maybe her teeth were going to rattle

330

right out of her head. Finn wiped the sweat-matted hair from her face and then pressed the cool washcloth to the back of her neck.

It was heaven.

He cracked a bottle of lime-flavored water with electrolytes.

"Where did you get that?" she asked.

"Willa. She has it in her shop. Says she gives it to the nervous dogs after they throw up."

"You told Willa I was throwing up?"

"She's in the kitchen making you soup for tomorrow when you feel better. Elle's bringing her a few ingredients she didn't have."

Pru managed a moan. "I don't want anyone to see me like this."

"You do realize that friends don't actually care what you look like," he said. "Take a sip, Pru."

She shook her head. She couldn't possibly swallow anything.

"Just a sip. Trust me, it'll help."

She did trust him. But drinking anything was going to be a disaster of major proportions.

He was moving her, using his shoulder to hold her head forward. It was take a sip or drown.

She took a sip.

"Good girl," he whispered and let her

settle back against him. They sat there, silent, for what seemed like days. Her stomach slowly stopped doing backflips.

"How do you feel?" he asked after a while. She had no idea.

When she didn't enlighten him, he took the washcloth from her neck, refolded it, and put it against her forehead.

"Eddie," she croaked. "He might be sick too —"

"I've got him covered. Spence is with him but the old guy's got a stomach of iron and doesn't appear to be affected."

She managed a nod, eyes still closed. She must have drifted off then because when she opened her eyes again the light was different in the bathroom, like some time had gone by.

Finn was still on the floor with her, only he was shirtless now, wearing just his jeans.

Oh yeah. She remembered now. She'd thrown up a bunch more times. She had her hands curled around his neck, clutching him like he was her only lifeline.

And he was. She stared at his chest. She couldn't stop herself. No matter how many times she saw his stomach, she wanted to lick it each time.

Not that she wanted to stop there either.

Nope, she wanted to lick upward to his

neck and then trail back down. She wanted to drop to her knees and slowly ease his jeans over his hips and —

"You okay?" he asked. "You just moaned."

Huh. Maybe she really was going to live. She dragged her back to his. His hair was tousled, his jaw beyond a five o'clock shadow, but he still looked hot.

She hated him. "You should go," she said knowing he either had to work or sleep.

He shook his head and brushed his lips over her forehead at the hairline. "It's been a couple of hours since you last got sick," he said. "Sip some more water."

Her stomach was much calmer now, but her head was beating to its own drum. She could feel it pulsating.

"You're dehydrated," he said. "You need the water to get rid of the fever and headache."

Too achy to argue, she nodded. She managed to take a few sips and then her body took over, demanding more.

"Careful," Finn warned, pulling it away when she started to gulp it. "Let's see how that settles first."

"Thor?"

"He's right here, sleeping on my feet. You want him?"

Yes. But she was in bad enough shape to

hug him too tight and the last time she'd done that, he'd gotten scared and bit her. She'd stick with just Finn for now. She was pretty sure Finn only bit when naked. Or on really special occasions.

She fell asleep on him again and woke up much later in her own bed. Willa was helping her change.

"That man is gone over you," Willa murmured, tucking Pru into bed.

"It's the damn fountain." Pru had to hold her head on, keeping her eyes shut even when Willa had paused.

"Fountain?" she asked.

Maybe if Pru hadn't been dying, she wouldn't have answered. "I wished," she said. "I wished for Finn to find love, but the fountain got it all wrong and gave *me* love instead. Stupid fountain. He's the one who deserves it."

"Honey," Willa said softly. "We all deserve love."

Pru wanted that to be true. God, how she wanted that . . .

"And how do you know the fountain didn't get it right?" Willa asked. "Maybe *you're* his true love."

Pru drifted off on that terrifying thought.

"You're going to want to sip some of this."

334

It was Elle. She sat on the bed at Pru's hip and offered a mug.

"What is it?" Pru asked.

"Only the best tea on the planet. Try it."

"I'm not thirsty —"

"Try it," Elle said again finally. "You're nearly translucent, you need fluids."

So Pru sipped.

"Now," Ella said calmly. "What's this I hear about the fountain and some wish going astray?"

Pru choked on her sip.

Elle rolled her eyes, leaned forward, and pounded Pru on the back.

"Willa told you," Pru said on a sigh.

"Yeah. She's cute but she can't keep a secret. She doesn't mean any harm, I promise. She doesn't have a mean bone in her body. Mostly she's worried about you and thought I could beat some sense into you."

Pru blinked.

"Metaphorically," Elle said. "And plus she wanted to borrow some change so she could go make a wish, seeing how it worked out so good for you."

"The wish was for Finn!"

"Uh huh."

"It was!"

"Well then, I'd say you got a two-fer."

Chapter 26

#WAXONWAXOFF

The next time Pru opened her eyes, the hallway light allowed her to see that someone was sprawled in the chair by her bed. That someone rose when she stirred and sat at her hip.

"How you doing?" Finn asked.

She blinked at the crack of dawn's early light creeping in through the slats of her blinds, casting everything in a hazy gold glow. From outside the window came the early chatter of birds, obnoxiously loud and chipper. She moaned. "I've never figured out if they're happy that it's morning or objecting to its arrival."

Finn smiled. "I vote for objecting."

Her too. He'd changed, she couldn't help but notice. Different jeans, a rumpled black T-shirt. Hair still tousled. Jaw still stubbled. Eyes heavy-lidded. He was without a doubt the sexiest thing she'd ever seen. Which told her one thing at least.

She hadn't died.

He propped her up in her bed, tied her crazy-ass hair back and brought her toast. Cut diagonally. She just stared up at him. Was he a fevered dream? "Tell me the truth," she murmured, her voice rough and haggard. "You're a fevered mirage, right?"

He frowned and leaned over her, one hand planted on the mattress, the other going to her forehead. His frown deepened and he leaned in even closer so that she caught a whiff of him.

He smelled like heaven on earth.

She did *not* smell like heaven on earth, and worse, she felt like roadkill. Like roadkill that had been run over, back upped on, and run over again. Twice.

But not Finn. She pressed in close and plastered her face to his throat at the same moment he pressed his mouth to her forehead.

"You don't feel fevered," he muttered.

"No, that's what happens when things are a mirage. In fact, last night never even really happened."

Pulling back, he met her gaze. "So I suppose you remember nothing."

"Nothing," she agreed quickly. "How could I? Nothing happened."

His lips twitched. "Nicely done."

"Thank you."

He smiled. And then dropped the bomb. "Tell me about the fountain."

"On second thought," she said. "Maybe I actually died. I'm gone and buried . . ."

"Try again."

She looked into his eyes, trying to decide if he knew the truth about her wish — in which case she might have to strangle Willa and Elle — or if he was just fishing. "Well," she said lightly. "It was built back in the days when Cow Hollow was filled with cows. And —"

"Not the fountain's history, smartass," he said. "I mean why you were muttering about it in your feverish haze."

Huh. So maybe Elle and Willa didn't have to be strangled after all. "I was feverish and delusional," she said. "You need to forget everything you heard. And saw," she added.

"You wished for love on the fountain?" he asked with a whisper of disbelief.

"What does it matter, you don't believe in the myth anyway, remember?"

"That's not an answer," he said.

"I don't believe in the myth either," she said, and he fell quiet, letting her get away with that.

Instead of pushing, he nudged the toast

her way. "Eat. And drink. You need to hydrate."

"You sound like a mom."

"Just don't call me grandpa." He got up to go, but she caught his hand.

"Hey," she said. "You went over and above last night. You didn't have to do that."

"I know."

It was hard to hold his gaze. "Thanks for taking care of me."

He just looked at her for a long beat. "Anytime."

By the next day, Pru was completely over the food poisoning and back to work, which was a good thing for several reasons. One, Jake desperately needed her.

And two, she needed to get over throwing up in front of Finn, and short of a memory scrub, working her ass off was the only way to do it. So she buried herself, banning thoughts of Finn, needing to build up her immunity to his sexy charisma.

This worked for two days but then her efforts to lay low failed when he showed up at the warehouse.

He was waiting for her between two tours, propping up a pillar in the holding area where passengers hung out before and after boarding the ships.

"What are you doing here?" she asked, surprised.

"Need a minute with you." He took her hand and pulled her outside. He was in low-slung jeans and a dark green henley the exact color of his eyes. His hair had been finger combed at best and he hadn't shaved, leaving a day's worth of scruff on his square jaw that she knew personally would feel like sex on a stick against her skin.

"You've been avoiding me," he said.

"No, I —"

He put a finger on her lips, his body so close now that she could feel the heat of him, which made her body shift in closer.

Bad body.

"Careful," he said quietly, dipping his head so that his mouth hovered near hers. "You're about to fib, and once you do, things change."

She absorbed that a moment, and wrapping her fingers around his wrist, pulled his finger away from her mouth. "What things?"

His eyes never left hers. "Feelings."

Any lingering amusement faded away because she knew what he was saying. He didn't believe in lying. Or in half-truths. Or fibs . . . And if he thought she was the kind of woman who did, then his feelings about her would change.

She'd known this going in, of course. What she hadn't known was how strongly it would affect their relationship.

Because he didn't know one important fact.

She'd been lying to him about something since the very beginning. She'd weaved the web, she'd built the brick wall, *she'd* created this nightmare of a problem and she had no idea what to do about it.

"Okay, so I've been avoiding you a little," she admitted, starting with the one thing she did know what to do about.

"Why?"

She stared at him. The truth shot out of her heart and landed on the tip of her tongue. She wanted to tell him. She wanted it out in the open in the worst way. Holding it in was giving her guilt gut aches. But they'd only known each other a few short weeks. She just needed a little bit more time. To charm him. To somehow get him to do what no one else ever had — fall hard enough for her to want to keep her.

No matter that she'd made a huge mistake. She needed to work him into that, slowly. "I'm not good with this stuff," she said quietly. Hello, understatement of the year.

"Going to need you to be more specific."

"I'm not good with . . . the after thing."
And so much more . . .

"The after thing," he repeated. "You mean after food poisoning? Pru, who *is* good at that?"

"No. I mean yes, and I don't know. But I was talking about the after sleeping with someone thing."

He looked more than a little baffled, and also somewhat amused. "So having sex isn't the problem, it's that we've actually slept together," he said.

Knowing it sounded ridiculous, she nodded.

She expected him to try and joke that away but he didn't. Instead, he wrapped his big hand up in hers and gave her a crooked smile. "I guess that makes us the blind leading the blind then. I don't do a lot of sleepovers, Pru."

"But you've been in a long relationship before," she said. "With Mellie."

He paused. "Someone's been telling tales."

"It's true though, right?" she asked.

"What is it that you're asking me, Pru?"

Okay, so he clearly didn't want to discuss Mellie. Got it. Understood it. Hell, she had plenty of things she didn't want to discuss either. "I'm trying to say that not only am I not good at sleepovers, I . . . haven't really

342

had any." She bit her lip. Dammit. That made her sound pathetic. She tried again. "It's more that you're my one and only —" Nope, now she was just making it worse. "Okay, you know what? Never mind." She started to walk off. "I'm going back to work."

He caught her and turned her to face him. "Wait a minute."

"Can't," she said. 'I've gotten —"

"Pru," he said with terrifying tenderness as he bulldozed right over her with his dogged determination, cupping her face. "Are you saying you've never —"

"No, of course I have." She closed her eyes. "It's just been awhile since Jake — and he wasn't a one-night stand. Or even a two-night stand. He was a week-long stand —" She covered her mouth. "Oh my God," she said around her fingers. "Please tell me to stop talking!"

He gently pulled her hand from her mouth. "You and Jake were together only a week?"

"Yes."

"And before that, you'd not been with anyone else?"

"I had a boyfriend in high school," she said defensively.

"But . . ."

"But he dumped me after my parents died," she admitted. "I was a complete wreck, and —"

"That shouldn't have happened to you," he said quietly, stroking her upper arms, his warm hands somehow reaching deep inside her and warming a spot she hadn't even realized was chilled. "That shouldn't have happened to anyone," he said very gently. "So other than your high school asshole boyfriend and one week with Jake, there's been no one else?"

If she'd ever felt more vulnerable or exposed, she couldn't remember it. It was horribly embarrassing, having her sexual history — or lack thereof — laid out, and with it came an avalanche of insecurities. She shook her head and stared at his throat instead of in his eyes, which was easier. Because he had a very sexy throat and —

"Pru. Babe, look at me."

She reluctantly lifted her gaze to his.

"I think I'm starting to understand more about what's going on," he said.

Oh good. Maybe he could explain it to her. That would be supremely helpful.

"What happened between us," he said, "it never occurred to me that you thought it was a one-night stand."

She stared at him, confused. "No?"

"Hell, no," he said. "Not with our chemistry. I knew from the beginning that one night wasn't going to be enough. Or two. Or ten. I thought you knew it too."

She swallowed hard. She did know it. That wasn't the problem. No, the problem was that the time they'd already spent together . . . it had to be enough. It was all she would, could, allow herself. "I didn't allow myself to think that far. Finn —"

"Look, I know we've done things ass-backwards, but I want to fix that." He smiled at her. "Go out with me tonight."

She stared at him. "Like . . . a date?"

"Exactly like a date."

"But —"

His mouth brushed along her jaw to her ear, his words whispered hot against her. "Say 'yes, Finn.' "

"Yes, Finn," escaped her before she could stop herself. Damn. Her mouth really needed to meet her brain sometime. But the truth was, she needed this, needed him. She wanted this moment and she wanted to enjoy it. Selfish as it was, she was going to think about herself for once, just for tonight. Besides, thinking was overrated. "You make it hard to think," she said.

She felt him smile knowingly against her skin. "Pru, I'm going to be so good to you tonight that there'll be no thinking required.

It's a good thing that thinking was over-rated.

He picked her up at six. She was nervous as hell, which was silly. It was Finn. And it was just a date.

At a red light, he glanced over at her and flashed a grin. "You look pretty."

She was in a simple sundress and flats. Hair down. "You've seen this dress," she said.

His eyes heated. Clearly he was remembering that it was the dress he'd made her hold at her waist while he'd had his merry way with her. "I know," he murmured. "I love that dress."

She blushed and he laughed softly.

"Where are we going?" she asked, needing a subject change.

"Nervous?"

Yes. "No."

He slid her a knowing glance. "It's a surprise."

That had her worried. But where they ended up made her smile wide and stare at him. "A Giants game?"

"Yeah." He parked at the stadium and pulled her from the car with a smacking kiss. "Okay with you?"

Was he kidding? For a beat, her troubles fell away and she grinned at him. "Very okay."

He brought her hand to his mouth and smiled over their entwined fingers.

She melted.

He fed her whatever she wanted, which was hotdogs and beer, and they both yelled and cheered the game on to their heart's content.

They sat next to a couple of serious Giants fans who were wearing only shorts — although the girl also wore a bikini top — and their every inch of exposed skin painted Giants orange.

The guy proposed between innings two and three, and it was nothing like the proposal on her ship. When these two hugged and kissed, there was love in every touch — although their carefully painted Giants logo smeared. The orange and white paint mixed into a pale color that actually resembled pink, making them look like a walking advertisement for Pepto-Bismol.

At the bottom of the fourth, the KISS cam panned the crowd and everyone went wild. It stopped on an older couple, who sweetly pecked. Next it stopped on two men who flashed their wedding rings with wide grins before giving the audience a kiss.

Everyone was still cheering when the KISS cam stopped on Pru and Finn. Pru turned to him, laughing, and he hauled her in and laid one on her that made her brain turn to mush and an entire inning went by before her brain reset itself and began processing again.

It was possibly the most fun date she'd been on since . . .

Ever.

After the game, Finn walked Pru to her door. She was a little tipsy so he held her hand, smiling as he listened to her singing to some song in her head that only she could hear.

She had a smudge of orange paint down her entire right side from the woman at the game. It'd drizzled for a few minutes in the eighth inning and her hair had rioted into a frizzy mass of waves.

He wanted to sink his fingers into it, press her back against her door and kiss her senseless. Then he wanted to pick her up so that she'd wrap her long legs around him.

He wanted her. Hard and fast. Slow and sweet. On the couch. In the shower. Her bed.

Anywhere he could get her.

And it wasn't just physical either. He'd

told her he didn't think love was for him, but he'd been wrong. At least going off the way his heart rolled over and exposed its tender underbelly every time she so much as looked at him. He wanted to claim her, wanted to leave his mark on her. On the inside. On her heart and in her soul.

But she wasn't ready. She was way behind him in this and he knew that. What they had between them scared her, and more than a little. She needed time, and he could give her that. *Would* give her that.

Even if it meant walking away from her tonight when she was smiling up at him, her eyes shining, her cheeks flushed, happy. Warm.

Willing.

" 'Night," he said softly. "Lock up tight."

"Wait." She blinked once, slow as an owl. A tipsy owl. "You're . . . leaving?"

"Yes."

"But . . ." She stepped into him, running her hands up his chest. "Aren't we going to . . ."

He went brows up, forcing her to be specific.

"I thought you'd come in and we'd . . . you know," she whispered, her fingers dancing over his jaw.

Catching her hand, he brought it to his

mouth and brushed a kiss over her palm. "No," he said gently. "Not tonight."

"But . . . when?"

"When you're ready to fill in 'you know' with the words," he said.

She stood there, mouth open a little, a furrow between her brows, looking bewildered, aroused, and more than a little off center.

Maybe she wasn't so far behind him after all.

" 'Night," he said, cupping her face for a soft kiss. Walking away was one of the hardest things he'd ever done.

When Pru's door closed, another opened and Mrs. Winslow poked her head out. "You sure you know what you're doing?" she asked him.

Hell no, he didn't know what he was doing.

She shook her head at him. "You sure don't know much about women, do you. You can't leave them alone to think about whether they need you, and do you know why?"

He shook his head.

"Because it's only in the moment that a woman will act impulsively. It's all the testosterone and pheromones that pour off you males, you see. Without you right in

350

front of her, that magic stuff wears off and she'll easily remember that she doesn't need you in her life."

"I'm going to hope that's not true," he said.

"You can hope all you want, but you'll be hoping alone in an empty bed."

CHAPTER 27

#SMARTERTHANTHEAVERAGEBEAR

Late the next afternoon, Pru was at work wishing she was anywhere but. She was in the middle of an argument with a guy who'd paid for a tour for him and his son the week before, but they hadn't shown up. Now he wanted a refund.

She'd only stepped behind the ticket counter as a favor to one of the ticket clerks who'd had to leave early. This guy was the last person she had to deal with before going home. She'd paused, looking for a credit option on the computer, when he decided she was dicking him around.

"Listen," he bit out. "I'm not going to deal with some homicidal, hormonal, PMS-y, minimum-wage chick who doesn't give a shit. I want the supervisor. Get him for me."

"Actually," she said. "You've got a supervisor right here. And no worries. I was homicidal hormonal last week. This week I'm good. Even nice, if I say so myself."

He didn't smile. He was hands on hips. "I want my money back."

Pru's gaze slid to the person who'd just come in behind him. Finn. He stood there quietly but not passively, watching. Pru turned back to Pissy Man and pointed to the large sign above her head.

No refunds.

The guy leaned in way too close. "Do you have any idea who I am?"

An asshole? A thought she kept to herself because she was busy noticing that Finn shifted too, until he was standing just off to her left, body language signaling that while he was at ease, he was also ready to kick some ass if needed.

She'd thought of him today. A lot. Last night after he'd left, she'd nearly called him a dozen times. He wanted words and she had them. She wanted to say "please come back and make love to me."

Because if she knew one thing, it was that what they'd done together wasn't just sex.

Dammit.

For now, her cranky customer was still standing there with a fight in his eyes. "I'm in charge of the budget for the city's promo and advertising department," he told her. "We make sure that your entire industry is listed in all the Things to Do in San Francisco guides. Without me, you'd be cleaning toilets."

Okay, now that was a bit of a stretch. "Listen, it wouldn't matter if you were POTUS. There are no refunds. I can get you a credit for another tour but you have to be patient with me while I figure out —

He slammed a hand down on the counter, but she didn't jump. She'd dealt with far bigger assholes than this one. Before she could suggest he leave, Finn was there.

He'd moved so quickly she never even saw him coming as he stepped in between her and the guy. "She said no refunds and offered you a credit," Finn said. "Take it or leave it."

"Leave it," the guy snapped.

"Your choice," Finn said. "But unless there's something else you'd like to say, and fair warning, it'd better be 'have a nice day,' you need to go."

The guy stared down Finn for the briefest of seconds before possibly deciding he liked his face in the condition it was in because he strode out without another word.

"Seriously?" Pru asked Finn.

He shoved his hands into his pockets. "What?"

"I had that handled."

He slid her a look. "You're welcome."

She let out a short laugh. "I was handling myself just fine." Always did, always would. Having been on her own for so long, she really didn't know any other way.

And yet he'd been there for her. When she'd been lonely. When she'd been sad. When she'd been sicker than a dog.

Whenever she'd needed.

"Pru," he said, "that guy was a walking fight. Where the hell's Jake?"

"Off today, and I didn't need him. It's not like he was going to take a swing at me. The only thing he was swinging was a poor vocabulary and a small dick."

His mouth twitched. "Okay, I stand corrected."

"And?"

"And what?" he asked.

"And you're sorry for stepping in and handling my fight for me?"

He just looked at her.

Nope, he wasn't sorry for that. Good to know. She took a longer look at his face and realized that not only wasn't he sorry, he looked a little tall, dark, and 'tude ridden. She'd seen him mad several times now so she recognized the stormy eyes, tight mouth, and tense body language. "So how's your day?"

He lifted a shoulder.

Okay. She reached out and put a hand on a very tense forearm. "Are you okay?" she asked quietly. "Because it doesn't feel like you are."

"I'm fine."

She gave him an arched brow.

He shrugged. "I just hate pushy assholes who think they can push someone around to get what they want."

She stared up at him, once again reminded that she wasn't the only one in this relationship-that-wasn't-happening with demons. "Because of your dad?"

"Maybe," he admitted. "Or maybe because I spent a good portion of my youth protecting Sean. He was a small, sickly kid with a big, fat mouth. It wasn't easy to watch his back and keep him safe because he attracted assholes and bullies." He scrubbed a hand down his face. "I guess I still get worked up about that. I saw that guy being aggressive with you and I wanted . . ."

"To protect me," she said softly.

"Yeah." He gave her a half grimace, half smile. "Not that you can't do it yourself, but emotions aren't always rational."

With her hands still fisted in his shirt, she gave a gentle tug until he bent enough that she could kiss him softly. And then not so softly. "I know," she whispered. She kissed him again.

"What was that for?" he asked when she pulled free, his voice sexy low and gruff now.

"For being the kind of guy who can admit he has emotions."

He cupped her face. "We don't have to tell anyone, right?"

She smiled. "It'll be our secret." But then her smile faded because she wasn't good at secrets.

Or maybe she was too good at them . . . "I'm not helpless," she said. "I want you to know that."

"I do know it." He paused, looking a little irritated again. "Mostly."

"Good," she said. "Now that's settled, you should know, the caveman thing you just pulled . . . it turned me on a little bit."

He slid her a look. "Yeah?"

"Yeah."

Looking a little less like he was spoiling for a fight, his hands went to her hips and he pulled her in tighter.

What the hell was she doing? Clearly, she wasn't equipped to stay strong, and who could? The guy was just too damn potent. Too visceral. Testosterone and pheromones leaked off of him. She dropped her head to his chest. "Ugh. You're being . . . you."

"Was that in English?"

"This is all your fault."

"Nope. Definitely not English."

"You're being all hot and sexy, dammit," she said. She banged her head on his chest a few times. "And I can't seem to . . . not notice said hotness and sexiness."

He smiled. "You want me again."

Again. *Still* . . . She tossed up her hands. "You wear your stupid sexiness on your sleeve and you don't even know it."

His smile widened. "All you have to do is say the word, babe. Or preferably words. Dirty ones are encouraged."

When she blew out a sigh, he laughed.

"You really can't say the words, can you," he said, sounding way too amused about that, the ass. He flung an arm around her. "Cute."

Cute? She had mixed feelings about that. On the one hand, she'd rather he found her unbearably sexy. But on the other hand, he was already more than she could handle. Maybe cute was just right.

She gave him a push and strode around, locking up.

He followed, still looking pretty damn smug, waiting patiently.

"Where do you want to go?" he asked.

"Who says I'm going anywhere with you?"

"Your body."

She realized she'd plastered herself to his front again. "You're not working tonight?"

"Later. I worked all day and have a full crew on now. They'll be fine for a few hours on their own."

Oh God. How was she going to resist? "Are you going to take me out on another date and then dump me at the door?"

"Depends."

"On?" she asked.

He just smiled mysteriously as he slid his fingers into her hair, letting his thumb stroke once over her lower lip so that it tingled for a kiss.

His kiss.

He wanted her to say the words and she knew what words too. *Make love to me . . .*

"You've got choices," he said. "You can pick a place, or let me surprise you."

His bed. She picked his bed.

She retrieved Thor from his nap spot in Jake's office and then Finn drove them out of there, his hands as sure on the wheel as they always were on her body.

Stop looking at his hands!

He took her for drinks at a cute place in the Marina, where they sat at a small table on the sidewalk with Thor happily at their feet watching the world go by.

Finn paid. He always paid. And he was sneaky about it too. She never even saw the check before he had it handled.

After, they headed to Lands End, a park near the windswept shoreline at the mouth of the Golden Gate Bridge.

The three of them followed a trail along a former rail bed to the rocky cliffs that revealed a heart-stopping, stunning three-hundred-and-sixty-degree vista of the bay. The wild blue ocean below was dotted with whitecaps thanks to the heavy surf of the early evening.

"Wow," she whispered. "Makes you realize that the whole world isn't centered around your own hopes and dreams."

He looked out at the view. "What are your hopes and dreams?"

She glanced at him, startled.

"I know you love being a boat captain," he said. "But what else do you want for yourself? To own your own charter business? To have a family?"

He was serious, so she answered truthfully. "I do love my job but I don't want to run an empire or anything. I'm happy doing what I do. And . . ." Her heart was suddenly pounding. "I do want a family." Because his eyes felt like mirrors into her own soul, she turned to the water again.

"Someday," she whispered.

His hand slipped into hers, warm and strong.

She held on and breathed for a moment. "And you?"

"I love my job too," he said. "And I want to keep the pub for as long as it works. But I don't want to live in the city forever. I want a family too, and I'd rather have a yard and a street where they can ride their bikes and have other kids nearby . . ."

She smiled. "You want a white picket fence, Finn?"

"It doesn't have to be white," he said and made her laugh.

And yearn . . .

Thor enjoyed himself thoroughly, chasing after squirrels until one of them turned on him and chased him right back into Pru's arms.

Finn shook his head. "He's missing something."

"He doesn't have the killer gene," she admitted, giving the mutt a squeeze.

"I was thinking balls . . ." But he took Thor and carried him for her, letting the dog nuzzle at the crook of his neck.

Pru rolled her eyes, but inside, secretly, she wanted to nuzzle there too.

"Look," Finn said, grabbing her hand with

his free one, pointing with their joined fingers to the hillside below of cypress and wildflowers every color under the sun.

"Wow," she whispered. "Gorgeous."

"Yeah," he said, looking at her.

She laughed. "That's cheesy."

He grinned. "You liked it."

"No, I didn't."

He peered at her over his dark sunglasses, letting his gaze slip past her face.

She followed his line of sight and realized that her nipples were pressing eagerly against the thin white cotton of her shirt. "That's because I'm cold," she said and crossed her arms over her chest.

He laughed. "It's seventy-five degrees."

"Downright chilly," she said, nose in the air.

Grinning, he reeled her in, and with Thor protesting between them, he kissed the living daylights out of her.

Then he tugged her down the trail, heading for the epic ruins of Sutro Baths.

She'd never been here before. Even better, they were alone. Pru had no idea why, maybe because it was the middle of the week, or just late enough in the day, but they had the place to themselves.

They walked through the ruins and Finn showed her a small, rocky cave. It was cool inside. Quiet.

Finn brought her over to a small opening that allowed her to see out to the rocky beach. Standing inside the cave, surrounded by the cavernous rock and way-too-sexy man, she could not only see the water but feel it in the cool mist that blew into the cave and stirred the hair at her temple.

Thor wriggled to be freed and Finn set him down, where he immediately scampered to a pile of rocks to explore.

This left Finn's hands free to tug Pru into him. "I should probably admit," he said, his mouth at her ear, "being alone in here is giving me ideas."

She bit her lower lip. Her too!

Laughing quietly at her expression, he fisted one hand in her hair. The other slid down and squeezed her ass. "You too?"

Okay, yes, so maybe she had a secret fantasy about doing it somewhere that they could maybe get caught, but she wasn't about to tell him so. Absolutely not. "I have a secret fantasy about doing it somewhere where we could maybe get caught," she said. *Dammit, mouth!*

His grin was fast and wicked, assuring her he was absolutely up for the challenge. She laughed again, nervously now. "But I'm pretty sure it's just a fantasy," she said quickly, putting her hands on his chest to keep him at arm's length.

Or to keep him close. She hadn't quite decided.

The hand on her ass shifted up a little and then back down, slipping inside the back of her pants. "How sure is pretty sure?" he asked, his fingers stroking the line of her thong, but before they could slip beneath, she laughed again and pulled free.

"Pretty, *pretty* sure," she said shakily.

His gaze slid down her body. "I suppose you're cold again."

Well aware that her greedy nipples were still threatening to make a break right through the material of her shirt, she scooped up Thor and clutched him to her chest.

Thor seemed to give her a long look like *please don't make me wait while you two do disgusting things to each other.* "Don't worry," she muttered to the dog. "I've got a handle on things now."

"I've got something you could get a handle on," Finn said.

She rolled her eyes. "Weak."

"It's not weak."

She laughed. "I remember."

"So if we're not making fantasies come true, how about dinner?" he asked.

Dilemma. She couldn't take him home, she'd sleep with him again. "Pizza," she said, thinking a crowded Italian joint should be safe enough.

"Sold," Finn said.

They left the cave and walked along the rocky beach for a few minutes. The tide was out, the water receded a hundred yards or more it seemed. Pru managed to trip over a rock and then her own two feet, dropping Thor's leash to catch herself. So naturally Thor took off directly toward the waves at the speed of light, barking the whole way.

"Thor!" she yelled. "He can't swim," she told Finn. "Sinks like a stone."

"Trust me, he'll swim if he has to."

But she couldn't be so calm. Her baby was racing right for the waves. She started after him much slower, having to be careful on the rocks.

"Don't worry," Finn said. "He'll be back as soon as his paws get wet."

But Thor hit the water and kept going, right into a wave. And then the worst possible thing happened.

He vanished.

"Oh my God." Pru took off running down the rocky beach, heading directly for the spot where Thor had vanished. She kicked off her sandals and dove in.

The next wave crashed over her head and smashed her face into the sand. Gasping, she pushed upright, swiping the sand from her face to find . . .

Thor sitting on the shore staring at her, his tail whipping back and forth, his mouth smiling wide, proud of himself. Dripping wet, he barked twice and she'd have sworn he said, "Fun, right?"

Finn laughed and picked the dog up. Thor wriggled to get free but Finn just tucked the dripping wet, very-proud-of-himself dog beneath one arm and reached for Pru with the other, a wide smile on his face.

Pru went hands on wet hips. "Are you laughing at me? You'd better not be laughing at me."

"I wouldn't dream of it."

She narrowed her eyes.

Finn did his best to squelch his smile and failed. "I told you he'd be fine."

"Uh huh."

His laugh drifted over her. "I'm guessing that this time you really are cold instead of just pretending to be."

She looked down at her shirt. Yep, plastered to her torso and gone sheer to boot, making her look more naked than she would be without a stitch of clothing. She narrowed her eyes at him but he just kept smiling. So she took a step toward him with the intention of wrapping her very wet self around him until he was just as wet as she.

But he dodged her and held up a hand. "Now let's not get crazy —"

She flung herself at him. Just took a running step and a flying leap.

He was a smart enough man to catch her, and in spite of the fact that it meant she drenched him with seawater, he hauled her in and held her close.

"Got you," he said, and melted away her irritation in a single heartbeat. Because he always did seem to have her, whether it was soothing her after *she'd* hit *him* with a dart, or when she'd been upset about her grandpa, or sick with food poisoning . . . He had her. Always.

It was as simple and terrifying as that.

Chapter 28

Finn bundled both the wet dog and the even wetter woman into his car. He pulled a blanket from his emergency kit and tucked it around them.

"I'm f-fine," Pru said, teeth chattering, lips blue.

Uh huh. In other words, "back off, Finn." Not likely. But he wasn't surprised at the attempt. Every time they got too close she seemingly regretted their time together.

He regretted nothing. Not the way she'd felt in his arms and not the way he'd felt in hers. From the beginning, there'd been a shocking sense of intimacy between them, one that had momentarily stunned him, but he'd gotten over it quickly.

He wanted even more but he was smart enough to know a reticent woman when he saw one. She was still unsure. She needed more time.

And he'd already made the decision to

give it to her. "Your teeth are going to rattle right out of your head," he said, cranking up the heat, aiming the vents at her.

Clearly freezing, she didn't utter a word of complaint. Instead she seemed much more concerned that he would skip the afore-promised pizza. "It takes calories to keep yourself warm," she said. "Pepperoni and cheese calories. A lot of them."

"I'll call it in and have it delivered while you shower," he assured her.

"No!" She paused, clearly searching for a reason to ditch him. "Lefty's won't deliver."

"Then we can call Mozza's," he said.

She managed a derisive snort in between shivers. "Mozza's isn't real pizza."

"Okay." He pulled into the back lot of Lefty's. "Stay here, I'll just run in and get it real quick."

But she was right behind him, emergency Mylar blanket wrapped around her and all.

Waiting in line, he slid her a look. "You didn't trust me to pick the right pizza."

"Not even a little bit."

Lefty was taking orders himself, he loved people. Smiling broadly at Pru, he said, "Hey there, cutie pie. What happened, you get pitched overboard? Not a good day for a swim, it's kinda brisk."

"Don't I know it," she muttered. "I had to

save Thor. Life or death situation."

Finn grinned and Pru turned a long look his way, daring him to contradict her story.

Finn lifted his hands in surrender and Lefty went brows up. "Sensing a good story here. Someone start talking."

"Would love to," Pru said. "But you've got a long line waiting, so —"

"They'll wait." Lefty set his elbows on the counter and leaned in. "Is it as good as you trying to kill our boy here with a dart?"

She whirled on Finn. "You know that was an accident! You've been telling people I tried to kill you?"

Lefty laughed. "Nah, he didn't say a word. Never does. Willa told me. Oh and Archer's guys too, Max and the scary-looking one with the tattoo on his skull."

Pru smacked her forehead. "How is it possible that the people in our building gossip more than a bunch of guys in a firehouse?"

"Don't you mean a bunch of girls in junior high?" Lefty asked.

"No," she said, glowering. "Girls have got nothing on guys when it comes to gossip." She sent a long look at Finn, daring him to disagree.

"One hundred percent true," he said and paid for their food. And then because she seemed skittish about going back to her place, he brought her and Thor to his.

As they got out of the car, Pru muttered something that sounded an awful lot like "just keep your clothes on and you'll be fine."

Finn hid his grin. "Problem?" he asked her.

She scowled. "Just hungry."

He let them inside. His phone buzzed an incoming call from Sean and he turned to Pru. "Help yourself to my shower to get warmed up."

When she'd shut herself in his bathroom, he answered his phone.

"We're filled to capacity," Sean said.

"Great. And?"

"And," Sean said, sounding irritated. "We need you."

"You're fully staffed. The pub doesn't need me."

There was a silence, during which Finn could hear Sean gnashing his teeth together. "Okay, I need you," he finally said, not sounding all that happy about the admission. "There's a bachelorette party here and the bridesmaids are *insane,* man. They've pinched my ass twice. I've also got a birthday party for some guy who's like a hundred and he's got a bunch of old geezers with him and they're doing shots. What if one of them ups and croaks on us? And then there's the fact that Rosa's sick and says she has to go home early. Code for her boyfriend doesn't have to work tonight and she wants to go see him."

Finn heard the shower go on down the hall. He hadn't had a woman here in this house . . . ever. Not once. The relationships in his life had all been short-lived ones, all existing away from home. He tended to keep his personal life out of his sex life.

And his personal life hadn't been a priority, in any sense of the word. His brother and the pub had been his entire world for a damn long time, which meant that Pru had been right when she'd told him that first night in the bar that he hadn't been living his life. It had been living him.

He wanted to change that. He wanted what he'd been missing out on. He wanted a relationship.

And he wanted it with Pru.

"Are you even listening to me?" Sean asked, clearly pissy now. "I need you to get your ass down here and help me with this shit."

"No," Finn said. "You're in charge."

"But —"

"Figure it out, Sean," Finn said and disconnected. He filled a bowl of water for

Thor, and since the little guy was looking a little waterlogged, he wrapped him up in a blanket and made him comfortable on the couch.

Thor licked Finn's chin and closed his eyes, and was snoring in thirty seconds flat.

"If only your owner was as easy to please," Finn said.

Thor smiled in his sleep and then farted.

Pru stood under Finn's heavenly shower until she'd thawed. Then she wrapped herself up in one of his large, fluffy towels and went looking for him, hoping he had a pair of sweats she could wear while her clothes dried.

She found Thor asleep in the middle of Finn's comfy-looking couch. The sliding glass door was open so she left the dog to his nap and poked her head out. The deck there was small and cozy and completely secluded by the two stucco walls on either side.

There was a tiny table, two chairs, and an incredible view of Cow Hollow, and beyond it, the Golden Gate Bridge and the bay.

Finn came out. She heard him set the pizza and drinks on the table and then he came up behind her where she stood hands on the railing staring out at the view. His hands covered hers. She could feel the warmth of his big body seeping into her. And something else. Hunger. Need. He always invoked those emotions in her, and if she was being honest, far more too. "I was hoping to borrow some of your clothes," she managed.

"Anything."

He had her caged in and she liked it. When he lowered his head to nuzzle the side of her throat, she nearly turned into a happy little kitten and began to purr.

"I like you like this," he said huskily. "Just warm, soft, delicious, naked woman in my towel."

"How do you know I'm naked under here?" she heard herself ask daringly.

Taking the challenge, he slid a hand up her thigh, letting out a low, sexy, knowing laugh when she squeaked.

"Clothes," she demanded.

"Sure." But instead of backing off, he lifted a hand to point to Fisherman's Wharf, where if she squinted, she could just make out Jake's building. "Sometimes I stand right here and look for you," he said.

She closed her eyes and let her body follow its wishes, which meant she rested her head back against his chest.

Finn brushed the hair from the nape of

her neck and slid his mouth across the sensitive skin there, giving her a full body shiver of the very best kind.

"You always smell so damn good," he murmured against her skin, his mouth at her jaw now while his hands slid over her body, revving her engines, firing up all her cylinders. "And now you smell like me. Love that. You make me hungry, Pru."

"Good thing we have pizza," she said breathlessly.

"It's not pizza I'm hungry for." His hands skimmed over her towel-covered breasts, skipping her nipples which were dying for his attention.

She made a little whimper of protest and felt him smile against her neck.

"You're teasing me," she accused.

"No, if I was teasing you, I'd do something like this . . ." And he dragged hot, open-mouthed kisses down her throat, his hands continuing to tease until she whimpered in frustration. *"Finn."*

"Tell me."

Stay strong, Pru. "I need you," she whispered. "I need you so much."

"Right back at you, Pru." And then he whipped her around and lifted her up onto the rail. "Hold on tight," he said against her throat.

Not having a death wish, she threw her arms around his neck. This had the towel loosening on her. But left with the choice of holding onto it or Finn, she did what any red-blooded, sex-starved woman would do — she let the towel fall.

Finn kissed her and then pulled back just enough to take a good, long look at her, letting out a rough groan. "You take my breath, Pru. Every fucking time. You're so beautiful."

She opened her mouth to tell him ditto but his mouth covered hers before she could speak as his hands began a full assault on her now naked body. It took him only a few beats to have her writhing under his ministrations, straining for more, and his hot gaze swept over her, heating her up from the inside out. "You're not cold?"

He was really asking this time and she managed to shake her head. "Not even a little."

With a smile, his mouth worked its way southward. As for Pru, she kept a monkey-like grip on him, her head falling back. "Oh my God," she whispered. "We're *outside.*"

His mouth curved against her bare shoulder. "Do you want me to stop?"

"Don't you dare —" She broke off and sucked in a breath as he gently captured her

376

nipple with his teeth.

Mindless now, she rocked up into him. "Please don't let go of me."

"Never." He sucked her into his hot mouth making her moan and clutch at him. He had one arm tight to her back while his free hand danced its way up the inside of her thighs. The flat of the railing that she was balanced on wasn't quite as wide as her ass but he had her, and in spite of joking that she didn't trust him to pick the pizza, she did.

Truth was, she trusted him one hundred percent, with her pizza, with her body, and if she was being honest, with her heart too.

It was a shocking thought but she didn't have the brain power to lend to it at the moment. She was far too busy being taken apart by Finn's fingers as they stroked knowingly over her. But in the vague recesses of her mind, she was aware that if she trusted him one hundred percent, she needed to trust him with the facts of who she was.

And she would. It was just that things between them had heated up so quickly and unexpectedly in their short time together, and had become so unexpectedly complicated. She wanted to tell him everything, and soon. But it hadn't really been all that long — only been two weeks — and she needed a little more time to figure it all out first.

The early evening's breeze floated over her bare skin, along with Finn's heated gaze. Every inch of her was crying out for his touch, needing him more than she'd ever needed anything in her life. *"Finn."*

"Don't let go of me," he said and tugged a gasp from her when his fingers went from teasing to driving her right to the edge, moving in beat with her heart. Suddenly she no longer cared if she was in danger of plummeting to her death because she was too busy coming apart.

When she could hear past the roar of her own blood in her ears, she hoped like hell that his neighbors hadn't been able to hear her cries. "Were we loud?" she whispered.

He grinned. "We?" he asked, laughing when she smacked him in the chest.

He caught her hand, kissed her palm, and then tore open a condom packet. Protecting them both, he plunged into her as his mouth claimed hers again.

Good God. She wasn't going to die from a fall. She was going to die of pleasure, right here . . .

The week went by in a blur for Pru. It was a rare blue moon — two full moons in the same calendar month — so SF Tours held a special moonlit cruise week.

Which meant that Pru and the other boat captains worked during the day, crashed for a few hours on whatever horizontal surface they could find in the building, and then went back out at night on the water.

This went on for three days.

On the fourth day, she crawled home and into bed right after grabbing dinner — Frosted Flakes. But she came awake some time later in her dark bedroom to find someone in it with her. Then that someone pulled his shirt over his head and shucked his jeans.

She'd recognize that leanly muscled bod anywhere and swallowed hard at the gorgeous outline of him bathed in nothing but moonlight. It didn't matter how many times she saw him in the buff, he never failed to steal her breath. With her still blinking through the dark trying to see his every sexy inch, he slipped beneath the covers with her.

Naked.

"Chris Pratt?" she asked. "Is that you?"

"You don't need Chris Pratt," Finn said as he pulled her into a heated embrace.

He was damp and chilled. "Hey!" she complained.

"It's raining sideways," he explained, wrapping himself around her. "Nasty storm. Your bed was closer than mine. And mine was missing something."

"What?"

"You."

Aw. Dammit. "How did you get in?" she asked. "I mean, your hands are magic but not *that* magic."

"Your hidden key." His magical hands began stroking her, while at the same time he pressed hot kisses against the back of her neck. "Do you mind?"

She loved being in the circle of his arms. Loved the way he touched her so knowingly and sure, and since he was actually licking her now, she couldn't concentrate on anything beyond his tongue. Did she mind? "Only if you stop."

His hands were hypnotic, his palms a little

rough with calluses, his long talented fingers tracing over her breasts, teasing her nipples.

One thing she'd come to know about him, he was incredibly physical. Whenever they were together like this, he wanted to touch and taste and see . . . everything. There was no hiding, not that she could remember to. He was an incredibly demanding lover, but also endlessly patient and creative. She never knew exactly what to expect from him but he always left her panting for more. "Aren't you tired?" she asked.

"I can sleep when I'm dead." He slipped his fingers inside her panties to cup and squeeze her ass, and then wriggled them to her thighs.

And she was a goner.

"Missed this," he murmured in her ear.

She'd been hoping for sleep. Now she hoped for this to never end. "It hasn't been all that long," she managed. "A few days."

"Four. Too long." Her T-shirt and panties vanished and then his hand was back to its serious business of driving her out of her mind. In less than a minute she was thrusting against his fingers. And in the next, she came so fast her head was spinning.

"God, I love watching you come," he said, and then proceeded to show her what a true force of nature could accomplish.

Mother Nature had nothing on him.

Later Pru lay in Finn's arms, her head on his shoulder, her face pressed into his throat, knowing by the way he was breathing that he was out cold, dead asleep. Poor baby, being a sex fiend was exhausting.

He'd left work and had come here, to her. And there in the dark, she smiled, her body sated, her heart so full she almost didn't know what to do with herself.

Had she ever felt like this? Like she just wanted to climb into the man next to her and stay there?

Being with Jake had been good. She'd had no complaints, but she wasn't for him. When they'd split, he'd moved on with shocking ease.

And in truth, so had she.

But it'd left her feeling just a little bit . . . broken, and more than a little bit unsure about love in general.

But then Finn O'Riley had come into her life. She knew that she had no business feeling anything for him at all. But apparently, some things — like matters of the heart — not only happened in a blink but were also out of her control.

She felt her heart swell at just the thought and before she could stop herself, she mouthed the words against his throat. "I love you, Finn."

She immediately stilled in shock because she hadn't just mouthed the words, she'd actually said them.

Out loud.

She remained perfectly frozen another beat, but Finn didn't so much as twitch.

It took a while but eventually she relaxed into him again, and there in the dark, told herself it was okay. He didn't know.

He didn't know a lot of things . . .

The panic that was never far away these days hit her hard. She'd been telling herself that she'd waited to tell him the truth in the hopes he'd understand better once he knew her. But deep down, she wasn't sure she'd done the right thing. Telling him now was going to be harder, not easier.

And the outcome felt more uncertain than ever.

As always, Pru woke up just before her alarm was due to go off at the shockingly early hour of oh-dark-annoying-thirty. But this time it wasn't thoughts of the day ahead that woke her. Or the knot of anxiety wrapped in and around her chest.

It was the fact that she was wrapped around a big, strong, warm body.

Finn had one hand tangled in her hair and the other possessively cupping her bare ass, and when she shifted to try and disentangle herself without waking him, he tightened his grip and let out a low growl.

Torn between laughing and getting unbearably aroused — seriously, that growl! — she lifted her head.

And discovered she wasn't the only one wrapped around Finn like a pretzel.

Thor was on the other side of him, his head on Finn's shoulder, eyes slitted at her.

And she did laugh then because it'd been Thor who growled, not Finn. "Are you kidding me?" she whispered to her dog. "He's *mine.*"

But no he's not, a little voice deep inside her whispered. *He doesn't yet know it but you wrecked this — long before it'd even begun.*

Pru told the little voice to *shut up* and concentrated on Thor. "I found him first," she whispered.

Thor growled again.

Thor didn't look impressed in the least. She opened her mouth to further argue but Finn spoke, his voice low and morning gruff. "There's plenty of me to go around."

Pru felt the pink tinge hit her cheeks and she shifted her focus from Thor to Finn.

Yep. He was wide awake and watching

and, if she had to guess, more than a little amused that she'd been willing to fight her own dog for him.

"He's mine?" Finn repeated.

"It's a figure of speech." She grimaced at the lameness of that but he smiled.

"I like it," he said. "I like this. But mostly, I like where we're going."

If she could think straight, she'd echo that thought, but she couldn't think straight because every moment of every single day she was painfully aware she'd built this glass house that couldn't possibly withstand the coming storm . . .

"Pretty sure I just lost you for a few beats," Finn said quietly, eyes serious now, dark and warm and intense as he ran a finger along her jaw. "Was it what I said about liking where we're going thing?"

She tried to play this off with her customary self-deprecatory humor. "Since where we're going is always straight to bed, I can't do much complaining about that, can I," she said in a teasing voice, desperately hoping to steer the conversation to lighter waters, because one thing she couldn't do was have the talk with him while naked in his arms.

But she should have known better. Finn couldn't be steered, ever.

"This is more than that," he said, voice low but sure, so sure she wished for even an ounce of his easy confidence. "A lot more."

His gaze held hers prisoner, daring her to contradict him, and she swallowed hard. "It's only been a few weeks," she said softly.

"Three," he said.

"It just seems like we're moving so fast."

"Too fast?" he asked.

She gnawed on her lower lip, unsure how to answer that. The truth was, she'd already acknowledged to herself how she felt about him. And another truth — she wouldn't mind moving along even faster. She wanted to leap into his arms, press her face into his neck, and breathe him in and claim him as hers.

For always.

But she'd gone about this all wrong, and because of that she didn't have the right to him. Not even a little.

His fingers were gentle as they traced the line of her temple. "Babe, you're thinking too hard."

She nodded at the truth of this statement.

"You're scared," he said.

Terrified, thank you very much. She nodded again.

"Of me?"

"No. *No,*" she said again, firmly, cupping

his face. "It's more than I'm scared of what you make me feel."

He didn't seem annoyed or impatient at her reticence. Instead he kept his hands on her, his voice quiet. "I'm not saying I know where this is going," he said. "Because I don't. But what I do know is that what we've got here between us is good, really good."

She nodded her agreement of that but then slowly shook her head. "Good can go bad. Fast." As she knew all too well.

"Life's a crapshoot and we both know it," he said. "More than most. But whatever this is, I can't stop thinking about it. I can't stop wanting more. I think we've got a real shot, and that doesn't come around every day, Pru. We both know that too." He paused. "I want us to go for it."

Heart tight, she closed her eyes.

He was quiet a moment, but she could feel him studying her. "Pru, look at me."

She lifted her gaze and found his still warm, but very focused. "Say the word," he said seriously. "Tell me that this isn't your thing, that you're not feeling it, and I'll back off."

She opened her mouth.

And then closed it.

His fingers on her jaw, his thumb slid over

387

her lower lip. "You're the self-proclaimed Fun Whisperer," he said. "You're the one preaching about getting out there and living life. So why are you all talk and no go, Pru? What am I missing?"

She choked out a laugh at his sharpness and dropped his head to his chest.

"Tell me what you're afraid of," he said.

Her words came out muffled. "It's hard to put words to it."

He wasn't buying it and slid his hands into her hair and lifted her face. "Fight through that," he said simply. "Fight for me."

Of course he'd say that. It was his MO. Want something? Get it. Make it yours. Go for it, one hundred percent.

Which brought home one hard-hitting point — she needed to adopt that philosophy and do what he'd said, fight for what she wanted. Fight for him.

She'd left her cell on the kitchen counter the night before and from down the hall, it rang. She ignored it but once it stopped, it immediately started up again. Not a good sign so she slid out of bed. Realizing she was very, very naked, she bent to pick something from the pile of discarded clothes and heard a choked sound from the bed.

She turned and found Finn watching her every move, eyes heavy-lidded but not with sleepiness.

He crooked his finger at her.

"Oh no," she said, pointing her finger back at him. "Don't even think about waving your magic wand and —" Shit. "I didn't mean *wand* as in . . ." Her gaze slid down past his chest and washboard abs to the part of him that never failed to be happy to see her. "You know."

He burst out laughing. "Babe, if my 'wand' really was magic, then you'd be on it right now."

She felt herself blush to the roots, which only seemed to amuse him all the more. She actually took a step toward him when her phone rang yet a third time. With a sigh, she slipped his shirt over her head and padded out of the room.

Three missed calls, all from Jake. She tapped on the voicemail he'd just left, hitting speaker so she could make some desperately needed coffee as she listened.

"You're either still sleeping or hell, maybe you're out playing fairy godmother before work," he said, sounding disgruntled. "I heard from a little birdie that you got Tim a place to live."

Damn. Not a little birdie at all. Nick had spilled the beans on her. Again.

"I don't know how long you intend to go

around fixing wrongs that aren't yours to fix," Jake said. "But at some point you're going to have to let go. You know that, right? You can't go on keeping track of everyone from the accident and righting their worlds. The seed money for what's-her-name —"

"Shelby," she said, as if Jake could hear her.

"Then there was the place to live for Tim. The job for Nick. And how about what you did for F—"

At the sound behind her, Pru hit delete at the speed of light.

Because she knew the rest of Jake's sentence.

The beep of Jake's message being deleted echoed in the room as she turned to face Finn, wearing only his jeans, unbuttoned.

"What was that about?" he asked.

"Oh . . ." She waved her hand. "You know Jake, sticking his nose into everything."

"Sounds like he thinks you're the one sticking your nose into everything."

She took a deep breath. *Be careful. Be very careful unless you're ready to give up the fantasy right here, right now.* It needed to be done. She knew that now more than ever. She'd do it tonight after work, when they had time to talk about it. *And after you figure out how to make him realize you'd only meant to help.*

Even if in her heart she knew that was no way to make him understand. He was smart and resourceful and sharp, and he was standing there steady as a rock.

Her rock.

Waiting for answers.

"I do tend to stick my nose into things," she said as lightly as she could. "I've got to get to work . . ."

"Or you need to change the subject."

Her smile faded. "Or that."

"You know . . ." He stepped into her, slid his hands to her hips and ducked his head to meet her gaze. "You once told me I needed to let stuff go."

She choked out a low laugh and stared at his Adam's apple. "Haven't you heard, swallowing your own medicine is the hardest thing to do?"

He wrapped her ponytail around his fist and gently tugged until she looked up at him. "What's going on, Pru?"

"What's going on is that I need to get ready for work —"

"In here." He slid his free hand up and tapped a finger over her temple.

She managed another smile. "You'd be

surprised by how little's going on in there
—"

"Don't," he said quietly. "If you don't want to do this, you only have to say so."

She hesitated and he took a step back. "Wow," he said, looking like she'd sucker punched him.

"No," she said. "I —"

He'd already turned and headed into her bedroom. She started to follow, but he came back out again, holding his shoes. Still no shirt, since she was wearing it. "Finn."

He headed to the door.

"Finn."

He stopped and turned to her, eyes hooded.

"Can we talk about this tonight?"

"Sure. Whatever." He started to leave but stopped and muttered something to himself. He then came at her, hauled her into his arms and kissed her. When his tongue stroked possessively over hers, her knees wobbled, but far before she was ready, he let her go.

He stared down at her for a beat and then he turned and left, shutting the door quietly behind him.

She moved to the door and put her hands on it, like she could bring him back.

But it was far too late for that.

Chapter 30

#JUSTTHEFACTSMA'AM

Outside Pru's front door, Finn stopped and shook his head. She was holding back on him, big time. But he knew something else too.

So was he.

Because as long as she wasn't one hundred percent in, it felt . . . safe. The crazy thing was that he wanted her to be one hundred percent in. He wanted to do the same.

But he wasn't going to beg her. He wanted her to come to him on her own terms. Until she did, he could hold back that last piece of his heart and soul and keep it safe from complete annihilation.

He was good at that.

He dropped his shoes to the floor and shoved his feet into them. He'd just bent over to tie them when Mrs. Winslow opened her door.

"Whoa, good thing my ovaries are shriveled," she said. "Or you'd have just made me pregnant from that view alone."

Finn straightened and gave her a look that made her laugh.

"Sorry, boy," she said. "But you don't scare me."

With as much dignity as he could, he hunkered down and went back to tying his shoes, attempting to keep his ass tucked in while doing it.

When he'd finished, he stood up to his full height to find her still watching. "You're a nice package and all," she said, "but I like 'em more seasoned. Men are no good until they're at least forty-five."

"Good to know," he muttered and started down the hall.

"Because until then," she said to his back. "They don't know nothing about the important things. Like forgiveness. And understanding."

He blew out a breath and turned to face her. "You're trying to tell me something again."

"Now you're thinking, genius," she said. "If you were forty-five or older, you'd have already picked up on it."

He went hands on hips. "Got a busy day ahead of me, Mrs. Winslow. Maybe you could come right out and tell me what it is you want me to know."

"Well, that would be far too easy," she said and vanished inside, shutting her door on him.

Finn divided a look between her door and Pru's before tossing up his hands and deciding he knew nothing about women.

Finn strode into the bar. His morning crew cleaners Marie, Rosa, and Felipe all lifted their heads from their various tasks of mopping and scrubbing and blinked.

Shit. He forgot that he was making the morning walk of shame.

Shirtless.

It was Felipe who finally recovered first and gave a soft wolf whistle. "Nice," he said with an eyelash flutter and a hand fanning the air in front of his face.

Finn rolled his eyes in tune to their laughter. Whatever. He strode to his office and — as a bonus annoyance — found Sean asleep on his damn couch.

In Finn's damn spare shirt.

He kicked his brother's feet and watched with grim satisfaction as Sean grunted, jerked awake, and rolled off the couch, hitting the floor with a bone-sounding crunch.

"What the fuck, man?" Sean asked with a wide yawn.

"I need my shirt."

"I'm in it," Sean said. Captain Obvious.

Fine. Whatever. Finn slapped his pockets for his keys. He'd just drive home real quick and —

His keys weren't in his pockets. Probably, given his luck, they were on the floor of Pru's bedroom. He walked out of his office and strode through the pub.

"Just as nice from the rear," Felipe called out.

Finn flipped him off, ignored the hoots of laughter, and hit the stairs, knocking on Pru's door.

From behind him he heard a soft gasp and a wheeze. Craning his head, he found Mrs. Winslow once again in her doorway, this time with two other ladies, mouths agog.

"You were right," one of them whispered to Mrs. Winslow, staring at Finn. She was hooked up to a portable oxygen tank, hence the Darth Vader–like breathing.

"I haven't seen hipbones cut like that in sixty years," the other said in the same stage whisper as her friend.

"You realize I can hear you, right?" Finn asked.

The women all jumped in tandem, snapping their gazes up to his. "Oh my god, he's *real*," the woman with the oxygen tank said — wheezed — in awe.

Mrs. Winslow snorted. "You'll have to excuse them," she said to Finn. "They probably need their hormone doses checked."

Finn decided the hell with waiting on Pru to answer her door. He'd slept with her. He'd tasted every inch of her body. She'd done the same for him. So he checked the handle, and when it turned easily in his palm, he took that as a sign that the day had to improve from here.

When Finn had left, Pru stood there in the kitchen, shaken. She grabbed her phone because she needed advice. Since she was still wearing only Finn's shirt, she propped her phone against the cereal box on the counter so that when the FaceTime call went through to Jake, he'd only see her from the shoulders up.

No need to set off any murder sprees this morning.

When he answered, he just looked at her.

"Hi," she said.

"Hi yourself. You think I don't know your thoroughly fucked face?"

She did her best to keep eye contact. "Hey, I don't point it out to you when *you* get lucky."

"Yes you do. You march your ass into my office, pull out your pocketknife, and make a notch on the corner of my wood desk."

"That's to make a point," she said.

"Which is?"

"You get lucky a lot."

He arched a brow. "And the problem?"

Well, he had her there. "I need your advice."

"Why now?"

"Okay, I deserve that," she said. "But remember when you were worried that Finn was the one who would get hurt?" She felt her eyes fill. "You were off a little."

"Ah, hell, Pru," he said, voice softer now. "You never did know how to follow directions worth shit."

She choked out a laugh. "I know this is a mess of my own making, I totally get that." She closed her eyes. And I've got no excuse for not finding a way over the past few weeks to tell Finn sooner." Well, she did sort of have one — that being she was deathly afraid to lose him when she'd only just found him.

Not that Finn would take any comfort from that.

Jake sighed. "Chica, the mistake's been made. Shit happens. Just tell him. Tell him who you are and who your parents were. Get past it. Stop hiding. You'll feel better."

No, she wouldn't. Because she knew what

came next.

Finn would be hurt.

She'd been so taken aback by the speed of events between the two of them, at how fast things had gotten out of her control, that she was scared. Terrified, really. Because hurting him had been the last thing she'd ever wanted. She opened her mouth to say so but at the sound of footsteps coming toward the kitchen, not hurried or rushed or trying to be stealthy, she whirled around, already knowing who she'd be facing.

Finn, of course. Still shirtless, face carefully blank, he strode to the table and picked up his forgotten keys.

Shit.

God knew how long he'd been there or how much he'd heard. It was impossible to tell by his expression since he was purposely giving nothing away.

Which really was her answer.

He'd heard everything.

"Finn," Jake said, taking in his shirtless state with a slight brow raise.

"Jake," Finn said, either not noticing the unspoken question from Jake or ignoring it completely.

Then they both looked at Pru, to their credit both doing so with a mix of affection and concern. With good reason, as it turned out, because she suddenly felt like she was going to be sick.

Go time, she thought.

"Pru," Finn said quietly. Not a question really but a statement. He wanted to know what was going on.

Oh God, this was going to suck. And the worst part was she'd started all of this with the best intentions. All she'd ever wanted was to fix a wrong that had been done to him, a terrible wrong that she regretted and had carried around until she'd been able to do something about it.

And she'd righted wrongs before, successfully too. But she'd crossed the line this time and she knew it.

And now she had to face it head on.

"Trust him, chica," Jake said from her phone. "He deserves to know and you deserve to be free of this once and for all. If he's who you think, it'll be okay."

And then the rat fink bastard disconnected.

"Pru?" Finn brought up his free hand and slid his fingers along her jaw, letting them sink into her hair. His expression was wary now, but that didn't stop him from standing in her space like they were a couple. An intimate one.

Her heart tightened. It'd been everything

she'd ever wanted.

Only a few moments ago he'd been looking morning gruff and deeply satisfied. Now there was something much more to his body language and — Oh good Lord. He had a bite mark just to the side of his left nipple. She felt the heat rise up her cheeks.

"I have another on my ass," he said, his tone not its usual amused or heated when discussing their sex life. "We'll circle back to that. Talk to me, Pru."

Her heart was pounding, her blood surging hard and fast through her veins, panic making her limbs weak. She looked at her phone but Jake was long gone and in the reflection of the screen she could see herself.

She hadn't gotten away from last night unscathed either. There was a visible whisker burn on her throat and she knew she had a matching mark on her breasts.

And between her thighs.

Finn had brought her pleasure such as she'd never known, both in bed and out.

And now it was over . . . "I'm so sorry," she said. "I've kept something from you."

"What?" There was some wariness to his tone now, though he still spoke quietly. Willing to hear whatever she had to say.

She immediately felt her blood pressure shoot through the stratosphere.

"Just tell me, Pru."

Well, if he was going to be all calm and logical about this . . . She inhaled a deep breath. "It's about my parents. And their accident."

His eyes softened with sympathy, which she didn't deserve. "You never say much about how it happened," he said. "I haven't wanted to push. You don't push me on my dad's shit and I appreciate that, so —"

"It was a car wreck." She licked her suddenly dry lips. "They . . . caused other injuries." She paused. "Life-altering injuries."

His eyes never left hers. "And?"

"And I . . . got involved."

"You've been . . . helping them?"

"Yes, but only in the smallest of ways compared to the damage my parents caused."

He looked at her for a long moment. "That's got to be painful for you."

"No, actually, it's healing."

He looked skeptical.

"I had to," she said softly. "Finn, my parents are the ones in the car who killed your dad."

His brow furrowed. "What are you talking about? The man driving the car that hit him

402

was some guy by the name of Steven Dalman."

"My dad," she said quietly. "My mom never took his last name. Her family was against the match every bit as much as his. She gave me her name, not his . . ." She trailed off when Finn abruptly turned from her.

He shoved his fingers into his hair and didn't say a word. She wasn't even sure if he was breathing, but she couldn't take her eyes off him. Off the sleek, leanly muscled lines of his bare back. The inch of paler skin low on his waist where his jeans had slipped.

The tension now in every line of his body. She tried to explain. "I just wanted . . ."

Finn whipped back around. "Want what? To satiate your curiosity? See if Sean and I were as devastated as you? What exactly did you want, Pru?"

"To make it better," she said, throat tight. "That's all I've ever wanted, was to make it better. For both of you, for everyone who my dad . . ." She covered her mouth.

Destroyed.

"I see," he said quietly. "So that's what I was to you, another pet project like the others you collected and fixed their broken lives."

"No, I —"

"Truth, Pru," he said, voice vibrating with fury. "You owe me that."

"Okay, yes, I needed to help everyone however I could. I needed to make things right," she reiterated, swallowing a sob when he shook his head. She was losing him. "So I did what I could."

"I didn't need saving," he bit out. "Sean and I had each other and we were fine —" He stilled and his eyes cut to hers, sharp as a blade. "It was you. You got us that money that was supposedly from a community fundraiser. Jesus, how did I not guess this before?" His gaze narrowed. "Where did that money come from? Is that why you sold your childhood home? To give it to us?"

"No, the money from the house went to the others. For you and Sean, I used my parents' life insurance policy."

He stared at her. "Fuck," he said roughly and turned to go.

She managed to slide between him and the door. "Finn, please —"

"Please what?" he asked coldly. "Understand how you very purposely and calculatedly came into my life? Moved into this building? Sat in my pub? Became my friend and then my lover? All under the pretense of wanting me, while really you were just trying to assuage some misguided sense of guilt." He stopped and closed his eyes for a beat. "Jesus, Pru. I never even saw you coming."

Having her crimes against him listed out loud made her feel sick to her soul. "It wasn't like that," she said.

"No? You sought me out, decided I needed fixing, slept with me, probably had a good laugh over me telling you how much you meant to me . . . all without telling me why you were really here — to ease your damn conscience." He shook his head. "Hope you got everything in that you wanted because we're done here."

"No, Finn. I —"

"Done," he repeated with a terrifying finality. "I don't want to see you again, Pru."

And then he walked out, breaking the heart she hadn't even realized she had inside her to break.

CHAPTER 31
#MISSEDITBYTHATMUCH

Weighted down by so many emotions that she couldn't name them all, Pru called in sick, letting Jake think she'd gotten her period and had debilitating cramps.

Since she'd never used such an excuse before, had in fact never missed work at all, she didn't feel in the least bit sorry.

Her ovaries had to be good for something, right?

She marathoned *Game of Thrones* and never left the couch. Every time her mind wandered to Finn, her heart did a slow somersault in her chest, her lungs stopped working, and her stomach hurt, so she did what anyone would do in the throes of a bad breakup.

She ate.

The next morning she was jerked out of her stupor when someone knocked on her door. She blinked and looked around. She was still dressed, still on her couch, surrounded by empty wrappings of candy bars and other varieties of junk food — the evidence of a pity party for one. She grabbed her phone but there were no missed calls, texts, or emails from Finn.

And why would there be? He'd been pretty clear.

He didn't want to see her again.

The knock came again, less patient now. She got to her feet and looked out the peephole.

Willa, Elle, and Haley.

Elle was front and center, her eyes on the peephole.

"I'm not feeling very sociable," Pru said. "In fact, I'm feeling pretty damn negative and toxic so —"

"Okay, listen, honey," Elle said. "Life sucks sometimes. The trick is not letting negative and toxic feelings rent space in your head. Raise the rent and kick them the hell out. And I've brought help in that regard." She lifted a bag.

Tina's muffins.

Pru opened the door.

Elle handed her the bag.

Haley handed over a very large coffee.

Willa smiled. "My job is to be supportive and get you to talk."

"Way to be subtle," Elle said.

Ignoring that, Willa hugged Pru. "Okay, so I missed the subtle gene," she said. "But you should know, we are unbelievably supportive."

"Even if I screwed up?"

"Even if," Willa said.

"I'm not going to talk about it," Pru warned, barely able to talk past the lump in her throat. "Not now. Maybe not ever."

Seemingly unconcerned by this, they all moved into Pru's apartment and eyed the scene of the crime.

Willa picked up an empty bag of maple bacon potato chips. "They make bacon chips?" She looked into the empty bag sadly. "Damn, I bet they were amazing."

"How did you know something was wrong?" Pru asked with what she thought was a calm voice.

"Because you missed Eighties Karaoke and didn't answer any of our calls last night," Elle said. "And you'd told me you wouldn't miss it unless Chris Evans came knocking at your door." She looked Pru over, her rumpled sweats and what was undoubtedly a bad case of bedhead hair. "And I think it's safe to say that didn't happen."

"It could have," Pru muttered and set the coffee down to dive into the bag of muffins.

She started with a chocolate chocolate-chip.

Haley reached to put her hand in the bag and Pru clutched it to her chest with a growl that rivaled Thor's.

Haley lifted her hands. "Okay, not sharing. Got it." She turned to Elle and Willa. "I think we've verified the breakup rumor."

Pru froze. "There's a breakup rumor?"

Willa lifted her hand, her first finger and thumb about an inch apart. "Little bit."

Pru sank to the couch, still clutching her muffins. "I'd like to be alone now."

"Sure," Elle said. "We understand." And then she sat on one end of the couch and picked up the remote to turn the volume up. "Season three, right? Love this show."

Eyes on the screen, already enraptured, Haley sat on the other end.

Pru opened her mouth to complain but Willa took the floor, leaning back on the couch, leaving a spot right in the middle for Pru.

She blew out a breath and in the respectful silence that she appreciated more than she could say, she wasn't alone at all.

Two days later Pru walked to work. In the rain. She knew she was bad off when Thor didn't complain once. He did however, keep looking up at her, wondering what their mood should be.

Devastated. That was the current mood. But she didn't want to scare him. "We're going to be okay."

Thor cocked his head, his one stand-up ear quivering a little bit.

He didn't believe her.

And for good reason. She hadn't slept. She'd called in sick again and Jake had let her get away with that.

Until this morning. He'd called her at the crack of dawn and said, "I don't care if your uterus is falling out of your body, take some Midol and get your ass into work. Today."

She wasn't surprised. And to be honest, she was ready to get back to it after a two-day pity party involving more ice cream than she'd eaten in her twenty-six years total. She'd run out of self-pity stamina. Turned out it was hard to maintain that level of despair.

So with it now at a dull roar, she'd showered and dressed and headed to work. "I just feel . . . stupid," she told Thor. "This is all my fault, you know."

"Honey," a woman said, passing her on the sidewalk. "Never admit that it's all your fault." She was wearing the smallest, tightest red dress Pru had ever seen, and the five-inch stilettos were impressive.

"But this time it really is," Pru told her.

"No, you're misunderstanding me. Never admit it's your fault, *especially* when it is."

The woman walked on but Thor stopped and put his front paws on Pru's leg.

She picked him up and he licked her chin.

Her throat tightened. "You love me anyway." She hugged him, apparently squeezing too tight because he suffered it for about two seconds and then growled.

With a half laugh and half sob, she loosened her grip. When she got to work, she walked straight through the warehouse to the offices. She passed those by too and headed back to the area where Jake lived.

He was lifting weights, the music blaring so loud the windows rattled. She turned off the music and turned to face him.

"You okay?" he asked, dropping the weights, turning his chair to face her, his face creased in worry.

She'd planned what she would say to him. Something like *I know, you told me so, blah blah blah, so let's not talk about it, let's just move on.* And she opened her mouth to say just that but nothing came out.

"What's going on?"

She burst into tears.

Looking pained, he stared at her. "Did you forget the Midol? Because I bought

411

some, it's in my bathroom. I've had it for over a year, I've just never figured out how to give it to you without getting my head bit clean off."

She threw her purse at him. "I didn't get my damn period!"

"Oh shit," he said, blanching. "Oh fuck. Okay, first I'll kill him and then —"

"No!" She actually laughed through her tears. "I'm not pregnant."

He let out a long breath. "Well, Jesus, lead with that next time."

Pru shook her head and turned to go, but he was faster than her even in his chair. He got in front of her and blocked the door.

"Talk to me, chica," he said.

"You done being a stupid guy?"

"I'll try to be." He said this quite earnestly, his gaze on hers. "You did tell him then."

She nodded.

"And . . . it went to hell?" he guessed.

"In a hand basket," she agreed.

"I'm sorry."

She shook her head. "Don't be. I was a dumbass. I should have told him from the get-go like you said a million times."

Jake let out a rare sigh. "Look, chica, yeah, you made a mistake. But everything you did was for the right reasons. You should feel good about that. You set out to help everyone from the accident and now you can say you did that. In a big way. In a much bigger way than anyone else I know would have."

She thought about it and realized she did feel good about that part. "So it's mission accomplished," she said softly.

"Yeah." He smiled. "Proud of you."

The words were a balm on her broken heart. The ache didn't go away and she wasn't sure if it ever would. Loss was loss, and Finn no longer being in her life was a hard pill to swallow. But she'd survived worse and she'd come back from rock bottom.

She could do it again.

Well . . . next time maybe tell him who she was before sexy times and getting hearts involved . . .

The first two days were a complete blur to Finn. On day three, he stood in his shower contemplating the level of suckage his life had become until the hot water ran out. He stood there as it turned cold and then icy, completely forgetting that they were on a water watch and he'd pay a penalty if he went over his allowed usage for the month.

He was sitting on his couch staring at the still-off TV when Sean called. "I'm taking tonight off," Finn said.

"Oh, hell no you're not," Sean said. "Three fucking nights in a row? I can't do this by myself, Finn. This is a damn partnership and you need to start acting like it."

Finn dropped his head, closed his eyes, and fought the laugh. "Are you throwing my words back in my face?"

"Hell yes." Sean paused. "Is it working?"

"I think you owe me more than a few nights."

Sean blew out a breath. "Yeah." He paused again, this one a beat longer. "What's wrong?"

"Nothing."

"Bullshit," Sean said. "You take time off never. Let me guess. You're . . . running away from home? No, it's worse than that. Shit. Just tell me quick, like ripping off a Band-Aid. You're dying?"

"I'm not dying. Jesus, you're such a drama queen."

"Right, then what?" Sean demanded. "Are you dumping me, is that it?"

Finn pinched the bridge of his nose. Sean's greatest fear was being dumped, and to be fair, he'd earned that particular anxiety the hard way from their parents. Pulling his head out of his own ass was hard but Finn managed for a second to do just that. "I can't dump you," he said, "you're my brother."

"People dump their family all the time," Sean said, and then paused. "Or they just walk away."

Finn softened and let out a sigh. "Okay, so yeah, I suppose I *could* dump you. And don't get me wrong, there are entire days where I'd like to at least strangle you slowly. But listen to me very carefully, Sean. I've honestly never, not once, wanted to dump you from my life."

There was a long silence. When Sean finally spoke, his voice was thick. "Yeah?"

"Yeah. I'd do anything for you. And I'll never walk away from you." And up until a few days ago, he'd have given Pru that very same promise.

And yet he had walked away from her.

At that thought, the first shadow of doubt crept in, icy tendrils as relentless as the afternoon fog.

"Are you going to tell me what's up?" Sean asked. "If it's not me and the pub's okay, then what? You mess up with Pru or something?"

"Why would you say that?" Finn demanded.

"Whoa, man, chill. It's a matter of elimination. Other than work, there's nothing else that could get to you like this. So what

415

happened?"

"I don't want to talk about it."

Sean was quiet a second. "Because of Mellie? I apologized for that like a thousand times but I'll do it again. I was an asshole and an idiot. And drunk off my ass that night. And it was a long time ago. I'd never —"

"This has nothing to do with Mellie," Finn said.

"Then what? Because Pru's pretty damn perfect."

Finn sighed. Not perfect. But perfect for him . . . "Why does it have to be anyone's fault?"

Sean laughed wryly. "It's just the way of the world. Men screw up. Women forgive — or don't, as the case often goes."

Finn blew out a breath. "I walked away. I had my reasons but I'm not sure I did the right thing." It was a hell of an admission considering he rarely second-guessed himself.

"If I've learned one thing from you," Sean said, "it's to suck it up and always do the *right* thing. Not the easy thing, the right thing."

Finn managed a short laugh. "Listen to you, all logical and shit."

"I know, go figure, right? So . . . you going to do it? The right thing?"

Finn sighed. "Who are you and what have you done with my brother?"

"Just hurry up and handle it and get your ass back to work."

"There he is."

CHAPTER 32
#TAKEMETOYOURLEADER

When Finn finally made his way to the pub that night, he stood in the middle of the bar as music played around him. His friends and customers were all there having fun, laughing, dancing, drinking . . .

The pub was a huge success, beyond his wildest imagination. He'd never really taken the time to notice it. But he was noticing now that his heart had been ripped out of his chest by a gorgeous dynamo of a woman with eyes that sucked him in and held him, a sweet yet mischievous smile that had taken him places he'd never been . . . then there was how he'd felt in her arms.

Like Superman.

And he'd dumped her. Roughly. Cruelly. And her crime? Nothing more than trying to make sure he was okay after a tragedy that hadn't even been her fault. Not in the slightest.

Hating himself for that, he stopped right

in the middle of the place. He wasn't in the mood for this. He needed to think, needed to figure out what the hell to do to alleviate this pain in his chest and the certainty that he'd walked away from the best thing that had ever happened to him.

But everyone was at the bar, waving at him. Bracing himself for the inquisition, he headed that way.

"Rumor is that you've been a dumbass," Archer said.

Finn stared at him. "How the hell did you know —"

"The girls and I stopped by Pru's place," Willa said.

"Is she okay?"

"She looks and sounds like her heart's been ripped out." Willa met his gaze. "She'd clearly been crying."

Shit.

Elle squeezed his hand. "Whatever you did, it's not completely your fault. You're a penis-carrying human being, after all. You're hard-wired to be a dumbass."

"Sit." Spence kicked out a barstool for him and poured him a beer from the pitcher in front of them.

Finn took a second look at him. "You're wearing glasses."

Haley grinned proudly. "Do you like

them? I picked them out for him."

"No, you didn't," Spence said. "I did."

Haley patted him like he was a puppy. "You were impatient as always and grabbed the first pair off the display you could. It took you less than two seconds. I waited until you'd left and put them back and picked you out a better pair that would better suit your face."

Spence pulled his glasses off and stared at them. "I liked the other pair better."

"Yeah?" Haley asked. "What color were they?"

Spence paused. "Glasses color."

Haley rolled her eyes. "Just like a man," she said to Will and Elle, who nodded.

Archer shook his head at Spence. "This is why you're single."

"You're single too," Spence said.

"Because I want to be."

Spence closed his eyes. "We were going to rag on Finn, not me. Let's stick with the plan."

"Right," Archer said and looked at Finn. "Tell us all how you messed up so we can point and laugh."

"And then fix," Willa said, giving the others a dirty look as she patted the empty seat. "Come on now, don't be shy. Tell us everything."

"Yes," Ella said. "I want to hear it all, because that girl? She's not just yours, Finn. She's ours now too."

"She's not mine," Finn said.

Everyone gaped at him.

Elle narrowed her gaze. "Does this have anything to do with that wish she made for you on that damn fountain? You know about that, right?"

Finn blinked. "She wished for *me*?"

"Have you ever heard of being gentle?" Archer asked Elle. "Even once?"

Elle sighed. "Okay, so he didn't know. Sue me." She shot Archer a dirty look. "And like you know the first thing about being gentle."

"Didn't know what exactly?" Finn demanded, refusing to let them go off on some tangent. "Someone needs to start making sense or I swear to God —"

"She made a wish for you to find true love," Willa said. "I was never clear on why she wished for you and not for herself. Probably because that's who she is, down to the bone."

Spence sucked in a breath. "I've been by that fountain a million times. It never once occurred to me to make a wish for someone else. That's . . ."

"Selfless," Willa said. "Utterly selfless.

And, by the way, it's also something that *none* of us would've thought to do. So it's not just Spence here who's an insensitive ass."

"Thanks, Willa," Spence said dryly.

She turned expectantly to Finn. "So? What happened?"

A terrible knot in his chest twisting, Finn snatched Spence's beer and knocked back the rest of the glass, not that it helped.

"Sure, help yourself," Spence muttered.

Everyone was looking at Finn, waiting.

He shook his head. "I can't. It's . . . private. What happened between us stays between us."

"Hey, this isn't Vegas," Spence said, and earned himself a slap upside the back of his head by Elle.

"Do you love her?" Willa demanded of Finn.

At the question, that knot in his chest tightened painfully. "That's not the problem. She . . . kept something from me."

"That sucks," Archer said, as Finn knew, understanding all too well the power of secrets and how they could destroy lives.

"No," Elle said, glaring at Archer. "No, you don't get to blindly side against her. She maybe had her reasons. Good ones," she said very seriously.

Something they knew that Elle understood *all* too well. She had secrets too, secrets they kept for her.

Archer met Elle's gaze and something passed between them. The fight might have ratcheted up a notch but Willa, always the peacemaker, spoke up. "Do you love her?" she repeated to Finn firmly.

Finn's mind scrolled through the images he had. Pru coming into the pub drenched and still smiling. Pru dragging him away from work to a softball game. Comforting him after a fight with Sean. Clutching a photo of her dead parents and still finding a smile over their memory. She'd brought a sense of balance to his life that had been sorely missing. It didn't matter whether she was standing behind the controls of a huge boat in charge of hundreds of people's safety or diving into a wave to save her dog, she never failed to make him feel . . . alive.

Just a single one of her smiles could make his whole day. The sound of her laugh did the same. And then there was the feel of her beneath him, her body locked around his when he was buried so deep that he couldn't imagine being intimate with anyone else ever again . . .

"Yes," he said quietly, not having to speak loud because the entire group had gone silent waiting on his answer. "I love her."

"Have you told her?" Willa asked.

"No."

"Why not?"

"Because . . ." Yeah, genius, why not? "And exactly how many people have *you* told that to?" he asked.

"Good one, going on the defensive," Elle said, not looking impressed.

Willa agreed with an eyeroll. "I mean I get that when you're playing sports or bragging to the guys and you need a six-foot-long dick," she said. "But this is Pru we're talking about."

"Six-foot-long dick?" Spence asked, grinning.

Willa waved him off and spoke straight to Finn. "Whatever she kept to herself, you did the same, Finn. You always do, even with us. You held back. You think she didn't feel that? Pru keeps it real and she's tough as nails, but she lost her family," she said, unknowingly touching on the very subject of the breakup. "She lost them when she was only eighteen and it left her alone in the world. And as you, more than anyone else knows all too damn well, it changes a person, Finn. It makes it hard to put yourself out there. But that's exactly what she does every single day without complaint, she puts herself out there."

I love you . . . Pru had whispered those words to him when he'd been drifting off to sleep that last night, and he'd told himself it was a dream. But he knew the truth. He'd always known.

She had more courage than he'd ever had.

"So presumably there was a fight," Elle said. "And then what? She walked?"

"And you let her?" Willa asked in disbelief. "Oh, Finn."

"You can fix it," Haley said softly. "You just go to her and tell her you were wrong."

Archer, eyes on Finn, put his hand on Haley's, stopping her. "I have a feeling we've got things backwards," he said.

"Ohhhh," Willa said, staring at Finn. "*You* walked."

Finn nodded. He'd walked. And she'd let him go without a fight.

Not that he'd given her any choice with the *I don't want to see you again* thing . . . *Fuck.* Willa was right. He'd been wielding around a six-foot dick, which made *him* the six-foot dick.

Willa looked greatly disappointed. "I don't understand."

Finn shook his head. "I know. But I'm not going to tell you more." He might have turned his back on Pru, but he wouldn't

425

have these guys doing the same. She deserved their friendship. She deserved a lot more than that, but he was still so angry and . . . *shit.* Hurt. He pushed away from the table. "I've gotta go."

He hoped to be alone but Sean followed him back to his office. "What aren't you telling me?" he asked. "What is it she did that was so bad?"

Finn shook his head.

"Just tell me," Sean pushed. "So I can tell you that you're being an idiot and then you can go make it right."

Finn stared at him. "What makes you believe that this can be made right?"

Sean lifted a shoulder. "Because you taught me that love and family is where you make it, with who you make it. And even in this short amount of time, Pru's become both your love and your family."

That this was true felt like a knife slicing through him. "Sean, her parents were the ones in the car that killed dad. Her dad was the drunk driver."

Sean stared at him. "Are you shitting me?"

"I couldn't have made that up if I'd tried."

Sean sank to the couch. "Holy shit."

"Yeah. Listen, this stays right here in this room, yeah?"

Sean lifted his gaze and pierced Finn.

"You're protecting her."

"I just don't want to hurt her," he said. At least not more than he already had . . .

"No, you're protecting her." Sean stood again. "The way I bet she was trying to protect you when she didn't tell you who she was."

Finn shook his head. "What are you saying?"

"That *you're* the dumbass, not her." Sean shook his head. "Look, I've got to get back out there. One of us has to have their head in the game, and trust me, no one's more surprised that it's me." He stopped at the door and turned back. "Listen, I get that you're too close to see this clearly, but take it from someone who lost as much as you did in that accident . . . we didn't lose shit compared to what Pru lost. She doesn't deserve this, not from you. Not from anyone."

And then he let himself out and Finn was alone. He went to his desk and pushed some paper around for half an hour, but it was useless. He was useless. He'd just decided to bail when Archer walked right in. "Ever hear of knocking?"

Archer paced the length of the office and then came to him, hands on hips.

"What?" Finn asked.

"I'm going to tell you something," Archer said. "And I don't want you to take a swing at me for it. I'm feeling pissed off and wouldn't mind a fight, but I don't want it with you."

Shit. "What did you do?" Finn asked wearily.

Archer grimaced. "Something I once promised you I wouldn't."

Finn stared at his oldest and most trusted friend in the world and then turned to his desk and poured them both some whiskey.

Archer lifted his glass, touched it to Finn's, and then they both tossed back.

Archer blew out a breath, set the glass down and met Finn's gaze. "I looked into her."

Archer had programs that rivaled entire government computer systems. When he said he'd looked into someone, he meant he looked *into* them. Inside and out. Upside down and right-side up. When Archer looked into someone, he could find out how old they were when they got their first cavity, what their high school P.E. teacher had said about them, what their parents had earned in a cash-under-the-table job four decades prior.

Archer didn't take this power lightly. He had a high moral code of conduct that didn't always line up with the rest of the world, but he'd never — at least not to Finn's knowledge — looked into his friends' pasts or breached their privacy.

He had, however, looked into Willa's last boyfriend, but that had been for a good reason.

"When?" Finn asked.

Archer gave him a surprised look. "Shouldn't the question be *what*? As in what did I find out?"

"You know who she is."

"Yes," Archer said. "Do *you*?"

"Why the fuck do you think I'm standing here by myself?" Finn asked.

Archer looked away for a beat and then brought his gaze back. "There's stuff you might not know."

"Like?"

"Like the fact that she's spent her life since the accident trying to right that wrong to everyone who was affected. That she, anonymously through an attorney, gave every penny she was awarded in life insurance to the victims of that accident, including you and Sean. She not only kept zero for herself, she sold the house she was raised in and used that money to help as well. She kept nothing, instead dedicated the following years to making sure everyone else was taken care of, whatever it took. She helped them find jobs, stay in college, find a place to live, everything and anything that was needed."

Finn nodded.

"You know?" Archer asked in disbelief. "So what happened between you two? She came clean and . . ."

"I got mad that she lied to me."

"You mean omitted, right? Because not telling you something isn't lying."

Finn swore roughly but whether that was because he was pissed or because Archer was right, he wasn't sure. "It was more than that. She had plenty of opportunities to tell me. If not when we first met, then certainly after we —"

Archer let that hang there a moment. "I'm thinking she had her reasons," he said quietly. "And it wasn't all that long. What, three weeks? Maybe she was working her way up to it."

Finn shook his head.

"Look, I'm not excusing what she did," Archer said. "She should've told you. We both know that. But we also both know that it's never that easy. She had a lot working against her, Finn. She's alone, for one. And she's got the biggest guilt complex going that I've ever seen."

Finn swore again and shoved his fingers in his hair. "She shouldn't feel guilty. The accident wasn't her fault."

"No," Archer said. "It wasn't. So I'm going to hope like hell you didn't let her think it was, no matter how badly she stepped on your ego."

"That's completely bullshit. This isn't about my ego."

"Your stupid pride then," Archer said. "I was with you when your dad died, don't forget. I know how your life changed. And I realize we're talking about a soul here and I don't like to speak ill of the dead, but you and I both know the truth. Yours and Sean's life changed for the better when your father was dead and buried."

Finn let his head fall back and he stared at the ceiling.

"You know what I think happened?"

"No," Finn said tiredly, "but I bet you're about to tell me."

Archer smiled grimly, and true to his nature, didn't hold back. "I think you fell and fell hard, and then you got scared. You needed an out and she gave it to you. Hell, she handed it to you on a silver platter. Well, congrats, man, you got what you wanted."

At his silence, Archer shook his head and headed for the door. "Hope you enjoy it."

Finn sat there stewing in his own frustration, both bad temper and regrets choking him. Enjoy it? He couldn't imagine enjoying anything, ever again. He looked around him. In the past, this place had been his home away from home.

But that feeling had migrated to Pru's place two floors up.

Just as his emotions had migrated to the same place, over softball, darts, hikes, and long conversations about what they wanted out of their hopes and dreams, often chased by the best sex he'd ever had.

He hadn't realized just how far gone he was when it came to her. Or how lost in her he'd allowed himself to become.

But he was. Completely lost in her, and lost without her.

He hadn't seen that coming. He'd assumed they'd continue doing what they'd been doing. Being together. Hell, it'd been so easy it'd snuck up on him.

And he'd fallen, hard.

That wasn't the surprise. No, that honor went to the fact that in spite of what she'd done, he was *still* in love with her.

And, he suspected, always would be.

CHAPTER 33
#LIFEISABOWLOFCRAZY

Pru was up on the roof with Thor, watching the fog roll in when she felt someone watching her. "I'm not going to jump, if that's what you're worried about," she said.

Archer stepped into her line of sight and crouched at her side. "Of course you're not, you're stronger than that."

She felt a ghost of a smile cross her lips. "You sure about that?"

"Very."

She turned her head and met his gaze, and saw that he knew everything. She sighed. "For what it's worth, I realize that I should've told him from day one, but I thought if he knew, he wouldn't give me the time of day and I wanted to help him."

"He doesn't like help."

"No kidding."

Archer smiled. "Finn's got the world in black or white. Like . . . the Giants or Dodgers. Home grown or imported. Us or

433

them. For me, and for you too, I suspect, it's not so simple. He's a smart guy, though, Pru. He figures things out. He always does, in his own time."

She shook her head, kissed the top of Thor's, and rose. "That's sweet of you to say, but he won't. And I don't expect him to. I made a mistake, a really big one. And sometimes we don't get second chances."

"You should," Archer said.

"He's right." This was from Willa, who appeared from the fire escape and came over to them. "Everyone deserves a second chance."

"Where's Elle?" Archer asked.

"She couldn't climb the fire escape in her heels and she refused to leave them behind. She's taking the elevator."

Spence showed up next. He came from the fire escape like Willa and held Pru's gaze for a long beat before nodding and stepping out of the way, making room for the person hitting the rooftop right behind him.

Finn.

He climbed over with agility and ease and dropped down, coming straight for Pru without a glance at any of his closest friends.

Pru's heart stopped. Everything stopped including her ability to think. She took a step back, needing out of here. She wasn't ready to face him and pretend to be okay with the fact that they were nothing to each other now.

"Wait," Finn said, reaching for her hand. "Don't go."

God, that voice. She'd missed him so very much. Feeling lost, she looked at the others, who'd backed off to the other side of the rooftop to give them some privacy. "I need to go," she whispered to Finn.

"Can I say something first?" he asked quietly. "Please?"

When she nodded, he gently squeezed her hand in his. "You told me you made a mistake and that you wanted to explain," he said. "And I didn't let you. That was my mistake, Pru. I was wrong. We each made mistakes, not just you. And I get that we can't pretend that the mistakes didn't happen, but maybe we can use them to cancel each other out."

Her heart was a jackhammer behind her ribs, pounding too fast for her veins to keep up with the increased blood flow. "What are you saying?"

"I'm saying that I forgive you, Pru. And in fact, there was never anything to forgive. Can you forgive me?"

The jackhammer had turned into a solid lump, blocking her air passage. "It's . . ."

She shook her head and tried desperately to keep hope from running away with her goose sense. "It can't be that easy," she whispered.

"Why not?" He reached for her other hand, taking advantage of her being stunned into immobility to tug her into him. Toe to toe now, he cupped her jaw. "Our last night together, you said something to me when I was drifting off." His gaze warmed. "You said it and then I felt your sheer panic, so I let it go. Or that's what I told myself. But the truth is that I was just being a coward."

She had to close her eyes at his gentle touch because just the callused pads of his fingers on her felt so right she wanted to cry.

"I love you, Pru," he said quietly but with utter steel.

Her eyes flew open and her breath snagged in her lungs. She hadn't realized how badly she'd needed to hear those words but . . . "Love doesn't fix everything," she said on a hitched breath. "There are rules and expectations in a relationship. And there are some things you can't take back. What I did was one of those things."

He shook his head. "Life doesn't follow rules or expectations. It's messy and unpredictable. And it turns out love is a lot like life — it doesn't follow rules or expectations either."

"Yes, but —"

"Did you mean what you said?" he asked. "Do you love me, Pru?"

She stared up at him and swallowed hard, but her heart remained in her throat, stuck there with that burgeoning hope she hadn't been successful at beating back. "Yes," she whispered. "I love you. But —"

"But nothing," he said fiercely, eyes lit with relief, affection. *Love.* "Nothing else matters compared to the fact that I managed to get the most amazing woman I've ever met to fall in love with me."

She slowly shook her head. "I'm not sure you're taking my concerns seriously."

"On the contrary," he said. "I'm taking you and your concerns *very* seriously. What you did was try to bring something to the life of two guys you didn't even know. You set aside your own happiness out of guilt and regret, when you had nothing to feel guilt and regret for. You lost a lot that day too, Pru. You lost more than anyone else. And there was no one to help you. No one to try to make things better for you."

Her throat closed. Just snapped shut. "Don't," she managed to whisper. "We can't go back."

"Not back, then. Forward." He gently squeezed her fingers in his. "I was wrong to walk away, so fucking wrong, Pru. What we had was exactly right and I'm sorry I ever made you doubt it."

Eyes still closed, she shook her head, afraid to hope. Afraid to breathe. He brought their entwined hands to his heart so that she could feel its strong, steady beat, as if he was willing his calm confidence about his feelings for her to soak in.

She let it, along with his warmth, appreciating more than she could say what his words meant to her. She hadn't realized how much she'd needed to hear him say he didn't blame her, that she had nothing to feel guilty for . . . It was as if he'd swept up all her broken pieces and painstakingly glued them back together, making her whole again. "Finn —"

"Can you live without me?" he asked.

Her eyes flew open. "What?"

"It's a simple question," he said. "Can you live without me?"

She stared past him at the others. Elle had arrived and maybe they were on the other side of the rooftop, but they were making absolutely zero attempt to hide the fact that they were hanging on every word.

"Pru," he said quietly.

She met his gaze again, chewing on her lower lip.

"Not talking?" he asked. "Fair enough. I'll go first. I can't live without you. Hell, I can't even breathe when I think about you not being in my life."

"You can't?"

"No." He gently squeezed her. "I live pretty simply, always have. I've got these interfering idiots —" He gestured to his friends behind them.

"Hey," Spence said.

"He's right," Willa said. "Now shh, I think we're getting to the good stuff."

Finn shook his head and turned back to Pru. "I thought they were all I needed and I felt lucky to have them. But then you came into my life and suddenly I had something I didn't even realize was missing. Do you know what that was?"

She shook her head.

"It's you, Pru. And I want you back. I want to be with you. I want you to be mine, because I'm absolutely yours. Have been since you first walked into my life and became my fun whisperer. And you can't tell me it's too soon for a relationship because we've been in one since the moment we met. We're together, we're *supposed* to be together. Like peanut butter and jelly. Like French fries and ketchup. Like peaches and cream."

"Like titties and beer," Spence offered.

Archer wrapped his arm around Spence's neck and covered the guy's mouth with his hand.

"No," Pru said.

Finn stared at her. "What?"

"No, titties and beer don't go together," she said. "But also no, I can't live without you either."

Finn stared at her for a beat, his eyes dark and serious and full of so much emotion she didn't know how to process it all. And then suddenly he smiled the most beautiful smile she'd ever seen. He took her hand, brought it to his mouth and brushed a kiss over her fingers before hauling her up against him.

"You ready for this?" His voice was rough, telling her how important this was. How important *she* was.

"For you?" she whispered against his jaw. "Always."

Epilogue
#YOUHADMEATHELLO

Two months later . . .

Finn let out a long breath as he parked. Santa Cruz was south of San Francisco and thanks to traffic, it'd taken them over an hour to get here. He got out of the car and came around for Pru.

"Keep the blindfold on," he said, as he'd been saying the entire drive.

Her fingers brushed over the makeshift blindfold — a silk handkerchief that they'd played with in bed the night before — and smiled. "I'm hoping we're heading toward a big cake."

"I told you to aim higher for your birthday."

"Okay," she said. "A nice dinner first and *then* a big cake."

"Higher," he said.

She let their bodies bump and she rubbed her hips suggestively to his. "Dinner, cake, and . . . that weekend away you promised me?" she asked hopefully.

"Getting warmer." He gripped her hips, holding her close enough that she could feel exactly what she did to him.

She smiled warmly, sexily, gorgeous . . . his everything. "Can I peek yet?"

His gut tightened as he turned her so that she faced the small Santa Cruz beach cottage in front of them. "Okay," he said. "You can look."

Pru tore off the blindfold and blinked open her big eyes, which immediately widened as she gasped. She stared at the place in front of her and then turned her head and stared at him for a beat before swiveling back to the house. "Oh my God," she breathed and put a hand to her chest. "This is — was — my parents' house. Where I grew up."

"I know," he said quietly.

Pru stared at the tiny place like it was a sight for sore eyes, like it was Christmas and Easter and every other holiday all in one. "I haven't been here in so long . . ." She looked at him again. "It's ours for the weekend?"

He took both of her hands in his so that she faced him. "The owners had it in a beach rental program." He slipped a key into her right hand.

"You rented it for me?" she breathed.

"Yes." He paused. "Except I didn't rent it. I bought it. It's in your name now, Pru."

Her mouth fell open. "What?"

"The owners live on the other side of the country. They instructed the management program to sell it if the opportunity arose." His heart was pounding and he hoped like hell he'd done the right thing here, that she would take it in the spirit he intended. "The opportunity arose."

Looking shaky, she took the few steps and unlocked the front door. Then she stepped inside. He followed, slowly, wanting to give her time if she needed it.

The place was furnished. Shabby beach chic. Tiny kitchen, two tiny bedrooms, one bathroom. He already knew this from his previous visit to scope everything out, but he followed as Pru walked through, quiet, eyes shuttered.

The postage-stamp-size living room made up for its tininess with the view of the Pacific Ocean about three hundred feet down a grassy bluff.

Pru walked to the floor-to-ceiling windows and looked out.

Finn waited, willing to give her all the time she needed. He was prepared for her to be mad at him for overstepping, but when she turned to him, her eyes didn't hold temper.

They held emotion, overfilling, spilling down her cheeks.

"Pru." He stepped toward her but she held up a hand.

"Finn, I can't accept this. We're just dating, it's not right —"

"Yeah, about that just dating thing." He tugged her into him — where he liked her best. Cupping her jaw, he tilted her face to his. "I don't want to just date anymore."

She blinked. "You bought me a house and now you're dumping me?"

"I bought you a house and now I'm asking you to take us to the next level."

She just stared into his eyes in shock and he realized something with his own shock. "You expected me to change my mind about you," he said.

She shook her head. "More that I'm afraid to want more from you. I don't want to be greedy."

Finn cupped her face, keeping her chin tilted so that she had to look at him. He needed her to see how serious he was. "Pru, don't you get it yet? I'm yours until the end of time."

She relaxed against him with a small smile. "Okay, that's good," she said a little shakily. "Seeing as I want whatever of you that you're willing to give me."

He let out a low laugh. "Everything. I want to give you everything, Pru."

Her eyes shined brilliantly. "You already have," she whispered and tugged his mouth to hers, kissing him with all the love he'd ever dreamed of and more. So much more.

When they broke for air, her eyes were still a little damp but also full of affection and heat. Lots of heat. "Did you really mean *everything*?" she asked.

"Everything and anything." To prove it, he pulled a small black box from his pocket where it'd been sitting for a week and flipped it open.

With shaking fingers, she took out the diamond ring. "Oh my God."

"Is that 'oh my God yes I'll marry you, Finn O'Riley?' " he asked.

She both laughed and cried. "Did you doubt it?"

"Well, I still haven't heard 'yes, Finn.' "

With a laugh, she leapt into his arms and spread kisses over his jaw to his mouth. "Yes, Finn!"

Grinning, he slid the diamond ring onto her finger.

She admired her hand. "So how pushy would it be of me to ask for something else right now?"

"Name it," he said.

She put her mouth to his ear. "I'd like some more of what you gave me last night. Right here, right now."

Remembering every single hot second of last night, he smiled. "Yeah?"

"Yeah." She bit her lower lip again, which didn't hide her smile. "Please?"

"Babe, anything you want, always, and you don't even have to say please."

The employees of Thorndike Press hope you have enjoyed this Large Print book. All our Thorndike, Wheeler, and Kennebec Large Print titles are designed for easy reading, and all our books are made to last. Other Thorndike Press Large Print books are available at your library, through selected bookstores, or directly from us.

For information about titles, please call:
(800) 223-1244

or visit our Web site at:
http://gale.cengage.com/thorndike

To share your comments, please write:
Publisher
Thorndike Press
10 Water St., Suite 310
Waterville, ME 04901